The Hectic Headspace

Of

ABIGAIL SQUALL

Scott O'Neill

A *Cool Hat* Book

Published in Great Britain 2018
Copyright © Scott O'Neill

First Edition

The author has asserted their moral right under the Copyright, Designs and Patents Act, 1988, to be identified as the author of this work.

All characters in this publication are fictitious and any resemblance to real persons, living or dead, is purely coincidental.

All rights reserved.
No part of this publication may be reproduced, copied, stored in a retrieval system, or transmitted, in any form or by any means, without the prior written consent of the copyright holder, nor be otherwise circulated in any form of binding or cover other than that in which it is published and without a similar condition being imposed on the subsequent purchaser.

ISBN 9781983059612

www.scottoneill.net

For Theresa and Alex

CHAPTER ONE

SWITCH ON

Mrs Tully found herself in some difficulty. The difficulty in question was one of speed. An excessive amount of speed. Speed and gravity. Her black plimsolls motored to a blur under her new summer dress. A floaty light cotton number bursting with big red roses. Much like the cheeks on her shiny round face.

Slow down...!

The bags of groceries tugging heavily in each hand pulled her down the steep slope towards the bus stop like a pack of feisty hounds. Faster... faster...

Speed plus gravity. Multiplied by mass. It resembled the problems she used to map out on a whiteboard for her students with a squeaky red marker: E = mass (146 pounds of retired schoolteacher) times the speed of descent (approximately seven mph) squared. If she didn't solve this equation promptly she was in serious danger of overshooting the path and charging into the road where, instead of catching the Number Eight bus, she would end up being thoroughly squished by it.

(146 x 7 ÷ 8 = 0).

Too embarrassing to contemplate. A big fat zero? Never! Sensing the slope level out she swung her hefty bags to the left and used the momentum to slingshot her shuffling feet to the safety of the bus stop and away from the oncoming traffic.

Mrs Tully plunked her shopping on the ground and rested her plump frame against the timetable. She fanned her crimson face with both hands. Too old for such exertion! Too hot for such exertion! It had turned out to be yet another furnace of a day. She hadn't experienced a heatwave like this since the summer of '84. One of her favourite years. The class of '84 had proved to be a particularly fine vintage. Little Jonny Squall for example, had gone on to become a Professor of Astronomy no less. She squinted up at the sky. Not a fluff of cloud to trouble the vast spread of blue.

Pressing her spectacles snugly to the bridge of her nose she stooped to review the comings and goings. The next bus was due in four minutes. She hoped it wouldn't be late. She had to get home before the sun melted the mint choccy-chip. A treat for Bill. Her husband was no doubt pottering around in the garden. Watering, pruning and weeding. Hopefully the silly old fop had remembered to wear a hat. How many times had she warned him about the dangers of sunburn? Every time she'd applied the calamine lotion to his frazzled scalp and neck, that's how often. He had the complexion of a sheet of foolscap. A paleness only a factor fifty or above could protect. But he could never bring himself to apply the cream himself. Hated the sensation of greasy fingers. And no amount of lecturing would change his stubborn ways. Teaching that old dog new tricks had always been a far greater challenge than teaching all those young pups new sums. Bless him. He deserved a treat.

This summer! Proof, if proof were needed, that you can have too much of a good thing. So hot! The road surface shimmered in the heat. The dry, dusty throat of the drain by the kerb gaped thirstily. The bushes and the grass had pawned all their green for worthless gold. The whole town was wilting.

Her heart rate returning to normal, she glanced at her watch. Any minute now...

BOOSH!

Mrs Tully let loose a terrified yelp as a melon, as big and heavy as her head, exploded on the pavement spraying goo all over her exposed ankles and calves. Pressing a hand to her thumping heart, she looked up at the footbridge directly overhead. Three evil, badly maintained grins beamed down then dashed off laughing and sniggering towards the tenements on the far side.

Brats!

She took a tissue from her pocket and wiped a lump of mushy flesh from her toes.

Brats, brats, brats!

She stepped out of the splatter of honeydew carnage. Scattered islands of shrapnel, green and glistening in little pools of juice already drying on the warm concrete. They could have killed her with that great melon bomb! And what a waste of a fine piece of fruit. Brats! Ill-disciplined brats! If only she were still teaching. Then those boys would learn a thing or two about respect and responsibility. Schools these days were too soft. Too frightened to challenge indiscipline. That was the problem. Back in her prime a stern look was all she needed to put an unruly pupil in place. But those days were gone. Aim a stern look at a pupil these days and in all probability you would find yourself in court for breaching the poor little imp's human rights. And as an added bonus, you would undoubtedly find yourself drenched in a torrent of abuse from an irate parent or two, promising to remove your head from your shoulders for having the temerity to suggest their little angel was anything less than a heaven sent blessing in front of whom, all humanity should sink to their knees in worship.

Thuggish parents, unmotivated kids and endless Government interference had left the profession teetering on the brink. She changed her mind. Why on earth would she want to be a teacher nowadays? Thank God she had left all that behind her. Her and Bill both.

A diesel rumble approached. She binned the tissue and threw one last scowl up at the bridge before nabbing her bags and boarding the bus.

Brats!

CHAPTER TWO

RECEIVER

A big yellow sunflower.

Its petals glowed as she held it against the rising sun. Sunflower rise. Self raising flower. She smiled and lifted the bloom high into the bluest of skies. A bird flew higher still. Merrily singing for anyone who cared to listen.

It happened one year ago to the very day. On this very spot. The sky looked and sounded very different back then. Heavy with dark clouds and hissing with rain. A hiss loud enough to smother the sound of the marauding vehicle.

One year later and the sun had robbed the scene of all its menace and replaced it with a benign landscape of hedgerows, lush fields and hillsides dense with conifer plantations. Abigail Squall carefully laid the flower by the roadside and sat on the kerb next to her bicycle. Behind her the stalls filling the hangar-sized space of McGregor & Sons Wholesale Market buzzed with the colour and blether of local farmers and smallholders here to sell the fruits of their labour. A happy arena of fresh produce, tall tales, old jokes and hard cash exchanging hands. They all knew why she was here and respectfully left her alone with her thoughts. Smile fading, her gaze drifted through the shimmering heat haze rising from the surface of the road.

SLOW.

The word had since been painted on both sides of the road in thick white letters three-foot long. Too late. Far too late.

Oh God I miss you...

They came here so often together. Abigail and Sylvia. Her canny mother always driving a hard bargain with the sellers but never settling for anything less than the very best for her grocery. All stock had to be organic and, wherever possible, locally sourced. Everything from leeks to cherries chosen for quality not for their looks. Sylvia believed people should accept their food the way they accepted their friends, with all their wholesome imperfections. Quirky bumps, lumps and blemishes; all were welcome.

'Would you rather have a perfectly round, perfectly red, perfectly polished tomato that tastes as dull as tap water, or one that looks like a bobbly lumpy misfit yet tastes like heaven?' Sylvia once asked. 'And besides, don't they all end up looking the same once your teeth get to work? The world has an unhealthy obsession with perfection. We need to stop treating fruit and veg as if they're supermodels. All surface and no substance. Only fit for magazines and not for the plate. Who cares about looks? It's what's inside that matters. All that lovely flavour! Give me a sweet tasting carrot that looks like a mistake any day, I don't care. I want crops that please my taste buds, not my eyes. We should celebrate the imperfections. They add flavour. Something different. Let's banish the bland!'

Abigail stared at her plum coloured Doc Martens. Her mother had few imperfections. Sylvia was beautiful. She remembered her smile. It made her chest ache every time she realised she would never see that smile again. One year ago to the very day. And for it to happen on Abigail's birthday of all days...

She flattened her long mustard corduroy skirt against her thighs and squinted at the blazing sun. So hot. Too hot for boots really but they were so comfy. A perfect fit. Her only concession to the heat was a white sleeveless top with a big goldfish on the front accompanied by the slogan – *You Can Keep Your Long Term Memory*. Her bare arms glowed honey pale. The rainbow of plastic bracelets encircling her wrist slipped and clicked together when she lifted her hand to stroke the mole near her shoulder. One of her own quirky bumps, lumps and blemishes. Sylvia and Jonathan always complimented her on her looks but Abigail would not be fooled. Parents after all, were contractually obliged to tell their kids they looked handsome or pretty, weren't they? No parent would ever tell their child they looked like a woodland fungus even if they did have a nose like a puffball.

Abigail didn't like her nose. Too big. Or her ears. A bit sticky-out. Her eyes were chestnut. She would've preferred blue. Hair? An untidily cropped bottle-blonde mess. Yes. She liked her hair. And her chin. And her hands. Knees? Not so much. Best hidden under a skirt or jeans. Chest? Too small. Backside? Too big. Feet? Her toes pointed at a slightly weird angle otherwise they were fairly standard feet. Stomach? Flat, but could be flatter. She sucked it in and pinched her waist. Pleasingly taut. - *Seen more meat on my budgie's toothpick!* – her granddad used to say, somewhat cryptically. She lifted her top a few inches. Belly button? An innie. Good. Outies were a bit freaky. Unlike her younger brother she had no desire to puncture herself like a pincushion or turn her hide into a sketchbook. She stood and stretched. Good height. Average. Not too short. Not too tall. Just right.

Over all? Abigail felt comfortable in her own skin. Quirky lumps, bumps, blemishes and all.

Oh, but the ache at her core would not go. Exactly one year ago to the very day, a car came speeding round that corner and hit Sylvia. The driver did not stop. Instead, the car sped on and out of sight before Abigail realised what had happened. Exactly one year ago to the very day Abigail, on her sixteenth birthday, saw her mother sprawled right here on the sodden tarmac. The blood flowing from her head. The rain water rinsing it down the storm drain as Abigail raced to her side and cradled her mother in her arms. Even now she could still feel the dead, pressing, weight. She remembered the light dying in Sylvia's eyes as they looked despairingly into hers and the few final words uttered in a fractured, breathless wheeze.

'I love...? One love...? I love...? One love...?'

And then her eyes quivered briefly and closed for the last time.

Abigail watched the petals of the sunflower at her feet gently flutter in the warm breeze.

Let's banish the bland!

She stood, gripped the handlebars and cycled off following the coastal road back towards town.

*

Balemouth Bay. North-west Scotland. A seaside haven of nigh on four thousand souls, their homes hugging the horseshoe of the bay and spilling up and thinning out across the inland hills. The sunshine flared from the white regimented roofs of the *Thistledoo Luxury Caravan Park,* which filled several manicured acres beyond the southern end of the bay. The tourists flocking to the golden sands of the beach and thronging the promenade easily doubled the town's resident population. The hotels and the B&Bs appeared to be having a contest on who could boast the most stylish *'No Vacancies'* sign. From handcrafted oak boards dangling from custom-built arches to multi-coloured neon letters winking from generous bay windows. At the northern end, the River Bale which threatened so often to flood the town in winter, trickled lazily into the sea. A major worry for the Balemouth Angling Club whose members could not remember ever seeing the water level so low.

The gulls perched on the ornate Victorian lamp posts which fringed the curve of the waterfront, kept switching their ravenous eyes from the line of sweltering sun worshippers queuing patiently by the ice cream kiosk, to the teenagers plunging into the Art Deco fountain, to the crazy golfers, the bathers, the kayakers and… to the toddler holding the rapidly melting cone in his pudgy little grip…

Rush hour was approaching in Balemouth Bay. Out of season this would mean a six car tailback at the only set of traffic lights. Now, at the height of summer, the queue of traffic stretched all the way back to Mr Ginty's Gift Shop. Abigail stepped out. So hot! *Hot hot hot*! She donned her purchases; a pair of sunglasses framed in chunky white plastic and a wide-brimmed straw hat decorated with a band of purple ribbon. She dipped a hand into her skirt pocket and pushed the heavy packet of peanuts deeper inside.

Ready...

Abigail cycled on, weaving her way through the hordes of bare-limbed day-trippers, one hand on the handlebars while the other held her hat in place. Once she'd crossed the old stone bridge spanning the river, the crowds began to peter out and vanished completely when the sands to her left were replaced by a shoreline of ragged rocks. The road forked under the decrepit shadow of St Luke's. Weeds sprouting from its defiant spire, while pigeons flitted in and out of the yawning holes in the roof, the old church waited for demolition like a condemned prisoner at the gallows. Abigail turned inland and followed the road another half-mile until she arrived at her destination. Leaning her bike against a telegraph pole she sunk her hands into her pockets and, zigzagging her way through the car park, surreptitiously scattered nuts between the massed ranks of sun-scorched vehicles and abandoned shopping trolleys.

Homing in on the doors she tilted the brim of her hat down over her brow and adjusted her sunglasses. She knew her disguise wouldn't win any prizes at the Petty Criminal Of The Year Awards, but it would have to do. She breathed deeply, steeling herself as she entered the belly of the beast. The shiny new Goodsmart superstore...

EVERYTHING UNDER ONE ROOF!
BUY ONE GET ONE FREE!
GET YOUR LOYALTY CARD!
EARN REWARDS!

SALE! SALE! SALE!
PRICE MATCH GUARANTEE!
SAVE £££££s!
BE GOOD, BE SMART - SHOP GOODSMART!

The signs badgered her from every conceivable angle the moment she entered the cavernous space. Dangling from the ceiling, stuck on the floor, fixed to the walls, attached to trolleys, and pinned to the uniforms of the staff. The supermarket was huge. Perhaps not as massive as those in far bigger Highland towns like Fort William or Inverness but it certainly dwarfed every other retail outlet in Balemouth Bay. Abigail scowled under her brim. Goodsmart had more floor space than all the local food stores combined. A corporate giant sucking every purse and wallet dry leaving the rest of the competition to wither and rot. Abigail clenched her fists.

No! No! No!

This underdog has bite!

And a nose that's a bit too big.

Abigail collected a basket and marched onwards noting the security guard manning his station as she passed. Aisle upon aisle upon aisle, racked and stacked, deep and high. Where to start? Fruit and vegetables of course. Same as last time. The place bustled with tourists chatting in all manner of strange and wonderful accents. She didn't blame them. They didn't know any better. They were merely responding to the lure of the ritual, calling them through these doors to follow the same identikit shopping experience they enjoyed back home. Such was the power of huge advertising budgets and a buying power that left suppliers kowtowing to their every corporate whim. No, she couldn't blame these robotic consumers. Everyone loves convenience and the comforting blanket of familiarity but the town needed them to support the little guy, not this soulless multinational conglomerate dragon.

Banish the bland!

She headed for the carrots, glanced left then right and quickly snapped a few before someone else ambled along. Mushrooms next. Portobellos. As big as her hand. And every one the same boring uniform shape. She handled a few pretending to check their quality and freshness while digging her nails deep into their skins. Next, on to the bananas, which for some inane reason, were pre-packed in clear plastic bags. As if nature's own packaging wasn't enough! She clocked the CCTV camera above and made sure she had her back to the lens, hands concealed, before she started giving several bunches a damn good, bruising squeeze.

Leaving a trail of broken cucumbers, dented apples, traumatised strawberries and punctured potatoes in her wake, she moved on to the bread. Racks of soft rolls and cloned loaves, all the flavour of damp cardboard, gathered under a sign proudly proclaiming:

PREPARED BY OUR IN-STORE BAKER!

Nonsense! All this so-called in-store baker did was shove some pre-prepared dough spat out by a machine in some vast factory hundreds of miles away, into the oven. Not like Mr Zurawski and his son Henryk. They baked everything from scratch. Bread, cakes, muffins, scones, pies... The works. She managed to jab her thumb into a dozen or so baps before she noticed the security guard cruising down the aisle opposite. He glanced suspiciously in her direction. Time to move on. An old lady on a mobility scooter had a query for the guard. Abigail used this precious opportunity to snap a few stems and pluck a few petals from the flowers bunched in buckets next to the newspaper stand as she sashayed for the exit.

The automatic doors parted and Abigail stepped from the air conditioned coolness into a wall of intense heat. She swept through the car park avoiding the plague of gulls scooping up the peanuts she'd scattered on her way in. One shopper wheeled his trolley to the rear of his shiny Alfa Romeo just in time to see a big white splat detonate on the roof. He shook an irate fist at the squawking culprit swooping overhead. Abigail smiled. Plenty of other vehicles would be in need of a thorough sponging at Big Betsy's Car Bath before the day was through.

She opened her bicycle's pannier, pulled out a poster and a stapler and attached the A4 sheet to the telegraph pole:

BUY LOCAL – NOT GLOBAL!

Tipping her hat to the security guard staring at her from the entrance, she mounted her seat and cycled off. Another little victory for the *Goodsmart Bandito – The Banisher of the Bland!*

CHAPTER THREE

LONG WAVE

Jonathan Squall opened his wallet.

'Henryk you are a genius! How much do I owe you?'

'Seriously Mr Squall, you don't have to pay me. If it's for Abigail's birthday I'm just happy I could help,' said Henryk bashfully.

'And you'll be a whole lot happier with some well earned extra cash in your pocket. This is not open to debate. This kind of detailed repair work takes time. And no little skill. It looks as good as new!' Jonathan pulled out a pair of crisp twenty pound notes. 'Here, take it. I insist.'

'Thank you very much Mr Squall. That's more than generous.' Henryk, feeling his cheeks flush, accepted the proffered notes and quickly stuffed them in his pocket. He handed over a carrier bag in exchange and watched Mr Squall carefully lift out the newly refurbished radio.

Eyes beaming Jonathan studied his prize. The radio was a thing of rare beauty. A classic from the Sixties. Chunky. Angular. Gleaming red and gold with big touchy-feely dials. It used to belong to his father. Alexander Squall, or Sandy as he preferred to be known, passed away eight years ago but Jonathan always remembered how Abigail loved this old transistor. Back then, as part of their Sunday ritual, the Squalls would troop up Broomway Drive to visit Sandy where little Abigail spent many a contented hour listening to crackly foreign radio broadcasts from God knows where, while her granddad pretended to interpret what they were saying. He used to make up all kinds of fantastical nonsense, and little Abigail, sitting on his knee, believed every single word. Abigail was equally spellbound by the whoops, whistles and gurgles she'd hear as she worked the tuning dial through the spaces between stations. And again her granddad would find himself unable to resist the opportunity to fill her gullible head with the tallest of tales, merrily explaining that these noises were the songs and poetry of aliens broadcasting from the centre of the moon. Apparently the moon was much like the earth only inside out. The sky, the seas, the forests and the cities were on the inside. And if you looked carefully enough you could see the holes the aliens (or Moonlings) had drilled on the surface allowing the sun to shed light and warmth throughout their inverted world.

Then the unit developed a fault shortly before Granddad Squall died after which the radio spent its days gathering dust on top of Jonathan's wardrobe. Just another addition to his list of Things That Will Be Fixed One Of These Days.

And for the old radio, that day had finally arrived. Jonathan turned it over, admiring every polished side. He couldn't wait to see Abigail's face when he gave it to her. He hoped the gift would achieve its purpose and trigger memories of those happier times.

'She'll love it. You've done an amazing job, Henryk. Amazing.'

'Thanks. I completely gutted the inside. Replaced the circuit board and transceiver. I kept the original fan. All it needed was a dab of oil. I bolstered the power unit and installed a 24-bit digital receiver which I salvaged from the dump. People really have no idea what they're throwing away half the time do they? Anyway, basically it should pick up all the digital and analogue stations going,' Henryk explained, trying to contain his pride.

'You're right. I'm not giving you enough.' And before Henryk could protest Jonathan pressed another twenty into his hand. 'Digital *and* analogue stations you say?'

'Aye, everything. But obviously she won't hear a thing until they switch on the new transmitter tomorrow. Thank you for the money but this is really too...'

'Henryk, if you don't mind me saying, and no offence to your dad, but I can't help but think you're wasted working in a bakery. You should be out there training to become an engineer or something equally suited to this kind of talent.'

'Oh I don't know about that,' said Henryk, feeling his face blush again. 'I just like fixing things.'

A cyclist appeared on the footbridge pedalling leisurely towards the shops.

'Quick, she's coming! Give me the bag!' urged Jonathan. Henryk held the bag open while Jonathan quickly concealed the radio inside. 'Thanks again Henryk. We'll catch up later,' he added patting Henryk on the shoulder before darting inside The Green Grocery.

Henryk watched Abigail dismount and wheel her bike towards the racks. Heart fluttering, he hurried for the safety of the bakery and almost collided with PC Godwin exiting with a bagful of pastries. The burly constable smiled guiltily at the young baker's son.

'Hello Henryk. You caught me.' He held up a sugary pink confection then lowered his voice into a sinister American growl. 'I am become meringue – the destroyer of teeth.'

'Hello officer Godwin. Sorry, can't stop. Need to help my dad with the, with the...' Henryk stammered, racking his brain for a suitable excuse. 'Croissants! Aye, the croissants need, they need... They need to be straightened. They're far too bendy. Bye.'

Crunching into his meringue, PC Godwin stepped aside allowing Henryk to pass then continued for the shop next door.

Abigail hooked a D-lock around her bike frame and snapped it to the rack. Balemouth Town Square was a five-minute ride up the High Street from the seafront and occupied a small open space at the heart of the town's main residential jumble. The line of shops ran along the western flank, facing the car park and the new Community Hall and Arts Gallery to the east side. A smartly designed single-storey, slate and sandstone edifice, the 'Chag' had already firmly established itself as the venue of choice for any social function of note.

Abigail made her way along the tidy parade of independent, family owned businesses, each one displaying BUY LOCAL – NOT GLOBAL! posters in their windows and doors. First in line were the fine meats and quality cuts of Mr Banks the butcher. A lovely man. Always ready with a jolly smile and a wave of his cleaver as she passed. That's if she was unlucky enough to catch his eye. She always stepped up a gear when passing this particular window. Those poor animals! The sight of those red raw lumps piled high under a dangling grotesquerie of skinned corpses made her retch. And the smell! Flesh and sawdust; livers, hearts, kidneys, tongues, steaks and scratchings. Minced, chopped, sliced and diced...

And the sight of the blood smeared liberally all over his apron! Yuck! Yes, Mr Banks was a lovely man. Pity about his gruesome trade. Not a morsel of meat had passed Abigail's lips since the first time she peered in this very window, standing on tiptoes with Sylvia holding her wee hand and explaining in no-holds-barred detail, the process that took those unfortunate creatures from their fields, pens and sheds and into Mr Banks' house of horrors. Her poor fellow mammals! That was the moment she vowed, like her mother, never to eat anything with a face or a digestive tract. Unfortunately, despite her best efforts, the men of the Squall household remained committed carnivores to this day. Indeed, whenever she broached the subject at the dining table of the many downsides of a meat diet, they would invariably respond by jamming another fork loaded with beef into their salivating mouths, chew it extra slowly and with their eyes pressed shut, treat her to a chorus of exaggerated grunts and moans of pleasure. Cavemen!

Next came the only marginally less gory Fruits Of The Sea fishmongers with its display of dead, button-eyed fish, cephalopods, molluscs and crustaceans washed up on beaches of ice. One ugly brute of a gaping, needle-toothed monkfish, seemed for all the world to be screaming for help. Abigail hurried to the altogether more pleasing view offered by Bay Bouquets, the florists run by Helen and Robert. A big rainbow bang of vibrant blooms. She waved through to Robert busily whistling while he worked on a spectacular wedding arrangement and couldn't resist a sniff of the roses bunched on the shelves by the door.

A few more steps and she was outside Noach's Newsagent. A quick scan of today's headlines: *BRITAIN MELTS! – HEATWAVE TO LAST FOR WEEKS! - IT'S OFFICIAL: HOTTEST SUMMER EVER! - LOCK UP YOUR HOSEPIPES! – DROUGHT TO CONTINUE.* Squeezed in behind her counter, the voluminous Maggie Noach fanned herself with a copy of *The Sun - SCORCHIO!* - and returned Abigail's smile.

Then, eradicating the last few traces of dead animal stink from her nostrils, came the deliciously dizzying waft from the wonderful Zurawski Bakery. She closed her eyes and filled herself with a deep helping of the sweet air. Warm bread and cakes. The scent of heaven itself! Eyes open, she feasted on the glories behind the window. Cream filled pastries, fruit scones, chocolate twists, tarts, macaroons, doughnuts iced in yellow, pink, white, orange and filled with jams: custard, strawberry, lemon curd, chocolate... And on the shelves surrounding the little cafe area inside; baguettes, bloomers, croissants, baps and speciality breads in all shapes and sizes – all of these wonders lovingly created by craftsmen. They even made their own ice cream! All of it was so tempting. Abigail touched her belly. Flat, but could be flatter...

'Abigail! Good morning my dear!' she heard Mr Zurawski hail from within as he laid another tray of fondant fancies on the other side of the glass. This great bear of a man possessed a wonderful booming voice which, though he'd lived in Balemouth Bay longer than Abigail had been alive, still retained a Polish accent as rich and thick as any of his éclairs. His son Henryk looked up from the table where he was serving coffee and biscuits. Abigail smiled and nodded a greeting to him. Just a year or so older than Abigail, he was a born and bred local and as such, spoke with the far less exotic Highland lilt, much like herself. Though how he managed to stay in such fine, athletic shape when surrounded by all this temptation remained a mystery to her. Henryk smiled shyly and quickly returned his attention to his customers.

The Green Grocery, once owned by Sylvia Squall and now run by Jonathan with a little help from Abigail, represented the end of the shopping line. A line of old-fashioned businesses perhaps, in so far as every little endeavour prided itself on quality and customer service, yet together they represented the beating heart of the community. But now, thanks to Goodsmart, every one of them was under threat. And if these shops died and the people and characters and friends who bought, sold and smiled and laughed and gossiped all left? Well, it didn't bear thinking about.

Mr Zurawski turned to Henryk with a rueful smile. The boy is in love! What else could explain the heated cheeks and his sudden inability to speak or to perform even the most basic of motor functions? It reminded the baker of his own early yearnings for Halina and the seemingly unfathomable games of courtship they played out a lifetime ago back in Gdansk. He hoped Henryk never sought his advice on such matters. He still had no idea when it came to the workings of a woman's mind. Play safe son. The rules of baking were far easier to understand. The quality of the flour, the strength of the yeast, the consistency of the dough... Quality, strength, consistency; attributes which Halina also had in abundance. Along with a tablespoon of stubbornness, a cupful of mystery and a pinch of volatility. The finest ingredients. Truth be told, he would not have changed a single moment of his life with her. Not one moment. Married for thirty-eight years and he still gave her the first loaf, warm and fresh, direct from the oven every morning.

He caught his son craning his neck to see if Abigail was still out there. Hard working and a talented baker though he was, he could tell Henryk's ambitions lay elsewhere. Electrical engineering. The boy enjoyed nothing more than taking gadgets apart to learn the mysteries of their inner workings before putting them back together. Mr Zurawski felt a twinge of sadness knowing that the family business would almost certainly retire when he did. He picked up a sourdough baguette and poked Henryk in the ribs.

'For pity's sake son if you want to catch her heart you first have to catch her eye. So why don't you go and ask the girl out?'

'I can't. What if she says no?' asked Henryk in return.

Mr Zurawski rolled his eyes, 'Always the negative. The bread never rises in your world does it? It's the girl's birthday. Give her a cake. I have yet to come across a woman anywhere in the world who does not like cake. So pick a cake and give it to her.'

Henryk eyed the choice on offer. 'Which one? She might not like chocolate. Or what if I give her a Danish and she doesn't like cinnamon? Or raisins?'

Mr Zurawski made the decision for him, 'Here. A slice of kremowka never fails.'

Henryk took the cream-stuffed confection and put it in a paper bag. Heading for the door he paused, then plucked a Danish from under the counter and added it to the bag. 'Just in case she does like cinnamon.'

'Good idea son,' Mr Zurawski nodded. 'Choice is good. Women like choice. Now go!' He watched his son hurry to the shop next door.

Henryk found Abigail tending the fruit displayed outside The Green Grocery. Once she'd lovingly rearranged the melons, apples and oranges to ensure they looked their absolute best she then paid careful attention to the lemons and limes. She lined them up; green, yellow, green, yellow, green, yellow... The zests enticing and vibrant in the sunshine.

'Happy birthday Abigail,' he said quickly before his nerve failed him.

'Thanks Henryk,' she grinned. She leaned across to a box stored above the lemons and limes. 'Would you like to have a date with me?'

Henryk's eager heart wobbled. 'A date? Really?' His ardour promptly retreated back in its cage when she offered him a small wrinkly brown fruit. 'Oh, a *date*. Thank you.' Unsure what else to add he smiled sheepishly and found himself locked in her big brown eyes.

'Don't you like them? They're a good source of potassium,' said Abigail, popping one in her mouth.

'I love 'em. We use them in mazurek cakes. Did you know the chemical symbol for potassium is K? And its Atomic Number is nineteen?' said Henryk.

'I do now,' said Abigail, impressed.

His face burning with embarrassment, Henryk thrust the paper bag to Abigail. 'Cake?' The word almost stuck in his tightening throat.

'Ooh, thank you!' Abigail took the bag and peered inside. 'That Danish looks amazing. And, oh my God what's this one? Is this a mazurek cake? I'm getting fat just looking at it!'

'No, it's a slice of kremowka. Two layers of puff pastry filled with whipped cream, buttercream and vanilla pastry cream,' Henryk explained, happy to be on safe conversational ground. 'I doubt it contains much in the way of potassium though. Let me know if you like it. If you do, I'll make you another one.'

Abigail closed the bag and stared at him accusingly. 'You are pure evil. How could I *not* like it? Puffed pastry and whipped cream? You give me more of these I'll end up looking like a beach ball. Don't you think I'm fat enough?'

'You're not fat! And you could never look like a beach ball. You're perfect in every way.' Henryk bit his wayward tongue. The stupid fat flap had ignored the memo from his brain marked; *For Internal Use Only*. 'Sorry, I didn't mean to say that. That bit about you being perfect. I mean of course I meant it, don't get me wrong. It's just erm... What I'm trying to say is that even if you ate all the cakes in the world I don't think you could ever resemble a beach ball. Not to me.' Henryk now wanted to march his tongue to the butcher and allow Mr Banks to feed it straight into his mincer.

Abigail smiled. 'Thank you... I think.'

Henryk knew he could fry a full Scottish breakfast on his hotplate cheeks; eggs, bacon, square sausage, potato scones, black pudding, the full works. Time for a dishonourable retreat. 'I'd better get back to work.'

'Okay. Bye Henryk. Thanks for the Danish and the krema... kremoosh...'

'Kreh-MOOV-ka,' Henryk confirmed.

'Kre-moov-ka.'

'That's it. Bye Abigail.' Blushing like a Belisha beacon, Henryk hurried off kicking his idiot inner self all the way back inside the bakery.

Abigail had another look inside the bag. 'Kremowka,' she whispered to herself. She dipped a finger between the layers of pastry and scooped some cream into her mouth. Delicious.

A bright sparkle of light danced on the toes of her boots. She looked up at the polished steel apple hanging above the door to The Green Grocery, gently rotating in the merest breath of a breeze. Sunlight ricocheted from its silver surface and flickered over the fruit, the windows and the paving stones. Mouth full of sugary cream and eyes full of light, she opened herself to the sun's enfolding warmth. Abigail closed her eyes...

*

The garden shed doubled as Sylvia's workshop. To a five-year-old girl the term 'shed' in this instance, represented something of an understatement. This was way too big to be called a shed. She'd been to many of her friends' gardens and their sheds were small little huts where they kept their lawnmowers, paint cans and spiders. By comparison, the Squalls' shed could comfortably accommodate a family of giant spiders wearing paint cans for shoes while riding around on a lawnmower the size of Jonathan's old Audi. Well, perhaps it wasn't quite *that* big.

Sylvia Squall; mother, wife, and greengrocer was also a sculptress. Metal being her chosen medium. Little Abigail spent many a happy hour watching the sparks fly as her mother set to work cutting, welding and polishing her work. With all that heat and all those little flakes of flame it was a wonder Sylvia's dungarees never caught fire.

Perched at a safe distance on the bench by the wall, little Abigail waggled her feet completely engrossed in her mother's craft. Sylvia held up a metal leaf and fixed it to the short stalk poking from the top of a shiny steel apple. Work complete, Sylvia lifted her welding mask and gathered her daughter on her knee.

'Do you like my apple?' she asked.

'Shiny,' Abigail nodded. 'I can see me in it. Is it a Golden Delicious?'

'No, it's a wee Honey Pippin, just like you. It'll look perfect above the shop, don't you think? Can you imagine it hanging above the door?'

Abigail put her face close to the metal apple amused by her ever-widening grin, distorted and stretched across the mirrored surface. Her nose looked like a big pig's snout. She moved her eyes closer to the surface until they merged into the blinking mischievous stare of a cheeky young Cyclops. She opened her mouth wide and laughed at the huge dark cave reflected in the steel. There was a gap in the arc of chunky white stalagmites lining the floor of the cave. A huge slimy pink monster probed through. Abigail checked her pockets. The fifty pence piece the tooth fairy had left under her pillow was still there.

'When you're older I'll teach you how to sculpt things out of metal. Would you like that?'

'Can I make a pumpkin?'

Sylvia turned Abigail until they were face to face, eye to eye. 'You can make anything you want sweetheart. You can *do* anything you want. I don't care if you want to be a street-sweeper, an astronaut or a footballer, I'll help you. And I'll love you whatever you decide to do. And don't let anyone tell you that you can't do this or you can't do that. You're my little girl and you will be brilliant at whatever you turn your hand to. Do you hear me?'

'I don't like football.'

Sylvia laughed and hugged her tighter still.

*

Abigail opened her eyes. The apple above the door glinted and gleamed. The little girl's reflection had long gone. What became of her? Another bite and the cream pastry had gone too. Abigail pushed through to the shop.

'Is it really necessary to have all that produce on display outside? Perhaps if you didn't have their weapon of choice so readily to hand?'

Jonathan gazed accusingly at PC Godwin. 'And perhaps if you spent more time in the gym instead of the bakery you might catch the little bampots.' He tilted his head allowing Abigail to peck his cheek as she passed by on her way to the till. She noticed the demure, elegant and slimline Valerie Hobbs working hard to stifle a giggle as she deliberated over the plums.

Deeply affronted, the portly crime fighter tucked his bag of Zurawski treats under his arm. 'These aren't all for me you know. I intend to share them with the rest of the boys at the station... Hello Abigail by the way.'

'Hiya, Officer Godwin.'

'Yes well, the world is full of good intentions,' Jonathan persisted.

A frown crimped PC Godwin's reddening face. 'What's that supposed to mean?'

Sporting his cheesiest salesman's grin Jonathan held aloft an enticing basket laden with citrus. 'I mean why subject your colleagues to a bag stuffed full of type two diabetes when you can treat them to a nice healthy fruit basket brimming with zest and vitamins?'

Wrong-footed, PC Godwin's frown faded as he studied the contents. 'How much?'

'Normally six pounds and fifty pence but to an old school pal such as yourself let's call it six pounds.'

'Hold me back! A whole fifty pence off! Is there no beginning to your generosity?' PC Godwin took the basket and pondered the fruit with suspicion. 'The wife can have these.' He fished out a note. Abigail handed him a few coins in change. 'Take my advice Jonathan and stop making it so easy for them, that's all I'm saying,' he added, before taking what appeared to Jonathan, to be an overly defiant bite from a bright pink meringue. The policeman turned on his heel and headed for the door but with both hands full and the meringue disintegrating in his mouth, executing a dignified exit proved impossible. Jonathan stepped across and opened the door for him.

'Hank oo.'

'No, thank *you* Phil.'

The little bell chimed as the door settled once more.

Valerie set her basket on the counter for Abigail to weigh and bag. 'Is Phil giving you grief again Jon?' she asked.

'It's those Morton kids,' Jonathan sighed. 'Irritating bunch of degenerates. Wouldn't be surprised if their dad was also their uncle. They're out of control! I keep telling Phil it's high time he sorted the three of them out and put a stop to this stupid little game of theirs.'

'What stupid little game?'

'The one where they pinch a piece of fruit or veg from our tables outside, then run to the bridge where they drop said item on to some poor unsuspecting head below. After which, they run off giggling their runty wee scumbag heads off.'

'The wee swines,' Valerie concurred.

'They hit Father Stokes on the head with a satsuma yesterday. And the day before, they dropped a Granny Smith on Bob Collins. Ironic really, seeing as they hit old Granny Smith with a courgette. And only this morning poor Mrs Tully had a melon dropped on her. Where's it going to end? What if they start pinching even bigger items? Apart from squeezing my margins imagine the damage they could do with something like a pumpkin? I'm telling you Halloween will be no time to go walking under bridges. Maybe Phil does have a point. Perhaps I should stop displaying produce outside.'

'Oh no, you can't give in like that. It's traditional isn't it? For a grocer to have their goods on display? It's what people expect. And besides, it looks and smells wonderful out there. I'm sure it entices customers in. I know it always makes me want to pop in,' said Valerie, offering Jonathan a smile. The offer went unnoticed as Jonathan, eyes down and his mind seemingly elsewhere, stepped back behind the counter where he developed a sudden and minute interest in testing the efficacy of the weighing scales calibrations.

'And it's always a pleasure to see you,' said Abigail, slightly irked by her father's apparent lack of courtesy. 'Isn't that right Dad?'

'Sorry? Yes, of course. Always a pleasure to see you here, Valerie,' he said, huffing a breath on the scales before attacking them with a duster.

Abigail handed Valerie her fruit neatly packaged in a large brown paper bag. 'That's right. You're welcome to grab half a kilo of Dad's succulent Mirabelles any time you like.'

Jonathan groaned. 'And here we go with the plum jokes.'

Valerie choked back a laugh. 'Thanks Abigail. But between you and me, it's his purple sprouting broccoli I'd really like to get my hands on,' she winked.

'Understandable, though I'm told his Red Bartletts are a must,' said Abigail.

'Is that so? Well, apparently all the girls down at the hockey club cherish his prize-winning Maris Pipers.'

'This is true, but if it's a good soft mash you're after, then you can't beat his Jersey Royals.'

'Ladies? Do you mind? I feel like I'm stuck in a seventies sitcom here,' Jonathan whined.

'Do you think we're embarrassing him yet?' whispered Valerie.

'I think so,' Abigail whispered back.

'Good!' Valerie took her change. On the shelf behind the counter she noticed the flame of a tea light guttering gently inside the belly a handcrafted metal pear. 'What's the candle for?'

Abigail's smile slipped. 'It's for Mum. It was a year ago today.'

'Oh,' Valerie winced, not quite knowing where to look or what to say. 'I'm sorry.'

'No need,' said Jonathan. 'The Earth keeps spinning as they say. Hard to believe it's already been a year though.'

Valerie dared to focus on Jonathan. 'It is hard to believe. Strange how the older you get, the faster the years seem to speed by.'

Jonathan stopped polishing and held her gaze. 'Very true.'

'Well, I'll leave you both in peace. Keep well.' Valerie took her bag and made for the door.

'You too Valerie.' When the last ring died on the little bell dangling over the threshold, Abigail folded her arms and stared hard at her father.

'What? What is it?'

'Nothing.'

'Oh no you don't,' said Jonathan. 'There's definitely something. Whenever you have that funny little smile on your face there's definitely something. So come on. Spit it out.'

'Why are you men so rubbish at reading signals?' asked Abigail.

'What signals?'

'Valerie. Can't you tell? She wants more than half a kilo of fruit Dad.'

'Then why didn't she buy some veg as well then?' asked Jonathan.

'I give up,' Abigail sighed. She moved across the store and flipped the sign on the door from *Open* to *Closed*.

With the display tables stored safely inside, Abigail helped Jonathan pull down the shutters on The Green Grocery. A shabby VW Camper van pulled up. The whole rusting hulk reverberated to the heaviest of heavy metal raging within. Abigail waved to the handful of teenage heads banging and flailing inside, most of whom grinned and waved back. A van full of piercings, wildly coloured hair, distressed leather and tormented T-shirts. The driver thrust her tongue out at Abigail. Abigail cheerfully retaliated. The van's side door slid open filling the square with a frenzied blast of guitar fury. The surliest of the bunch sloped out to join Abigail and Jonathan.

'Hello Thomas,' said Jonathan.

Tom Squall grunted then aimed a half-hearted salute to the van as it tooted its horn and fled off down the street. The music slowly fading into the distance, Abigail gave her younger brother a hug. Tom stood stiffly until his sister finished the unwelcome embrace and climbed inside The Green Grocery delivery van. With Abigail in the back and Tom staring sullenly through the passenger window, Jonathan turned the key and steered them away from the shops.

Abigail spotted Henryk watching from the bakery and flashed a smile and a wave. In his eagerness to wave back, Henryk knocked the tray from Mr Zurawski's hands sending an avalanche of hot cross buns cartwheeling across the floor.

CHAPTER FOUR

FREQUENCY MODULATION

Sylvia Squall

Taken too soon

"This is not goodbye..."

Jonathan Squall watched his two children standing at the grave of his wife. He felt numb. Lost and helpless. The year had passed and passed so quickly. And what had he done with that year? What had he achieved? Nothing. He was treading water. Waiting for something to happen. Something to jolt him from this torpor, force his hand and propel his broken family away from this crippling loss to reclaim all their futures... *"This is not goodbye..."* Why had he chosen those words? A patent lie. Chiselled in marble. He wished he could turn that chisel on himself and chip away the stone cold numbness at his core. Something had to happen soon before the weight of it crushed him into oblivion.

Not a word had been exchanged on the ten-minute drive to the cemetery. Ten minutes of engine noise and gear changes. A quiet drive of repressed emotion and splintered thoughts. He tried to imagine the thoughts running through Abigail's and Tom's minds. To picture the desolation from their perspective. Why didn't he just ask them? Encourage them to open up, share their worries and concerns so he could do his duty and assure them all would be well in time? He knew they were suffering in there. He could sense it. He was supposed to be the one to pull them together, provide strength, comfort and guidance. To bind them tight. But in truth he was lost and had strayed far beyond his comfort zone. This was not his area. Sylvia was the glue. Not him.

She held everything together. She. Sylvia. The knot of guilt tightened. It was all slowly, inexorably slipping away. The memories. The impression of her. The things he took for granted. The details he would see every single day and never fully appreciated because he saw them every single day. The feel of her hair. The spark in her eyes. Her scent. Her clothes. Her joyous smile. The rings on her fingers and the lines on her hands. All that boundless enthusiasm and unpredictability. Her spur of the moment decisions to make something, or go somewhere, or burst into a song by one of those obscure bands she loved. He cherished all of those qualities. Yes, she had her annoying traits. That boundless enthusiasm and unpredictability could be frustrating at times. Times when he simply wanted to sit in silence. Sylvia had no time for stillness. But when everything was placed on the scales, the plusses utterly destroyed the minuses. He loved her. Didn't he? Yes... Once... For sure...

So why wasn't he crying? He should be crying. Or at least manfully holding back an onslaught of tears in an attempt to hide his emotions from the kids. But he didn't feel that tightening in the throat or that tell-tale pressure building behind the eyes. So what did he feel? A growing frustration. Forty-four years old and here he was, drifting aimlessly. He had become defined by her loss. He had spent the entire year doing 'the right thing'. He'd played the heartbroken widow and shown due mourning and even sacrificed the job he loved - Head of Astronomy at Inverness University - in order to take over Sylvia's shop and look after the kids. A year of condolences and pitiful looks and well-meaning but clumsily delivered platitudes had come to shape who he was. He had to get a grip! Tackle the issue head on. Move on somehow or before he knew it, he'd be mouldering under this grass himself. Problem was, he simply didn't know what to do. Except wait. Waiting had become his speciality.

Tom walked away from the grave. Eyes shielded behind sunglasses, he leaned against a tree. The sun betrayed him, glistening against the trails of moisture lining his face. Ripped black jeans, bulky black boots, black t-shirt and a ripped leather jacket in an ever so slightly different shade of black, emblazoned with patches of heavy metal bands and their logos. Most of whom Jonathan had never heard of. Who was he kidding? He'd never heard of a single one of them. His fifteen-year-old son was a patchwork quilt of satanic skulls and flayed bodies bellowing at him beneath names like; Cannibal Corpse, Knife Frenzy, Deathgasm, Slipknot and Bloodface. Tom's ears had been replaced with pincushions and his entire face would have completed the porcupine look had it not been for a prolonged Father/Son diplomatic summit of threat, counter threat and downright blackmail. The threat of economic sanctions forced a compromise and Tom agreed to settle for just the single stud piercing his chin. Jonathan couldn't dismiss the self-mutilation as Tom's way of dealing with his mother's death as he'd been this way, and had been listening to that infernal racket ever since he'd hit puberty. Sylvia even encouraged the boy. Sewing on patches, dying his hair (currently it was jet black with a dip of white at the fringe), strategically damaging his clothes and spray-painting his boots. If this was merely a phase it was a record breaker.

Abigail kneeled in front of the headstone. Only eighteen months separated her from her brother but they looked worlds apart. There was so much of Sylvia in her. So much positivity and light. Not to mention the stubbornness and the at times, frankly mystifying logic. She placed a bouquet at the grave next to a more permanent memorial - a metal rose sculpted by Sylvia herself. Abigail drew a single bloom from the bunch and held it against the sun where the petals glowed a vivid blue.

He watched a tear wend its way down the side of her nose as she placed the flower on top of the headstone and stood back. Jonathan couldn't believe how she'd managed to stay sane. After what she'd witnessed it was astonishing she hadn't ended up in an institution. Several times he'd tried to persuade her to open up and share her feelings regarding the events of that fateful morning but she refused every time and even now, one year later, she had yet to utter a single solitary syllable about the crash.

The crash... The sense of rage welled up again as it had so often over the past year. The rage against the driver of that car...

Finally, the lump pressed at Jonathan's throat. He turned his gaze to his, or rather Sylvia's, delivery van parked by the cemetery gates. The sun flared violently from the windscreen...

*

'Can I open them yet?'

'Not yet. A few more steps... Here. Okay... Open them.' Jonathan took his hands away from Sylvia's eyes.

'What have you done?' she yelped, astonished.

'I bought you a new van,' he said, enjoying his wife's reaction as she performed a circuit of the shiny little combi van.

'We can't afford this!'

Jonathan beamed with pride. 'Oh, yes we can. You are now married to the University's new Head of Astronomy.'

'You got the promotion?' Sylvia wrapped him in an ecstatic hug. 'I knew you would. It was never in doubt Starman.'

Jonathan dangled the keys in front of her eyes. 'With the extra responsibility comes a nice fat bump in wages. Enough for the odd little luxury. They did a fine job on the livery, don't you think?'

Sylvia took the keys. Cheshire cat grin fixed all the way, she traced her fingers along the van, following the loop and flow of every big green letter: *The Green Grocery* - and underneath in a smaller typeface – *Food For Life!* – A big basket brimming with fruit and vegetables adorned the rest of the available space. The same logo decorated the bonnet and the rear doors.

'It's beautiful,' she said finally.

'I don't know about beautiful. Functional, certainly. I only hope it's big enough,' said Jonathan, helping her open the back. Sylvia clambered inside, took Jonathan's hands and pulled him in.

'It's beautiful, functional and plenty big enough. Much like yourself,' Sylvia said, eyes glinting with mischief as she pushed him to the floor. 'And, as your local greengrocer, it is my duty to provide you with your five portions a day.'

'Shouldn't we park up somewhere quieter?' he asked while Sylvia whisked off his tie and unbuttoned his shirt.

Sylvia reached over to close the door. 'Here will do just fine. Don't worry professor, I'll be gentle with you,' she whispered. 'Or we could turn the radio up full blast and just go for it. Test the suspension. What do you say Starman?'

'I am at your mercy. But I have to say, I really don't think I could manage five portions a day.'

Sylvia unfastened her dungarees and peeled her t-shirt over her head. Curls falling over his face, she lowered her smile to meet Jonathan's.

'No harm in trying is there, Professor?'

*

'Happy birthday.'

The first words any of them had said since returning home from the cemetery, were uttered by Tom. Grease-stained pizza boxes and slowly congealing dips littered the dining table while the scent of warm cheese, pepperoni and garlic bread hung in the air. The mood remained sullen. Abigail could only stomach two slices of her margherita. Jonathan thought the packaging looked more appetising in all honesty. Some birthday treat. On the drive home he'd offered to take them to a proper restaurant, somewhere decent, but no-one was in the mood.

Tempted by the crumbs Abigail had thrown out, a sparrow hopped up to the open patio doors where the warmth of the evening sun flooded inside and shadows stretched across the garden beyond.

Tom pulled an envelope from his pocket and pushed it across the table to his sister. Abigail opened it and pulled out a handmade card. She smiled at the suitably demonic greeting - *Have A Hellish Birthday!* The words dripped blood over a drawing of the devil chomping into a gigantic chocolate cake ablaze with candles. On closer inspection, she realised the candles were actually a ring of mutilated partygoers trussed to stakes with their heads on fire. Genuinely impressed she left her seat to hug her brother who, failing to see the need for this second unnecessary physical encounter of the day, shrank deeper into his own.

'It's perfect. Thank you.'

'I would've bought you a present but I'm a bit short just now,' Tom mumbled, eyes fixed on the glass table top.

Abigail returned to her seat pushing the food aside to give the card pride of place. 'I don't need a present. This is more than enough. How did you manage to make the melting flesh on those candles look so real?'

Jonathan leaned forward to his son. 'You could always earn some cash by helping out in the shop for a few hours at the weekends. When I was your age I was out working every weekend and most evenings topping up whatever pocket money my parents gave me,' he said, tapping a finger on the table in emphasis before suddenly feeling deflated by the sound of his own voice. - *When I was your age* – He sounded depressingly like his own father.

'Here we go again,' Tom huffed rising from his chair.

'Oh for the love of God Thomas, will you quit scowling! You want money? Then earn it! Meanwhile, spare me the *life's a bitch* attitude,' Jonathan yelled as Tom left the room. He leaned back with a heavy sigh, shaking his head in time to the petulant rhythm of Tom's feet clumping up the stairs until they disappeared behind the slam of his bedroom door.

'I don't know what to do with him, I really don't.'

'He'd be no good in the shop Dad. He doesn't like dealing with people.'

'I have to say, he's inhabiting the wrong planet if he doesn't like dealing with people. Is there anything he does like?'

'He loves his music.'

'*Music*? That's not *music*. That's a form of sonic torture. The Americans have been using it for years in Guantanamo. Very effective at making the prisoners ears bleed.' Jonathan leaned forward ready to continue his tirade when his eyes fell on a photo of Sylvia fixed to the fridge by an *I Love Balemouth Bay* magnet. He slumped back in his chair and inhaled a deep calming breath. 'Sorry. This isn't what I intended. You shouldn't have to put up with the two of us whining and bitching on your birthday.' He rose from his seat, retrieved a gift-wrapped box from the top of the fridge and handed it to Abigail. 'Happy birthday Abi. Sorry about the wrapping. Bit of a rush job. Got a bit carried away with the sticky tape.'

Abigail gleefully flayed the gift wrap in record time revealing a plain cardboard box. Working her overexcited fingers under the flaps, she tore it open. Her eyes lit up at the prize nestled inside.

'Granddad's radio!' she gasped. She freed the red and gold Bakelite unit and rested it in on her lap.

'I know how much you loved that thing when you were wee,' said Jonathan, buoyed by Abigail's obvious joy. 'Well, it's finally mended. I've had it completely refurbished. New circuit board, transceiver thingy-ma-bob, everything. It can even pick up digital stations now. Think of all the stuff you'll be able to hear when they switch on the new transmitter tomorrow. You'll be able to listen to the whole world with that. You do like it don't you?'

Abigail couldn't take her eyes off the radio. Speechless, she replied instead with an ecstatic nod before rushing to kiss her father on the forehead and bouncing upstairs to her room.

Closing the door behind her, Abigail sat on the edge of her bed holding the precious radio in her hands Stroking the edges, the buttons and the dials. Memories flooded back. Afternoons spent at Granddad's house listening to wild stories of how he used to work as a safari guide in Cameroon where he'd gained the respect and awe of the local tribesmen with his ability to subdue even the most ferocious man-eating lion with his secret, silent, two-tone whistle technique. But this was nothing compared to his career as a top notch consultant for the Venezuelan Space Authority, where he designed and built deep space craft capable of shooting through black holes powered by nothing more than a pair of AA batteries. And then he would boast of being the world's leading breeder of dustbirds. Rare little birds with beaks like vacuum cleaners through which they'd suck up dust, their only source of food. This, apparently, was why his shed was always so spotless and clean. Strangely, Abigail never set eyes on a dustbird. 'Awfie shy and elusive creatures they are,' Granddad would explain.

All of these achievements paled into insignificance when he discovered how to run car engines on a single squirt of lemon juice – a discovery he was forced to keep under wraps once the oil companies learned of its existence. Shell, BP and Total had operatives combing the globe with orders to track him down, *'retire'* him, and destroy the blueprints for his internal lemon combustion engine.

These tales were usually relayed as he tended his allotment, with Abigail helping to plant seeds or reap the harvest, while his wonderful wireless chattered and sang in the background.

She placed the radio on the room's only shelf and switched it on. Twisting and turning the dials proved fruitless. Nothing but frustrating hiss. Abigail's eyes dropped to the cork notice board fixed to the wall below. The only item pinned to the board was a newspaper cutting with the headline:

LOCAL POP HERO TO HIT THE SWITCH

Underneath the headline, two pictures accompanied a short article. The first featured a pouting pop singer by the name of Tony V and the second showed the brand new transmitter perched expectantly on the summit of Thrapsay Hill, an imposing peak which overlooked the entire district. Tony V would be performing his new single as part of the big "switching on ceremony" tomorrow at two p.m. Looking at Tony V's perfect face prompted more memories. Abigail dived under her bed and pulled out an old shoebox covered in stickers and stars. The box contained a host of keepsakes and mementos including;

photos, badges, shells, sea glass, her diary and a beautifully wrapped, unopened gift. She found what she was looking for buried at the bottom of the box; a CD by her one-time favourite band *Hi-Jump!* called *Girl Trouble*.

She smiled at the cover finding it hard to imagine why, just a few short years ago, she dedicated so much time and effort into following every move *Hi-Jump!* made. Slavishly poring through all the glossy teen zines, swooning over every photo spread, adding every TV and radio appearance they made to her YouTube playlist, buying every single calendar, pencil case, t-shirt, badge, key ring, tote bag, mug and all manner of tat. She religiously practiced drawing the band's logo, complete with obligatory exclamation mark, until she could literally do it blindfolded. She knew everything there was to know about each individual member of the quiffsome quartet; everything from how they took their tea, their shoe size, their scariest nightmare to their favourite marsupial. She would hang on their every word as if they were divine nuggets of wisdom retrieved from Mount Sinai itself. Most of the trashy merchandise had long since been binned along with her devotion to *Hi-Jump!ism*. Only this CD remained, tucked inside an age-yellowed magazine cutting proclaiming: *Hi-Jump! Split!* - Heartbreaking news to the then twelve-year-old Abigail.

She studied the bronzed faces of Billy J (milk, two sugars), Bobby Q (size 9½), Tony V (drowning in peanut butter!) and Jake C (wombat). Billy J had always been her favourite, though she could never quite fathom why. Maybe it was because he looked slightly dishevelled compared to the rest and always gave the distinct impression that he wanted to be somewhere else and that somehow he had been chosen for this band by mistake. Bobby was a little too muscly. Jake too plasticky. And Tony's tan tended to make him look like a carrot in a suit. But Tony V was a bona fide local hero. Balemouth Bay born and bred. The first proper star ever to hail from this insignificant backwater. Legend had it that one evening, after a hard day's work in the tourist office, Tony joined his pals for karaoke night at the Marina Hotel where a top London Svengali, who happened to be enjoying a driving holiday through the Highlands, spotted his potential and lured him off to the bright lights with promises of fast money, fast cars and even faster women.

And tomorrow Tony V was coming home to switch on the all new, all singing, all dancing, transmitter. Abigail couldn't wait! She fed the CD into the player and peered out of her window...

Girl take a stand,
Girl give me a hand,
Girl I feel such a clown,
Cos our love's broken down,

So girl push me hard, with all your heart,
Cos I need a Jumpstart, Jumpstart,
Quick smart, You're a work of art,
Jumpstart, Jumpstart,

The cheesy boy band anthem made her toes curl. How could she ever have enjoyed such rot? How could a*nyone* enjoy such rot? Still, it had been fun at the time. And what was so wrong with that? She followed the horizon to the distant hilltop stained orange by the setting sun. And there at the summit stood the transmitter. Waiting...

Closing one eye and squinting through the other, she reached out a hand and held the teeny mast between her forefinger and thumb. So much promise...!

The CD moved on to track two – *Lovegun...*

Release the safety switch,
Pull my trigger,
Take another bullet babe,
From my lovegun,
Lovegun! Lovegun!
It's fully loaded,
And plastic coated,
Lovegun! Lovegun!

That was it. Enough. Jeez! *Plastic coated? Really?* She ejected the disc and tucked it safely back in its jewel case out of harm's way.

Now all she could hear was the muffled throb of metal thudding from Tom's room on the other side of the wall. The vibrations tickled her feet and gently buzzed the objects lining the shelf. A picture slipped from the shelf and fell to the carpet. The thudding stopped after a fist pummelled Tom's door.

'Will you turn that bloody racket down? ... Thank you so much!'

Abigail listened to Jonathan retreating back downstairs. She retrieved the picture. A quick inspection revealed no damage had been done to the framed photo of Abigail aged four, caged in Sylvia's arms. Both smiling. Both happy. Abigail lay down on her bed to take a closer look at the image. She couldn't remember the moment the photograph was taken. Taken presumably, by her dad. It was sunny in the picture, as sunny as today had been. A beach and rocks in the background. Balemouth Bay. Sylvia, her hair tied back in a headscarf, wearing a Joy Division t-shirt, cut-off jeans and pink flip-flops. A jangle of multi-coloured plastic bracelets adorned her wrists. The very same bracelets now encircling Abigail's wrists. She held the picture tight against her chest. The ache squeezing her heart like a sponge, she sank her face into the pillow and let the tears flow.

Waiting patiently on the shelf, the radio continued its soft, unwavering hiss...

*

The rain fizzed from the thick grey duvet smothering the early morning sky. Heavy and persistent. The torrent flowed under the kerbside wheels of Sylvia's van and swirled into the retching throat of an overworked drain.

'*Here comes the sun, doopy doo doo...*' Sylvia sang, hair soaked and matted to her forehead as she battled to make room in the back for one last consignment of grapefruit. 'There. That should do it. Oh, mangoes! Did we get mangoes?'

Adjusting her grip on the clear plastic umbrella which continued to prove itself singularly ineffective against the horizontally propelled rain, Abigail consulted the list she'd jotted in the margin of a newspaper.

'Um... check.'
'Mushrooms?'
'Check.'
'Kiwi fruit?'
'Check.'

'Cherries?'
'Check.'
'Peppers?'
'Check.'
'Bananas?'
Silence.
'Did we get bananas?' Sylvia repeated.

Still no response. Sylvia stepped from the rear of the van and found Abigail, her brow furrowed with concern, staring at the newspaper.

'Abi? What's wrong?'

'Listen to this: "After months of wrangling, planning permission for the new Goodsmart superstore has finally been granted. Work will begin next month to develop the old fish processing factory site on the outskirts of town." – How can they do this? It'll kill our shop!'

Sylvia took the newspaper and quickly skimmed through the story. 'Bloody council! Idiots! I thought they'd put an end to this nonsense once and for all. Just goes to show what a brown envelope stuffed with twelve pieces of silver can do. Don't you worry. We'll show them. We can beat Goodsmart! We might not be able to match their prices but we can certainly kick them squarely in the walnuts when it comes to taste, customer service and quality. Let them peddle their bland flavourless gunk. We'll fight our wee corner to the end. Quality and flavour versus banality and unexpected items in the bagging area. What do you say? Me and you? Ready for the challenge? Ready to banish the bland!'

Abigail remained a little unsure at first until Sylvia's ultra confident smile worked its magic and evaporated all doubt. 'Bring it on!'

'Good! Team Squall versus Goodsmart. I almost feel sorry for them. Besides…' said Sylvia handing back the newspaper and pointing to another article further down the page as she did so. 'I thought you'd be more worried about this story.'

Abigail angled the damp paper under the van's interior light for a closer look:

> *Hi-Jump! Split! Again! After a string of sold out concerts and their greatest hits album 'Jumpcharts!' still in the top ten, the*

boy band sensations who include Balemouth Bay's very own Tony V, have decided to pull the plug on their short-lived comeback. 'It really is the end this time,' the group's chief songwriter Jake C explained. 'Finito. This time it's for good. We all feel it's time to move on and pursue our own projects. It's been a blast!' Rumours continue to persist that this latest split is the result of an ongoing feud between Tony and Jake, rumours which initially surfaced when Tony took to the stage sporting a black eye at the O2 Arena last month. 'All nonsense,' according to Jake. 'We love each other like brothers. Tony's a top man and I wish him all the best in whatever he does next.'

'You used to love them didn't you? I remember all those posters in your room. Plastered all over the walls, the ceiling and over your door…'

'I used to. I didn't even know they'd got back together,' said Abigail with an embarrassed glance at the preening, silver-suited pouts accompanying the article. 'And yes, we do have bananas.'

Sylvia closed the van's rear doors. 'I remember when Bros split. Very nearly rang the Samaritans. But then I found a Milky Bar in the fridge and suddenly the world was a place full of joy and magic once again. Just remember sweetheart boy bands come and boy bands go but chocolate never lets you down. Speaking of which,' Sylvia dipped a hand into her dungarees and handed Abigail a caramel wafer. 'Happy birthday!'

'Thanks. It feels a bit squishy.'

'Sorry. It's been in my pocket a couple of days. Forgot I had it. Stick it in the fridge when you get back. It'll be fine. And don't panic. Your real present is ready and waiting at home. But you must promise me you won't open it till I get back tonight.'

'I promise.'

Sylvia pressed a finger to Abigail's chest. 'And no peeking!'

'No peeking.'

Sylvia studied her daughter's face for a moment, gave a little shake of her head then wrapped Abigail in a tight hug. 'Look at you. You're all grown up! Can you really be sixteen already?' she asked.

'Fraid so.'

Sylvia pulled back with mock surprise on her face, 'But I'm too young to have a sixteen-year-old daughter surely?'

Abigail tapped her toes in the puddle forming at her feet, 'And yet here I am. Getting wet.'

Sylvia pecked Abigail's cheek then ushered her towards the front of the van, 'You're right. Let's get going before the whole town floods.'

As Sylvia hurried to the driver's side, Abigail quickly folded the umbrella. Her fingers gripped the cold wet door handle. The newspaper fell to the kerb. She stooped to pick it up and saw the lights swoop and glitter, bleaching a white arc across the wet black sheen of the tarmac. Brighter and brighter. And then came the sound. An awful nauseating screech knifing clean through her bones and into her marrow... The shriek of the brakes. And the scream... And then a thud. Something hard striking something soft... Her stomach twisted noose tight. The screeching stopped. And the roar of an engine tore through the curtain of rain. An engine anxious to escape. To run and hide. Abigail straightened up. The sodden newspaper rolled and flipped towards the drain. Through the thick baubles of rain collecting on her lashes, she saw the vehicle accelerate through the gloom. Tail lights a smear of red. Too quick to capture details. It looked big. Bigger than the van. The scarlet smudges hared round the sharp bend and the great growling monster vanished leaving a twisting vortex of rain in its wake.

Water dripping from her face, Abigail stared into the space it left behind. Time slowed. And the sky darkened. It seemed to take forever to run to the other side of the van.

Sylvia lay sprawled on the road. A broken star of limbs. Her left leg buckled horribly under her. She still had the van keys clutched in her hand. Sylvia's mouth hung open but no words came. Abigail collapsed to her knees and crawled in close beside her.

'Mum?'

And then she saw the blood leaking from the mushy dent at the back of her head. There was a lump of fleshy pulp trying to leave her skull. It looked like a burst fruit. The crimson river trailed swiftly towards the drain.

'Mum!'

Sylvia's eyes tremored and rolled, struggling to focus. Abigail gently lifted her mother's head on to her lap, one hand cupping the wound's soft warmth while the other pushed the matted hair from her face.

'Mum?'

Sylvia's eyes finally met Abigail's. A wheezing breath clambered from her throat.

'I love...? One love...? I love...? One love...?' she gasped in broken fragments. Her body fell limp. And then the light dimmed from her eyes. Sylvia was gone…

Abigail doubled over her dead mother and screamed until her lungs ached. Until her whole being collapsed in on itself. She became vaguely aware of movement. Of the figures running from the wholesalers and the hands lifting and pulling her away...

*

Abigail woke. Darkness. Beyond the window a smiling moon adorned a clear sky, filled with stars.

'I love...? One love...? I love...? One love...?'

Sylvia's last words spun through her head for the millionth time.

'I love...? One love...? I love...? One love...?'

The inflection in Sylvia's voice haunted Abigail as much as the meaning of the words eluded her. She recalled the anguish in her mother's eyes as she exhaled those four fractured little gasps, remembering how they darted between the raindrops as though desperately seeking the correct answer to some vitally important question. But the answer remained infuriatingly just out of her reach. Abigail had tried so hard to understand the meaning behind those tortured scraps.

'I love...? One love...? I love...? One love...?'

If Sylvia was simply trying to use her final breath to tell Abigail how much she loved her, then why did she sound so unsure? At that moment, when faced with death, had she lost all confidence in the truth of her own feelings? None of it made any sense. Perhaps that was the point. It was nonsensical and therefore the most likely explanation had to be that there was no meaning or purpose behind those words. In all probability they represented nothing more than the workings of a mortally wounded brain picking through its library of scattered thoughts. Sylvia could have been thinking of tennis or squash or Bob Marley or any one of the countless things she loved; sculpture, apple pie and custard, her teddy bear Tansy, thunder storms, Nordic noir, the smell of pipe tobacco ... Anything.

Not that it really mattered. No. The thing that troubled Abigail far more, leaving a permanent bruise on her heart, was the fact she never had time to tell Sylvia how much she loved her in return.

Abigail gradually became aware of the strange noises emanating from her brother's room. It sounded like there was a wild animal trapped in there, jumping around in a frenzied attempt to escape back to the safety of the herd. Bounding and skidding, back and forth across the carpet, bumping against the walls and on to the bed.

Jump... jump... *sliiiiiide*... bump... squeak, creak... jump... jump...

Her stomach grumbled. Hungry. With any luck the remnants of her pizza would still be on the dining table and not in the bin. She swung her legs off the bed and replaced the precious picture of Sylvia and little Abigail back on the shelf.

Stepping out of her room, she crossed the landing and put her ear to Tom's door. She could hear the music rumbling from his headphones as he bounced around; a rapid series of muted *bup bup, bup bup bups...*

Bup bup, bup bup bup, bup bup...

CHAPTER FIVE

SHORT WAVE

Tom span, leapt and twirled like a whirling dervish to the brutal thrash metal of *Spiderglue* exploding from his headphones. Face hot, hair damp with sweat, the music's blistering wrath fired bursts of undiluted rage straight to his core. The fury powered him on and on until his burning limbs could take no more of the frenzy and, hurling his headphones aside, he flopped backwards across his bed exhausted.

Panting hard, his eyes wandered over the pleasingly grotesque posters and album covers papering the entire room. All the legends of heavy, thrash, doom and death metal. All meshing into one amorphous satanic mass thanks to the tears welling in his eyes.

What a tube! Crying like a baby! What for? Get a grip and grow a pair!

He angrily scrubbed the offending tears against the heels of his hands. Vision clear, he stared at the bass guitar standing proudly to attention in the corner. His most prized possession. His passport to a booze-soaked, drug-fuelled, women-saturated future of rock superstardom. It was a beautiful instrument. Made more beautiful by the strategically arranged scorch marks burned into the wood. His headphones continued to buzz on the floor close by, struggling to contain the thunder erupting from the hi-fi.

He leaned back, closed his eyes and listened... *bup bup, bup bup bup...*

*

Tom's amp throbbed in complaint as he thumped out another thunderous bassline. So loud he couldn't hear the fist pounding against his bedroom door. Jonathan stormed in, yanked the lead from the amp, grabbed the bass and swiftly stomped back out before Tom had a chance to fully grasp the Pearl Harbor seriousness of the attack.

'Hey!' he yelped and hurried after his kidnapped instrument. He reached the top of the stairs just in time to see Jonathan reach the bottom and stride on through to the rear of the house. 'Give it back!' Tom clattered down the stairs, nabbed the end of the banister and spun himself through the hall sliding across the tiles on his socks. Jonathan marched through the dining room and into the garden.

'I don't know how many times I've asked you to turn that bloody racket down! I've asked you politely, I've asked you nicely. I've been reasonable. I've been patient. Far too patient. But no more!'

'What d'you think you're doing? Give it back!' Tom demanded, closing the gap but not before Jonathan arrived at the brazier burning merrily in the middle of the lawn.

'This ends now,' said Jonathan. He lifted the bass guitar and dangled it over the hungry flames licking at the brazier's blackened lip.

Tom skidded to a halt both hands raised in surrender. 'No! Don't! Mum, tell him!'

Sylvia snipped the last unruly strand from the cotoneaster and calmly entered the fray.

'Jonathan, give the guitar back,' she said as the smoke curled around the strings and slithered along the neck.

Jonathan stood his ground, 'No. I've told him time and time again but he simply will not listen. I just have to accept that you cannot reason with the unreasonable.'

Tom dared to take another step closer, 'You're the unreasonable one, not me!'

'You see? He won't be happy until he's ruptured all our ear drums with this bloody thing!'

Sylvia placed her gloved hands on her hips and fixed Jonathan with a searching - *Who's the biggest kid here?* - stare. 'He just gets lost in his music sometimes and forgets everything else around him. Much like you do when you're gazing at your stars.'

'Music? That racket isn't music,' scoffed Jonathan, guitar starting to weigh heavy in his grip. 'Simply Red, Phil Collins, Dire Straits. *That's* music. Not that headbanging thrash, bash, crash, smash, or whatever they call it this week, metal nonsense of his!'

Sylvia glared at her husband in disbelief. 'Phil Collins? *Seriously?*'

Tom folded his arms defiantly. 'Go on then Dad. Burn it. See if I care. I can always get another one. Burn it! I dare you!' Tom's bravado evaporated the instant Jonathan dipped the bass closer to the flames. 'No! Please! Don't!'

'Aye! Please do! Do the whole street a favour!'

Sylvia turned to face the debate's latest contributor, their neighbour Mr Studley. A retired tobacconist, Mr Studley was a tall, rake thin man with a nose that forever seemed to be stuck in other people's business. Taking a break from tending his precious roses, he pointed his beak over the fence towards the smouldering guitar. His colourless mouth twisted in delight. Picking up her secateurs Sylvia approached Mr Studley and greeted him with the widest of smiles. Smile fixed all the way, she reached across the fence and lopped the head off his finest floribunda. Before he could splutter a syllable of complaint she opened the blades to another fine specimen and threatened it with the same fate.

'Thank you for your input George but I'm sure we can sort this out ourselves.'

Sour faced, Mr Studley took the hint and slunk off to prune the less vulnerable blooms on the far side of his garden. One problem solved, Sylvia collected a watering can, crossed the lawn to Jonathan and poured the contents into the brazier. A great plume of smoke engulfed her husband as the flames coughed and spat. She took the guitar from his raised arm leaving him standing there like the Statue of Liberty minus her stolen torch.

'You,' said Sylvia prodding him in the belly. 'Inside. Put the kettle on.' Jonathan sniffed and plodded back to the house. Sylvia turned to Tom. 'And you, in the workshop. Now please!'

Fearing a telling off Tom sloped inside the ivy covered outbuilding overlooking the rear of the garden. He sat sulkily on the bench surrounded by his mother's tools and sculptures. Some complete, some works in progress, and some no more than nascent heaps of raw material. Sylvia shut the door, flicked on the light and handed the guitar to Tom. He scoured the bass from every angle anxiously checking for signs of damage.

'Is he really my dad? You can tell me if he's not. I really won't mind?' he asked petulantly.

Sylvia, perched beside him. 'Give your old man a break will you, Tom?'

'Why should I? You saw what he tried to do. Look! The lacquer's blistered!' he wailed.

'Oh come on, it doesn't look too bad. Believe me, he didn't mean to do any damage. Not really.'

Tom picked off a flake of scorched varnish with a thumbnail and showed it to her. 'How can you say that? Looked like he meant it to me.'

'Listen, if he really wanted to, he could've dumped your guitar straight in the fire and walked away. This was your dad's stupid way of trying to grab your attention. The only reason it touched the fire at all was because he forgot how heavy the thing is. I'll admit he came across like a teething toddler with anger management issues but nevertheless, you have to agree he does have a point. You do play loud. Very loud.'

'Metal is loud!' Tom frowned. 'That's whole idea! What does he expect?'

'All he expects is a wee bit of consideration.'

'He never shows me any.'

'Are you sure about that?' Sylvia asked, looking him straight in the eye.

'Positive.'

'Okay, let me get this straight. You're absolutely positive your dad has never shown you any consideration whatsoever, is that correct?'

'Correct. Never.'

'Interesting,' said Sylvia. 'And here was me thinking you had an excellent memory. The best in the family. Looks like I was wrong doesn't it?'

'What d'you mean? There's nothing wrong with my memory.'

'Then remind me Tom, who bought you that guitar?'

Wilting under his mother's burning gaze Tom took a sudden interest in the guitar's tuning heads, all four apparently required some urgent tweaking.

'Tom?'

'He did,' Tom reluctantly admitted.

'And who bought you the amp to go with it?'

Tom squirmed. 'He did. But...'

'But nothing. I know it seems ridiculous but not everyone appreciates the finer points of thrash metal. You've seen his CD collection. It's an A to Z of tedium. Sad to say but music's just not his thing. Remember, he likes to spend his time quietly looking at the stars whereas one day you, if you keep practicing, will *be* a star.'

Tom's chest puffed with pride. 'D'you really think so?'

Sylvia ruffled the boy's hair. 'I know so. You already stand out from the crowd. Who else plays a fire damaged bass? Pretty cool for a metal band.'

Tom inspected his guitar in a new light. 'I suppose. Could use some more burn marks though.'

Sylvia leaned across her workbench, fired up a blowtorch and passed it to a wide-eyed Tom. 'Agreed. We need to make it look like it's been plucked from the jaws of hell.'

'But like you said, I need to practice and to do that, I need to play loud.'

'Then we'll get the workshop soundproofed for you. After which you can turn your amp all the way to eleven and rock like a screaming feedback demon for all I care. Meanwhile, get used to wearing these.' Sylvia pinged a pair of headphones over his ears. She stood back smiling while Tom set to work with the flame, eagerly adding a fresh latticework of scorch marks to his guitar.

*

Abigail watched Tom through the inch-wide gap in his bedroom door. He looked so sad. Lost in another world, her brother had been staring blankly at his guitar for minutes now. She wanted to talk to him. To see if he needed a sympathetic ear or even a hug but knew he'd zip up tighter than a scallop if she dared try. An abrupt shiver and Tom escaped his trance. He picked up his charred guitar, plugged in his headphones and started to practice, the strings producing a barely audible thrum. He was good though. No denying it. Not that she understood the whole metal thing.

Abigail closed his door and moved on down the hall.

'Abi! Come and have a look.' She looked up to see Jonathan poking his head through the loft hatch. 'Come on. Conditions are perfect!' he beckoned sounding a little on the tipsy side.

Abigail lowered the ladder and climbed up to the dimly lit roof space. The loft was Jonathan's pride and joy. His bolt-hole. Fully converted, floor panels laid, the rafters boarded and plastered. Every square inch decorated with glorious astronomical charts and atlases of the planets and moons. And at the centre of it all, his telescope, sleek and beautiful, its lens aimed through the skylight.

Jonathan swilled the glass of red in his hand, took a sip then poured one for his guest.

'It's a lucky night,' he said. 'You can see it clear as a bell. Look for yourself.'

Abigail put her eye to the telescope and saw something wonderful. A planet, still small in the viewfinder but with its rings clearly visible.

'Saturn!'

Jonathan nodded happily. 'I must have looked at it a thousand times but it never loses its power. Never.'

'It's so beautiful. How far away is it?'

Jonathan dribbled the last of the Rioja into his glass. 'At the moment? About seven hundred and ninety-four million miles away. Give or take.'

'Wow!' Abigail marvelled at the impossibly distant world gently quivering like a marble in a tiny hula hoop. 'How long would it take to get there?' she asked.

'Ah well, that depends on the size and mass of your rocket and what route you take. You could for example, speed things up with a helping hand from Jupiter's gravitational pull. For instance, it took Voyager One a little over three years to get there,' Jonathan explained sitting cross-legged on the floor to gain a better view of the wonder on Abigail's face.

'Three years...!' she whispered in astonishment.

'Travelling at the speed of light you could theoretically be there in under two hours. Imagine! Two hours! How pure dead brilliant would that be! Never mind a weekend break in Paris, let's go to Saturn!'

Abigail took her eye away just long enough to share a smile and sample the wine before gazing back to the majestic planet. Her head swam with the distances and the times involved. Saturn suddenly seemed such a lonely world. So far away. Stupidly so. Lonely and empty. A place where no-one has and probably never will visit. She couldn't bear the thought of it being so alone in all that endless darkness, in all that endless cold. With no-one there to admire its undeniable beauty and wonder.

'Two hours to reach Saturn? Is that all?' she asked.

'A mere blink of an eye when you consider that if we wanted to pay a visit to Polaris for example, even at the speed of light it would take us four hundred and thirty years to get there. We'd need to locate a wormhole to make that journey even remotely practich, praccy, pracatiball... possible,' Jonathan stuttered suppressing a burp.

So stupidly far away...

Unreachable...

Yet there it was, right in front of her eyes. Calling to her... daring her to come closer. To reach out and take it in the palm of her hand...

'So if Polaris were to explode right now, we wouldn't see it happen for another four hundred and thirty years?'

'Mind-bending isn't it?'

'Wow... four hundred and thirty *years*... And if Saturn is only two hours away at light speed... How far away is Polaris? I can't work it out.'

'Good grief. That'd be a difficult enough question when I'm sober...' Jonathan puffed his cheeks and rubbed his eyes while the numbers rattled through his brain. 'Six times four hundred and thirty...' he muttered, face creased in concentration. Problem solved he cheerfully raised his glass to toast the solution. 'Two thousand five hundred and eighty trillion miles!... Give or take.'

'*Trillions*... It doesn't seem possible,' Abigail whispered still enthralled by the minutely quaking jewel locked inside its bracelet. 'So when I look through here, I'm actually looking back in time?'

So stupidly far away...

Jonathan drained his glass and shook the bottle. Empty. 'Looking through a telescope is as close as you'll ever get to travelling in a time machine.'

Abigail's heart ached a little. 'Do you think we'll ever be able to travel at the speed of light or even faster? Fast enough to go back in time?'

'I don't believe so. Even if science cracked all the myriad theoretical problems the costs involved in turning the theory into a practicky, praciball... reality, would bankrupt the entire planet.'

'That's a shame. It would be nice to go back. Even for just a short visit,' she said joining her dad on the floor. Abigail shared some of her wine into Jonathan's grateful glass and together they settled back to enjoy the stars framed in the skylight.

'Do you think there's anyone up there looking down on us right now?' she asked.

'No. The International Space Station passed by twenty minutes ago.'

'I wasn't thinking about the space station.'

Jonathan scrunched his face as though the wine had suddenly developed a bitter aftertaste. One eye shut, he squinted drunkenly at Abigail. 'I know exactly what you're thinking Abi and I thought you'd grown out of all that God, angels and souls nonsense. I blame your Aunt. God bothering numpty. Never should have allowed Gemma to babysit for you kids. Shoes and feet have soles, nothing else... Apart from socks I suppose.'

'I don't understand how someone who spends so much time looking at all the wonders of the universe can think like that,' said Abigail with a note of disappointment.

'I've hardly looked at *all* the wonders of the universe Abigail. What I've studied probably equates to taking pinch of sand from Balemouth beach. And just because something is beautiful or wonderful isn't proof of some divine hand at work any more than something rotten or disfigured has some evil intent lurking behind it.'

'I don't believe in a bearded old man sitting on a white fluffy cloud any more than you do but there must be *something* behind all this.' Abigail waved a hand to the skylight.

'Such as?'

'Something... I don't know. Something *more*. Do you not think so?'

'No, I don't.'

'So when we die that's it, we literally have nothing to look forward to?'

'Precisely. Our bodies break down into their constituent parts. Dust and ashes. Elements and atoms. Nothing more,' said Jonathan stifling another belch. He saw the sadness and frustration cloud his daughter's eyes. 'I'm sorry. There was no need to be so blunt. But that's the danger of looking through a telescope. Where one person sees romance the other sees physics. I wish I could see what you see sometimes Abi honestly I do, and yes, I wish I could go back in time and change things but... I can't. It really is just me, you and Tom now.'

'I know,' Abigail sighed.

'We'll make it work, I promise. Things will be good again. Guaranteed. Or your money back.' He smiled plaintively. 'Meanwhile, let me raise a toast to the single most important thing in the universe right now.' Jonathan clinked his glass against Abigail's. 'Happy birthday Abigail.'

She rested her head against his shoulder, looked up to the rectangle of sky and concentrated on the brightest star until her eyes began to flood.

So stupidly far away...

CHAPTER SIX

VERY HIGH FREQUENCY

Notes of birdsong flurried in through the open window. The song repeated then flew away. A thin spear of honeyed light slicing under the skirt of the venetian blind, glinted against the radio on the shelf. Its speaker issued a soft spool of white noise. No louder than Abigail's measured breathing. She formed a sleeping S under the thin cotton sheet. Duvet long since tossed to the floor. Too warm on such a muggy night.

A shrill bullying siren kicked everything else aside. Abigail groaned, flopped out an arm and slapped the alarm clock. Rubbing her eyes, she caught the light needling from the radio's shiny dials and remembered with a thrill...

Yes! It's transmitter day! The big Switch On!

Quick shower. Then to the wardrobe. She swiftly swiped hanger after hanger along the rail. What to wear? Something to catch Tony V's eye? The red gypsy number? The polka dot blouse? The denim dungarees? How about the skinny-fit jeans and the tie-dyed tee?

Lifting the jeans free she suddenly stopped herself and put them back. *Why in God's name would I want to catch Tony V's eye? What a horrible thought!* - she shivered. Five or six years ago perhaps, when she was too young to realise what a supremely vacuous idiot he was, catching the plastic boy's eye would have been the absolute pinnacle of pre-teen Abigail's existence, but not now. Not today. Tony was merely the tiresome support act to the real star of the show. The transmitter.

She raised the blinds and stared through the window. There it was, a little black thorn poking through the distant hilltop to scratch the sky. Ready and waiting and full of promise. She couldn't wait to see it up close. To be there when it became alive and fired its invisible nets into the air, gathering a rich harvest of music and conversation flowing in from all over the globe. There was something magical about listening to the radio. Something you could never get watching television. Something about lying in bed late at night, listening to someone chatting away in a foreign tongue and not understanding a single word they were saying. And then there were those truly spellbinding moments when she'd twist the tuning dial through the static to come across a new song for the first time, the music making the hairs on her neck stand on end while she waited eagerly for the DJ to tell her who it was she'd just listened to.

Abigail remembered one of Granddad Squall's regular war cries and smiled: '*Take the wheel and set sail on those radio waves, Pookie! Take us on a voyage of discovery!*'

Back to the wardrobe. The lemon dress - *Yes, that'll do* - Ankle length and cool to the breeze. She slipped it over her head and gave herself a twirl in the mirror. A quick messing of her blonde crop, shades on, boots on and then for the door... But a tempting suggestion whispered by the juvenile Ghost of Abigail Past, persuaded her to stop and go back for the *Hi-Jump!* CD. She applied a touch of lipstick. What harm could it do? If she did catch his eye, unintentionally and through no fault of her own, then perhaps Tony V would sign it for her...

*

The entire population of Balemouth Bay seemed to be squeezing aboard the Number 6 bus. Giggling gaggles of teenage girls clutching pictures of Tony V and *Hi-Jump!* formed the bulk of the queue. Abigail attached herself to the end of the line and glanced up at the bridge. No sign of any fruit bombers. No sign of anyone at all. Not surprising as everyone was in this interminable queue. Another breathless duo of fans in *Hi-Jump!* t-shirts ran up behind her.

'I'm gonnae get him to sign ma boobs!' the redhead proclaimed, making her dark haired pal shriek.

'Never!'

'I am! I brought a permanent marker and everything!'

Abigail showed her pass to the flustered driver. 'Keep moving to the back of the bus please!' he barked.

Those standing duly obliged until the precarious line could shuffle no further. Every seat occupied. Every holding strap claimed. Jam-packed. The air rattling with breakneck chatter, dirty laughs and girly squeals all punctuated with disapproving tuts from a few of the town's elders, mortified by the amount of brazen flesh on show.

Abigail found herself pressed up against a fat wedge of a man. The continents of sweat mapped out on his beige shirt and the meaty waft of *Eau de L'Armpit* turned her stomach. His pudgy fingers gripped the handrail while, beneath a beetroot scalp suffering a serious case of deforestation, his eyes roved leisurely across her chest. She managed to retreat a few precious inches catching the attention of a trio of teenyboppers squeezed into the seat next to her. The girl in the middle cast a disparaging frown over Abigail's clothes and hair. Deciding Abigail was no threat, she resumed ogling the *Hi-Jump!* calendar held aloft by her freckly pal in the window seat. All three squealed and cooed as each turn of the month revealed a fresh posse of tanned six-packs, oiled and rippling above strategically unbuttoned trousers. December apparently, every bit as humid and sticky as June. The girl in the middle kissed Jake C's tight shorts setting off a volley of shrieks on either side.

The bus grumbled off with a jerk which sent the line of human dominoes crowding the gangway wobbling backwards. Abigail bumped against the Smelly Man.

'Sorry,' she said, anxious to peel away.

'Nae bother, hen,' he answered, pressing closer. He smiled like a lascivious toad eyeing a juicy bug. Or perhaps he had his eye on the small fly which had taken a liking to Abigail's nose. She blew the pest as hard as she could, sending the insect spiralling into an old dear's candyfloss hair.

Oblivious to the bug struggling to free itself from her bouffant, the old dear carried on gossiping to her equally wizened companion.

'... but it's like I said tae Mary, if you don't gie the boy a firm hand, he'll end up like his faither.'

'Ooh, yer right enough! Whit a terrible man. Wait, hang on a second Lizzie...' The eagle-eyed companion plucked the trespasser from her friend's hair and smeared it into the velour seat. 'Carry on...'

So hot and claustrophobic!

The journey soon became an endurance test. Mile after oven-baked mile of nattering old women and increasingly hysterical girls and now her backside was under attack from the Smelly Man's wandering hand. He did his best to disguise each touch as the unintentional contact of a fellow passenger merely trying to maintain his balance, but after his palm brushed her for the third time, Abigail fixed him with her fiercest glare. Feigning innocence, the Smelly Man suddenly developed a keen interest in the advert over her head...

- Get Buff for The Beach! Join Slim-N-Trim Gym Today! -

The bus suddenly lurched and juddered through a series of potholes leaving Abigail fighting to stay upright. The hand returned. This time the fingers treated themselves to a gentle squeeze.

Saved by the bell. The bus came to a halt triggering a mass of hormonally charged squeals harrying for the door. Abigail patiently allowed everyone in front to vacate their seats. Once she had a clear unobstructed run for the exit, she stamped her boot heel like a jackhammer hard and true into the Smelly Man's foot.

'Oh, I am sorry!' she said with mock apology as the man collapsed into an empty seat nursing his throbbing instep. Eyes shooting daggers at Abigail, his jowly face flared an alarming shade of puce. He opened his mouth ready to spew a stream of profanity but when Abigail made to stamp on his other foot he cowered against the window, pressing his eyes shut.

Stepping out in to the open and blissfully odour free air, she gave the Smelly Man a wave as the bus continued on its merry way. The man scowled at her.

'*Love Bubble! Love Bubble! I will never burst your Love Bubble!*'

Belting out the band's debut classic, a pair of heavily made-up *Hi-Jump!* devotees linked arms and set off towards a dusty dirt track where they merged into a gaudy raucous snake of singing, laughing teens, some accompanied by long-suffering mothers. Teetering in heels clearly not designed for hill walking, the girls lunged onwards eager to overtake as many of their fellow pop pilgrims as they could.

Abigail eyed the prize at the summit. The transmitter. Shiny and new. Making way for a fresh batch of aggressively determined fanatics all wearing skirts hardly longer than the belts holding them up, she joined the path threading through the trees and followed the hordes ever upwards.

*

Tony V paced nervously. Another quick swig from his hip flask. The cherry vodka burned sweetly. Nope. No effect. The nerves jangled as bad as ever. For the umpteenth time he used his little finger to gently edge a gap in the purple velveteen curtains. A gap just wide enough to let him focus on the baying, jostling mob pressed against the barrier protecting the small stage. Stage seemed too grand a term for the circular white dais. Rising merely a foot or two above the plateau surrounding the transmitter compound, it looked like a giant mint. The platform occupied a bald patch of gravel between the transmitter itself and a small, brick maintenance hut marking the end of the access road which ferried him to the hill's summit. Tony remembered playing up here on Thrapsay Hill when he was a kid. He and his little gang would plunder the forest, always on the hunt for rare eggs and the building materials necessary for their wildly ambitious dens, forts and huts. Tony specialised in wonky wigwams which invariably collapsed before the raiding cowboys had a chance to reload their BB guns. Happy days.

He still had a home here in Balemouth Bay. Not just any old home. He owned the handsome Inch Point Lighthouse with its adjoining keeper's cottage. A whitewashed Victorian complex, perched precariously on the spindly promontory which gave the place its name, a mile along the coast from the southern end of town. The perfect sanctuary for when the London mayhem proved too much. Remote. Out of the way. Didn't stop the odd fan from knocking on his door once in a while though. And some of these stalker type fans looked very odd indeed. Psychotically odd...

TONY! TONY! TONY...!

Jeez! It was like watching a pack of rabid hyenas closing in on a kill. He had a vision of the slavering hordes breaching the barrier and dragging him to open ground. Hundreds of clawing fingers unbuckling, unbuttoning, unzipping... Scores of biting mouths... Fangs slicing and dicing... A frenzied blur of painted nails and dental braces shredding his clothes and skin, mauling deep into his flesh to yank out his slimy, slippery organs, and toss his bones in a spray of blood, to the hot blue sky.

He felt his Calvin Kleins begin to stretch...

TONY! TONY! TONY...!

As long as the little maniacs showed the same frantic desire to get their paws on the new single, all would be well. He needed every penny their purses could muster. It was Jake's fault. Jake C. Obvious what the C stood for. Jake the complete C. How dare he take the lion's share of all the *Hi-Jump!* songwriting credits! Which meant the lion's share of the royalties. Bastard! Tony couldn't stomach the smug C endlessly bragging about his fully restored, seventeenth century windmill overlooking the Norfolk Broads. And seeing the place with its smarmy occupant filling every glossy lifestyle mag on the shelves left Tony with no option. Tony had to retaliate... with a lighthouse! Trump that Jake! Except the sense of triumph proved short-lived. Had *OK*, *Hello* or *Heat* deigned to feature his new pad in their hallowed pages? No, the bastards had not. Not so much as a sniff. Christ, he'd virtually had to beg the *Balemouth Courier* to do a spread - if you can call a rubbish black and white photo with a brief paragraph on page twelve under an advert for the local undertakers a spread. A bad omen for sure. The lighthouse had become a voracious money sponge. Endless repair bills; electrics, plumbing, plastering, roofing, a full security upgrade... And the place was a bitch to heat.

The vultures were circling. Everything hinged on this solo venture. The lighthouse, his Maida Vale flat, and his collection of wheels. From the temperamental Triumph Stag to the mighty Hummer. Luckily his dear old mum still lived in Balemouth Bay. She had kept his bedroom exactly as it was the day he left home. A comfort to know that if everything did land butter side down he could crash there if needed. But that scenario had to be an absolute last resort. Every time he heard Jake laugh that aggravating laugh, he wanted to spread his nose across his oh so pretty face. And Jake had been laughing non-stop since he split the band to pursue his annoyingly successful solo career. In comparison, Tony's annoyingly unsuccessful solo career was currently supping a pint of flat Hasbeen Ale in the Last Chance Saloon, while the jukebox played Jake C on a never ending loop. But no more! Time for the phoenix to rise! Tony point blank refused to gift the oily mollusc the opportunity to have the last laugh of all because if he did, well, he would have no option but to kill the C...

TONY! TONY! TONY...!

He looked at the retro, fifties style microphone waiting on its stand in the middle of the mint – the focal point for all those snarling, oestrogen raddled carnivores. Most of them were holding up photos of him and the band. Snippets of songs shrilled out from the shifting hormonally charged hubbub. A bunch right at the front were shrieking *Party Hard* at the top of their lungs:

'*I'm your star attraction!* –

I'm your best course of action! –

Top billing! – God willing! –
We'll be beer swilling! –
So let's Party Hard! – Party Hard –
Let's make this party hard!'
TONY! TONY! TONY!

A bored looking reporter from the local paper and his photographer sidekick covered their ears against this latest brutal chant.

TONY! TONY! TONY!

A duo of seen-it-all-before security beefers patrolled the inner side of the barrier poised and ready to flatten any desperate lunge for the stage.

Tony closed the curtain with a groan. He peered up at the transmitter looming over him. Another mighty swig drained the hip flask dry. Smoothing down his crisp black suit Tony turned to his manager, a greying cube of a man with a London accent husked by a forty-a-day habit and a lifetime spent selling dreams of superstardom for a mere twenty percent.

'This is a farce, Billy. What am I doing here under this bloody ugly chunk of metal?'

'Tony relax. This is ideal. As publicity stunts go this is a corker,' Billy Spink soothed. He tried to take a firm, calming grip of his star's shoulder, but Tony was in no mood for the same old pep talk.

'No Billy! It's utter mince. I'm switching on a transmitter for God's sake. A transmitter! How bloody boring is that? You'll have me opening poxy phone boxes next. Or how about parking meters? Is that what you think of me Billy? Am I the go-to-guy for the opening of dull new public service equipment? Oh, wait! I hear they've got a new electricity substation ready and waiting down at Plockton. Better book me in for that quickly, eh Billy?'

'Tony. Sweet Tony. You're nervous. That's understandable. It's a big week. New single's out. But these are exciting times. We're reaching for the sky, Tony. You're on the up. That's why we're here. The transmitter is symbolic of how your career's going my friend. Stratospheric!'

'Jake isn't doing this kind of crap is he?' Tony growled, emphasising his point by jabbing a thumb into Billy's barrel chest. 'Oh no! He's lording it up because he's number one with that twatty song of his. He's having more success solo than the band ever had!

Why's that Billy? Why is he swanning around bathing in the glory? Hitting the red carpets. Leicester Square premieres. Sold out shows at the O2. He's even been called the new George Michael! *I* want to be the new George Michael. Me! Without the gay stuff obviously.'

Billy Spink finally managed to grasp his protégé long enough to shake some sense into him. 'Listen, forget Jake. He's a flash in the pan. He's only having this success because he got his record out first. I've checked the numbers and all indications are you're gonna kick his garbage off the top spot. You Tony, will be Numero Uno! You're better than him in every department. You've got the looks and with this new material you'll have the kudos to back it up. Your solo career is a much sturdier beast. Built to last. And what better way to launch the new single than here, in your home town, in front of your own people. *Your* people! And playing gigs at altitude Tony, that's always been a winner. It worked for The Beatles on the Apple roof. It worked for U2 on that roof in America. And we're going one better Tony. Never mind roofs. We're on top of a hill my friend!'

Tony shrugged himself free. 'Bollocks to The Beatles and double bollocks to U2,' he griped. 'You're talking ancient history. Music for the hospice generation. I want to be for the *now* generation. Get it!'

'And what better way to show that you, Tony V, are at the cutting edge than by switching on this transmitter. This is state of the art technology. You are spearheading the digital revolution in your home town. The press will lap it up mate.'

'What bloody press? I can only see one photographer out there and I've got a funny feeling I went to school with him.'

'Trust me Tony,' said Billy. 'It matters not a jot how many hacks are here in person. The printing press is dead. The world *will* hear of this. The world will *see* this.'

'And how do you propose to make that happen Billy?'

'With my own little piece of advanced technology, my young Scottish friend.' Nodding in satisfaction at his own cleverness, Billy pulled a camcorder from the inside pocket of his cream linen jacket. He flipped open the viewfinder screen and powered the unit into life. 'I'm gonna film you knocking them dead out there. I'm gonna capture all your classic moves and all their orgasmic jailbait screams in full HD. Then we upload the footage to YouTube, the footage will go viral and you, Tony V, will be an internet sensation. You have the Billy Spink cast iron guarantee on that.'

Tony licked the last trailing drops from the mouth of his hip flask. 'You better be right.'

'Course I'm right.'

A tall grey, gangly man with an equally grey and gangly beard, strode towards them with a beaming smile. Tony shook his outstretched hand. The Mayor's palm felt a little too sticky for his liking.

'Mr T! Beautiful day is it not?' the Mayor gushed.

'Mr *V*. I'm Tony V. Not T.'

The mayor patted his ceremonial chain with a chuckle. 'I'm so glad you're performing for us. Our very own home-grown star! This is such an auspicious day for the town.'

'It's a joy to be here Mr Mayor. There's nowhere else in the world I'd rather be.' Tony's perfect smile slipped the instant he turned his back to take one last peek though the curtains at the increasingly excitable rabble beyond.

*

Abigail arrived at the summit. Finding herself taller than most of the tweenies thronging the barrier, she had a clear view of the makeshift stage and the purple curtain rippling softly in the warm breeze. With no desire to push through the crowd she contented herself with a spot near the treeline.

A newspaper reporter who appeared to be having the worst day of his life sidled past her talking into a voice recorder:

'So here we are on top of Thrapsay Hill waiting for Balemouth's very own Tony V. Local boy made good, making one last desperate attempt to claim his share of the teenybopper market who so adored the super shite and now thankfully defunct Hi-Jump! - and it doesn't get any more desperate than this. Miming his new single to a bunch of gum-chewing pubescents reeking of Clearasil and cheap nail polish, too young to realise that this is a man with all the charisma of a pouting puddle of piss. A man who, if you waved a fiver in his face, would attend the opening of an email.' Content with this summary the reporter clicked his recorder off, lit a cigarette and turned to watch his colleague zooming in on one particularly well endowed barrier hogger.

Abigail's gaze drifted up the latticed structure of the transmitter. Four chunky legs bending to meet at the tower's waist. The tower itself loomed higher and higher overhead. A hundred feet tall. It was an awesome sight. The sun glittered against the satellite dishes adorning its frame like strange silvery fruit. House martins zipped and swooped over the very tip. Higher still, a jet cut a slow white vapour trail through the solid blue. Unbearably hot though it was, Abigail shivered and rubbed the goose pimples rising over her bare arms. *So exciting!* Not long now. The sound of shrieking girls faded and for a moment Abigail imagined she could hear the swish of all those signals firing invisibly through that impossible blue, all rushing to be collected, interpreted and redistributed by that massive steel spike.

'Ladies and gentlemen!' the Mayor bellowed into the microphone rupturing Abigail's reverie. 'At long, long last thanks to this state of the art facility our wee town can now fully embrace the digital age. Now, thanks to this transmitter, every single one of us will be able to enjoy the wonders of digital broadcasting and communications in all their glory. Finally, we find ourselves rowing away from the analogue backwaters to join the rest of the modern world. No more lagging behind. No more fuzzy pictures or crackly sound. This is a new era of clarity and pin sharp resolution. The red buttons on our remote controls will no longer simply turn our televisions off. No! We too can now explore a host of interactive viewing options. Yes! We have finally taken the plunge and dived with both feet into the warm welcoming waters of the twenty-first century and it's one hell of a feeling. So what do you say? How about giving us three hearty, full-throated cheers for Balemouth Bay! Hip hip…!'

The Mayor smiled expectantly but his audience ignored the request and steadfastly upped the volume of their incessant chanting instead.

'*TONY! TONY! TONY! TONY! …*'

Disappointed, the Mayor pocketed his speech. 'Very well. I realise you're not here to see me so, without further ado, let me welcome our very special guest. Yes! It's our own, our *very* own... *Tony T!*'

No-one noticed the Mayor's faux pas as the noise surging across the barrier drowned him out long before he finished the introduction. Resisting the excitable cry from her inner pop geek to dash forward,

Abigail stayed put as the curtains swiped apart prompting a fresh deluge of ear-crunching screams. With a flash of genuine fear in their eyes, the bouncers came perilously close to being overwhelmed by the sheer force of raw teenage desire aimed at Tony V as he moseyed over to the Mayor. The Mayor led him to a big green button mounted on a pedestal. The photographer scurried into action, crouching, stretching and bending in search of the perfect shot to match the singer's flawless teeth and tan.

'It's green for GO people!' Tony yelled pumping one fist in the air while the other whacked the button. Disco lights whirled, span and strobed in sync with the backing track thumping from the PA system. Tony V twirled with a flourish to the centre of the platform.

'Come on! Sing it with me! This is *Bedtime Toy*!'

The bedlam somehow managed to intensify further. Abigail had to smile when the Mayor struggled to find his way back through the curtain while Tony danced and threw shapes tantalisingly out of reach of the hungry, snatching claws. She watched the younger girls all pressing, clutching, screaming, their eyes aflame, desperate to make contact with this preening superficial excuse of a man. And then Abigail realised with certainty; this was not for her. She wanted no part of it. Not anymore. Time to lay the Ghost of Abigail Past to rest.

Good luck to her.

She tapped the nearest girl on the shoulder and offered her *Hi-Jump!* CD. The girl ripped it from her hand without so much as a grunt of thanks. But Abigail didn't mind. The transmitter was finally alive! She walked away from the madness and began her descent. Halfway down the hill she stopped to admire the view of the town and the bay spread out below. The sea and sky merged on the horizon in a shivery burning haze. The water glimmered. Scores of little boats moved to and fro on its mirror-flat surface. The paddlers and sunbathers peppered the blazing sands of Balemouth Bay in tiny coloured dots. Moving inland the rooftops gleamed under the fearsome sunshine. It was a picture postcard scene of warmth and happiness. She traced the familiar topography until she fancied she could see her own bedroom window way beyond the river, beyond the playfields and the meadows. Glinting and waiting. Just like Granddad's radio...

The bus grumbled onwards leaving Abigail alone at the stop under the bridge. She studied her reflection in the bus shelter window. A vision in lemon.

Look at you. All grown up...

'Look at me,' she sighed.

She wiped her mouth smearing the lipstick over the back of her hand. She felt lighter somehow. And the ache bruising at her core eased... if only a little.

'Now!'

The voice came from somewhere over her head. Abigail looked up for the source.

A heavy yellow/green blur smacked her squarely on the crown. The world dimmed and smudged. Snickering laughter and pattering feet trailed off into the distance.

Eyes flittering, Abigail slumped to the ground.

The world darkened further...

And then the lights died completely.

CHAPTER SEVEN

WIRELESS

Silence...

A world of black... split... hesitantly... apart...

Abigail opened her eyes. A big, out of focus, yellow/green lump lay on the ground inches from her face.

So hot... and bright...

She felt the grit under her cheek and a dampness, cooled by the air, at her brow. Lifting her throbbing head, the pineapple became clear. The fruit lay bashed and leaking juice into the paving stones. It smelled sweet.

She became aware of other shapes surrounding the stricken fruit. Lots of colours. Maroon. White. Purple. Black. Orange. Brown... All in pairs. She blinked hard and focused. A circle of shoes. Shoes all around. All those toes pointing towards her; some encased in leather, some bare, some painted...

Silence...

She eased herself into a sitting position and stared up. A forest of anxious faces peered down at her, their mouths fluttering like skittish butterflies. She couldn't hear a word.

The crowd made room as she struggled to her feet. She felt a trickle wend its way down her forehead to the end of her nose. She collected the swelling drip on the tip of a finger.

Blood.

The top of her head felt matted and tacky to the touch. Bashed and leaking. Like the pineapple. Leaking her own red juice. She wanted to laugh but it hurt too much.

A woozy wave coursed through her body. Her legs buckled. Arms sprang out from the forest to prevent her falling again. One face leaned in closer than the rest. A kindly face. Mrs Tully's face. And her cherry red lips split open...

<GOOOALLLL! KANE SCORES! ENGLAND ONE KAZAKHSTAN NIL!...>

The cheers exploding from an army of rapturous football fans rattled Abigail's skull with such shocking violence, she almost fainted again. Frightened and confused, she couldn't understand where the noise was coming from. It was inconceivable that a circle of what amounted to no more than a dozen or so concerned bystanders, could produce such a ruckus. She vigorously wobbled her head hoping to shake it all away.

<TRAFFIC UPDATE: LONG DELAYS EXPECTED ON THE M6 AFTER A LORRY SHED ITS LOAD OF LAWNMOWERS JUST PRIOR TO JUNCTION FIFTEEN SOUTHBOUND...>

The voice sounded so excruciatingly *loud*! And crystal clear. As though she were wearing earbuds, expensive earbuds with the volume turned up to the max and rammed tight up against her cochleae. So loud and sore it made her vision quake. Abigail blinked rapidly at the people staring at her. Their faces an array of bewilderment, worry and fear.

Again Mrs Tully hove into view. She tried to say something but her words were obliterated by a sudden, stentorian blast of classical music. Abigail thought she recognised it. Forthright and strident. Tchaikovsky? It didn't matter what the hell it was. It was a symphony of pure pain. So loud and sore! As though the orchestra were literally performing right inside her head. Her ear drums bucked and thrummed to every crashing cymbal. The music raged on behind her smarting, pulsing eyeballs until it became impossible to distinguish one shape from another.

The circle of faces throbbed, melted and bounced in a smear of colour. She slapped her hands against her ears, desperate to make it stop but succeeded only in detonating a tumultuous medley of songs and voices, in every conceivable style, deep into her skull. Each individual radio signal squabbling for supremacy, demanding to be heard. It was an all-out blitzkrieg of sound. A shock and awe invasion of Abigail's headspace. Bombs of noise insisting on her unconditional surrender. Insisting on her full and undivided attention...

<*I WANNA KISS YOUR SWEET SUNSHINE SMILE*><TEMPERATURES WILL CONTINUE TO RISE AS HIGH PRESSURE BUILDS FROM THE WEST><*I WOULD DIVE TO THE DEEPEST DARKEST OoooCEAN*><THE GOVERNMENT NEEDS TO ACT AND THEY NEED TO ACT NOW!><*LITTLE ANGEL WON'T YOU LIGHT MY WAY?*><THE WEST INDIES HAVE WON THE TOSS AND HAVE CHOSEN TO BAT><*BABY BABY I WOULD GIVE EVERYTHING*><HAVE YET TO IDENTIFY THE MUTILATED REMAINS FOUND IN WOODS NEAR BRAINTREE LAST NIGHT><*THEY-HEY-HEY WILL MAKE THIEEEEEVES OF US ALL*><THE ACCEPTANCE OF GOD'S WILL IS AN EXTEMPORANEOUS CONCEPT

WHICH IN THESE MODERN TIMES ONLY SERVES TO REINFORCE THE NOTION><*YOUR HEART IS FULL OF PETALS AND THORNS*><YOUR LISTENING TO HIGHLAND RADIO 94.6FM!>...

Invisible fingers were digging messily into the soft blancmange of Abigail's brain, using the cortex as a tuning dial, twisting and tweaking through every available transmission. Blasts of crunching static separated each blistering snippet of voice or song. The surging volume bulged and pressed against the walls of her skull threatening to crack it like an egg. She threw her head back and forth and from side to side but the churning maelstrom thundered on.

<KISS ME, FEEL ME, SQUEEZE ME BABE, LET ME BE YOUR BEDTIME TOY>

With Tony V's latest bouncing around inside her screaming headspace, Abigail pushed through the crowd and ran off clutching her ears back up the slope towards the shops. The broadcasts flip-flopping with every other step:

<HAVE CALLED A TWENTY-FOUR HOUR STRIKE>< *IT'S SUCH A CRUEL, CRUEL WORLD*><AND ON OUR PANEL TODAY WE HAVE HARPER CROY, AUTHOR OF THE BESTSELLING TREEBONES TRILOGY><*I REMEMBER THE RAIN IN MISSOOOOOURIIIIIIII*>...

Vision distorted by the clamour pistol-whipping her skull, Abigail's palms slapped against the baker's window as she staggered by. Noticing her obvious distress, Henryk leapt over the counter and hurried out. Abigail stumbled headlong into the display of fruit and vegetables outside The Green Grocery and collapsed to the floor under a cascade of citrus. Jonathan rushed from his shop.

'Abi! What's wrong? What's happened? Oh my God she's bleeding. Quickly, call an ambulance!'

Henryk dug out his mobile and hit the nines. Abigail watched him through hazy eyes, his features fuzzy and vibrating in time with the noise punching at her cranium. She felt Jonathan's arms slide around her. She lifted her gaze to see the alarm on his face. Questions fell from his mouth asking her things she couldn't hear.

<...*AND EVERYTHING MARGARET OWNS FITS IN A LITTLE TIN BOX*><WITH THE PROSPECT OF FURTHER JOB LOSSES><*WHEN LIFE HAS DEALT SO MUCH PAIN THAT A*

LITTLE MORE WON'T HURT><ARE THE LATEST WATER COMPANY TO INTRODUCE A HOSEPIPE BAN><*I'M GONNA SET YOUR IVORY TOWER ON FIRE, AND WARM MY HANDS AS YOU BURN YOU FILTHY LIAR*><A POLICY WHICH COULD LEAVE THOUSANDS HOMELESS><*I LOST MY NERVE, I SPOKE LIKE A FOOL*><LARGE NUMBERS OF DISEASED CATTLE><*HAPPY WAYS TO SPEND HAPPY DAYS IN A HAPPY PLAAAACE*>...

The tuning mechanism went berserk, slamming each broadcast hard into the next. The flurry of radio signals flowing quicker and louder.

Abigail clung to Jonathan, her pleading eyes fading toward darkness. 'I can't hear you Dad. I can't hear what you're saying. Make it stop. Make this noise stop. Please…'

'Abigail! Abi...!'

'... Abi...'

Blue lights...

Sirens...

So much noise...

... Darkness...

<...THE TIME IS NOW FOUR SIXTEEN><*BOO BOO SHA SHA LA LA BA DING*><OUR QUESTION FOR TODAY: IS THE MONARCHY IN CRISIS?><*HE'S A SMOOTH TALKIN' DEVIL, AIN'T NUTHIN' ON THE LEVEL...*>

Abigail opened her aching eyes. Jonathan looked over her, his face etched with worry as he stroked her hair. Beside him a woman in a green uniform held a syringe. Her mouth fluttered…

<...OR CALL US NOW ON 0500><*YOU GOTTA SHAKE IT, GRIND IT, WORK IT*><HAD TO EVACUATE THEIR HOME AFTER A MASSIVE SINKHOLE><*SHE LIVED IN APARTMENT NUMBER NINE, SCENE OF A VERY PECULIAR CRIME YEAH OH YEAH...*>

Abigail sensed they were all travelling at speed. The space swayed to the left... and then to the right. Flat on her back. It was a bumpy ride. Why was everyone in such a hurry these days? The needle punctured her arm and the sedative flowed into her bloodstream. The signals clamouring in her vastly overcrowded headspace crackled, fizzed and hummed...

<...EXPLODED KILLING SEVENTEEN><*DANCE, DANCE, DANCE, KEEP DANCING, NEVER STOP, NEVER STOP, NEVER STOP DANCING...*>

... And the blissful empty blackness descended like a welcome, smothering blanket...

CHAPTER EIGHT

BANDWIDTH

*Welcome To MetalPedia.org!
Your online resource for all things metal.
Heavy, Death, Thrash or Nu,
It's all here just for you!*

Now let's ROCK!!!!!!!!

Search Results For:
The UnNamed.

THE UNNAMED:

The UnNamed are a thrash metal band from Balemouth Bay, Wester Ross, Scotland.
Formed by drummer Portia Wills (AKA Wizz) and her then lover vocalist Rick Chambers, the group were soon joined by guitarist Kris Grint but it wasn't until the supremely gifted bass player Tom Squall completed the line-up after answering an ad in the local paper, that the band truly unleashed their potential.

After surviving an early scare when Wills and Chambers' romance came to an abrupt end, The UnNamed grew in strength and perfected their trademark Devil's Fury sound; a monolith of noise built around a fast technical style supplemented by complex arrangements and howling feedback harmonics, all made possible thanks to Squall's extraordinary talent on the bass. The group's lyrics focus mainly on death, the empty despair of youth and (thanks to Wizz's insistence) feminism...

With four completed songs in their repertoire and a fifth approaching completion, plus two nearly sold out shows at the not quite 100 capacity Balemouth Youth Club, it's surely only a matter of time before The UnNamed find themselves at the centre of a multi-million-pound bidding war involving every major record label on the planet. With the awesome Tom Squall at their core the band are certain to enjoy a career littered with platinum albums, sell-out world tours, universal critical acclaim and an endless stream of obliging groupies...

'Tom! Wakey, wakey!'

Tom's obliging groupies disappeared in a blink. Arms folded across her snare, Wizz stared at him impatiently.

'Eh? Sorry,' he muttered adjusting the guitar strap across his shoulder.

'Okay people. From the top.' Wizz clacked her sticks, 'One! Two! Three! FOUR!'

The music howled like an agonised banshee in her death throes. The thrill of its rage filled Tom to the marrow. This was what he lived for. His fingers worked his bass in perfect unison with Wizz as she pounded and thrashed her kit, her blue and pink hair and flailing limbs a mere blur. Kris the guitarist had the distortion whacked up to the max, his wrist whisking a mesh of furious chords. And fronting this beautiful chaos, growling menacingly into the mic, stood Rick. The singer couldn't play an instrument to save his life but he sure knew how to handle a microphone and make it surrender to that meaty voice of his. Tom thought he sounded a bit like Bruce Dickinson which was meant to be a compliment but Rick took it as an insult. In Rick's world Iron Maiden performed Pussy Metal. A bunch of wimps compared to Megadeth or Rammstein. These were Rick's ultimate heroes. He wanted his band to sound like them. No, he wanted his band to sound even *heavier* than them.

And what a sound! Who needed drugs? This was the perfect high. Pure metal! So loud! He placed a foot on his battered second hand amp feeling it buzz wildly against the bassline underpinning the whole blissful surge of energy. He found himself staring at the strange regular growths covering the walls. Block after block of grey spongy spikes separated by deep pits, advancing upwards until they completely colonised the ceiling. They reminded him of massive egg cartons. Soundproofing. Installed as promised by his mother to stop the neighbours complaining. Tom still found himself amazed at how effective it was. He'd stepped outside once, while the others thrashed at full volume, and stood in the garden with the door shut. Hardly a murmur could be heard coming from within.

Thinking of Sylvia his eyes wandered across the area that was once his mother's workshop. Her old tools still stacked under the scorched tables and benches. The same tools she used to weld, melt and shape her sculptures. It was a perfect space, comfortably large enough for the band to rehearse, which they did several times a week and had done for nearly two years. Tom watched his bandmates with growing pride. They were good. No doubt about it. Tight, aggressive and fierce. They had their own songs now. Four complete, one almost ready and two more sketchy ideas in the works. Gone were the tedious yet crucial days spent learning and perfecting cover versions of Metallica and the like.

If only they could settle on a name. One on which they all agreed. Something punchy. Something to set them apart. Something to make people sit up and take notice. A mission statement. So far they'd been through half a dozen or more. All suffering from varying degrees of cheesiness or worse: The Balemouth Behemoths, Bodybag Raiders, Arterial Spray (dropped when a quick Google revealed another band had already nicked the name), The Stab Wounds, Viscera Etcetera, Putrefaction Action – none unanimously agreed on and all eventually dropped.

Now they were simply The UnNamed – 'It'll have to do until something better comes along,' Wizz had said. Wizz the Elder, the oldest of the group at nearly eighteen just ahead of Rick at seventeen and a half. Kris was a full year younger. And taking up the baby baton was Tom, sixteen next month.

However, Tom was not the youngest person currently in the room. He returned his attention to the pretty Goth girl sat on a stool watching them perform. She looked fantastic. Ripped tights, bulky boots, jet black hair, deep blue eyes lined kohl-black, black gypsy skirt, fingerless lace gloves and a tired old leather jacket. Black of course. But for some unknown reason Susannah, two months younger than Tom, was plainly depressed. And this was no Goth affectation. Normally she'd be thrashing around in front of them like a spinning top gone mental, smiling and whooping. But now she just sat there glumly tapping one mega-buckled boot.

The song *Meal Ticket To Insanity* ended in a screeching flourish of feedback.

'Yeah!' Wizz grinned, hair matted with sweat. 'Me and you,' she jabbed a stick at Tom. 'The rhythm section by which all others should be judged. Ace!'

Tom smiled and downed tools with the others, apart from Kris who, ever the perfectionist, methodically set about tuning his cherry black Schecter Hellraiser.

Rick nodded thoughtfully, 'Agreed. Tighter than Kris's G-string.'

'Ah, the old G-string gag,' Kris sighed. 'Someone take me to A and E. I think my sides have split.'

Rick snatched a crumpled sheet of paper and a pen from the floor. 'I need to have another go at these lyrics. They still need work.'

'Rick, they're fine,' said Wizz, grabbing one of the beers Tom was handing out. 'Nobody can make out a bloody word you're singing anyway. It's just noise. A bloody wonderful noise mind you. You could be singing the Spotify terms and conditions for all anyone would know and it'd still sound bloody great!'

'I suppose,' said Rick, happy to accept the praise. 'Didn't stop you making me alter *Satanic Bitch Blues* though did it?'

'The word "bitch" is banned. End of. All sexist terms are banned as you well know. There's enough rampant misogyny in the music business as it is. It's our job, no it's our *duty* to help redress the gender balance, especially in metal.'

'I have no idea what any of that meant but I totally agree with you,' said Rick.

A wise man, thought Tom. Always a good idea to agree with Wizz. The androgynous sticksmith had biceps of high-tensile steel. She possessed the kind of upper arm strength that could arm-wrestle them all at the same time. And win. Comfortably.

'What did you think sis'?' Rick asked turning to Susannah. 'Is this new song the best yet? Are we the mutt's nuts or what?'

'Heard worse,' she shrugged.

Wizz cracked open her can. 'What's up Susie girl? You've had a face on all day,'

'Nothing. I guess I just have a naturally miserable face.'

'Nope. Not having that,' Wizz insisted. 'Kris here has a naturally miserable face, not you. So come on? What's happened?'

'I don't want to talk about it.'

'The Morton brothers stole her phone and some money.'

Susannah glared at her older brother. 'Thanks Rick! What did I just say?'

'Why didn't you tell us Rick?' Wizz asked, firing a scowl at the singer.

'Because she made me promise not to tell anyone.'

'And thanks very much for breaking that promise,' Susannah sulked.

'Did you tell the police?' Tom asked, handing her a beer.

Susannah's scowl softened as she looked up at him. 'No. What's the point?'

'How much money did they take?' asked Wizz.

'Not a lot. Twenty pounds I think. Not bothered about the money. The phone was a present from Mum and Dad. Proper swish it was.'

'I can't believe you didn't tell us Rick,' Wizz frowned, prodding him with both drumsticks.

'Like I said, she made me promise not to talk about it,' he protested.

'Yes, I didn't want to talk about it and now *everyone's* talking about it!'

'Sorry sis' but isn't it good to talk about it? Get it out in the open?'

'No,' concluded Susannah firmly.

Wizz angrily bashed a cymbal. 'Those wee bastards! Why doesn't someone sort those tumshies out once and for all? Aren't they the ones that put your sister in hospital Tom?'

'Think so, but there's no real proof.'

'No proof? Who else could it have been? I'm surprised you haven't given those wee turds the gubbin' they deserve,' Wizz argued.

Uncomfortable at being the target of so many stares, Tom suddenly found the information printed on the rear of his beer can truly fascinating ... *Please drink responsibly...* The guilt grew as cold as the aluminium in his hand. Why hadn't he gone after them? They had hospitalised his own sister and he'd done nothing. He wasn't scared of the Mortons. Not really. Except maybe the oldest one, Jamie. He was positively unhinged. Tom hadn't even gone to visit his sister in hospital. Why? She was his flesh and blood. She was family. Or what was left of it. Didn't that count for anything? Abigail would have visited him in a flash. But they were different. He wasn't like her. What *was* she like? He didn't really know. Didn't really know his own sister. And whose fault was that? Did he even care? Did he even care what happened to his own sister?

'Tom's not the type to go gubbin' people. He's like me. He's a lover not a fighter. Is that not right Tom?' Rick said, raising his can.

Avoid alcohol if pregnant or trying to conceive...

'Trust me Rick, I wouldn't rely on your skills as a lover either,' Wizz smirked.

'Is that right? Never heard you complain. Besides, there's three of them don't forget.'

'And there's four of us isn't there?' Wizz countered. 'All I know is, if it were my sister I'd track 'em down and jam these sticks right up their jacksies!'

Tom winced at the sight of Wizz ramming her sticks deep and hard into an imaginary posterior.

'Wizz, you are one exceptionally scary female,' Rick conceded. 'But you're right. We should teach those retards a lesson. We should be like avenging demons from hell!'

'Aye, like avenging hell spawn,' Wizz agreed.

'Aye. Hell spawn avengers... Wait!' Rick suddenly stood, sloshing a little beer on to the concrete floor. 'That's a great name for the band! Hell Spawn Avengers. What d'you reckon?'

'Liking it,' grinned Wizz. 'Tom?'

Tom nodded his approval. 'It's good. Really good. It would look pretty swish on posters and T-shirts.'

'Bloody right it would. Motion carried!' said Rick clacking cans in celebration with Wizz and Tom. 'Right. We need to set up a website. Plus: Facebook, Twitter, Instagram and Pinterest accounts. Everything. Hey Susie, you're good at all that stuff. I'm putting you in charge of our online footprint. In fact, how do you fancy being our PR?'

'Okay,' said Susannah.

'We are no mere thrash metal band. We are Hell Spawn Avengers!' Wizz cried in triumph. She turned to the guitarist. 'Hey Kris! We are now called Hell Spawn Avengers! Cool or what?'

Kris continued to slide through the scales, fine-tuning his strings. 'Nice one.' Unhappy with the A-string he gave the tuning key a little tweak. A tweak too far. The string snapped. 'Oh bloody arse-wank! Not again. Poxy cock-splash!'

Tom couldn't help but laugh and even Susannah succumbed, breaking out one of her finest showstopper smiles. Their eyes met and Tom's heart bounced...

*

Welcome To MetalPedia.org!
Your online resource for all things metal.
Heavy, Death, Thrash or Nu,
It's all here just for you!

Now let's ROCK!!!!!!!!

Search Results For:
Hell Spawn Avengers.

HELL SPAWN AVENGERS:

Hell Spawn Avengers are a thrash metal band from Balemouth Bay, Wester Ross, Scotland.
Formed by drummer Portia Wills (AKA Wizz) and her then lover vocalist Rick Chambers, the group were soon joined by guitarist Kris Grint but it wasn't until the ultra brilliant bass player Tom Squall completed the line-up after answering an ad in the local paper that the band truly unleashed their potential...

CHAPTER NINE

INTERFERENCE

Jonathan Squall rubbed his aching back. The twisty route from Balemouth Bay to the big city lights took a pinch over an hour to drive on a good day. His spine twinged in complaint at having endured the ride half a dozen times in the forty-eight hours or so since Abigail collapsed. A quick assessment at Balemouth Health Centre concluded that Abigail required the kind of specialist treatment available at only one location in the Highlands: Raigmore Hospital, Inverness. He knew the route well enough. His old commute to the University.

'Look at these scans Mr Squall. I don't know about you but I've never seen anything like it.'

Jonathan stared at a pair of images attached to the wall mounted light box in front of him. Brain scans apparently. Blobs of colour and shadow. The tall wiry consultant stabbed at them with her biro as she attempted to outline the situation as if giving a lecture to a class of one.

'The one on the left is from a typical brain. Unremarkable I'm sure you'd agree. These red patches reveal normal levels of activity. Now, look at the one on the right - your daughter's. The entire brain is lit up. Every region from the medial posterior of the occipital lobe, all the way through to the anterior orbital gyrus of the frontal lobes. Extraordinary! Heaven only knows what's going on in there. Even under heavy sedation her mind is racing like a runaway train. Look here at the temporal lobe. Her primary auditory cortex in particular is busier than a hive of bees on a performance related pay scale. And all because she was hit on the head with a pineapple you say?'

Jonathan adjusted the duffel bag weighing heavily on his shoulder. 'That's right. And I swear if I ever get my hands on those bloody thugs I'll string them up by their primary genital lobes.'

'Quite so.'

'Jonathan! How is she?'

They turned away from the scans to see a middle-aged woman bustling towards them, her face furrowed with concern. Jonathan's heart sank. Gemma Hadley. Fussy, forceful and formidable. A soft shell with a hard core. Seeing her now, he instantly regretted informing her of Abigail's misfortune but he'd been duty bound. She was family after all. And if he hadn't told her, and Gemma had found out from another source, she would've made absolutely sure he'd never hear the end of it. This was a woman who knew how to hold a grudge.

'I'm still trying to establish that with the consultant Gemma.'

'Is this your wife?' the consultant asked cheerily. She offered Gemma her hand, an offer Gemma pointedly declined.

'I'm his sister-in-law. Are you taking good care of my niece? Is this hospital even *capable* of taking good care of my niece? Shouldn't she be somewhere better? Somewhere more suited to treating cases of this kind? And if you don't mind my saying so, you look a little on the young side. Do you have the experience to handle potentially serious head injuries?'

The consultant tilted her nose upwards. 'Your niece is in good hands.'

'I should certainly hope so.' Gemma turned to Jonathan changing her tone from stone to silk. 'How are you Jonathan? Are you coping? My word you look bedraggled. And no wonder with all this stress. If there's anything you need, all you have to do is ask. You're not alone. I'm here now. Anything at all. Ask.'

Jonathan stepped away to look through one of the windows lining the ICU where, on the other side of the glass, he saw Abigail lying in the room's only bed. She had sensors attached to her head feeding data into a monitor by her side and an intravenous catheter feeding fluids into her arm. Her red glazed eyes remained fixed on the ceiling. 'Is she in pain?'

The consultant moved beside him folding her arms. 'No, we've taken care of that. Has she managed to say anything to you since the incident?'

'She told me her head was full of noise. She said it was so loud it felt like her head was going to burst. Since then she's said nothing. Nothing coherent anyway. She sings to herself every now and then, just the odd line mind you. That's when she isn't muttering weird things about the weather or traffic congestion on the A9.'

Not content to remain on the sidelines, Gemma pressed between them. 'That can't be right! Be straight with us doctor, how serious is this? How worried should we be? She will recover from this won't she?'

Jonathan bristled at the supposedly comforting hand she placed on his shoulder.

'There are a few tests we need to perform,' the consultant answered, deliberately addressing Jonathan. 'Meanwhile, it may be beneficial if perhaps you could bring something in to remind her of home. Something she enjoys.'

'Would it be all right to leave this at her bedside?' He freed Abigail's radio from the duffel bag and showed it to the consultant.

'I don't see why not.'

Jonathan entered Abigail's room and quietly approached the bed. After carefully placing the radio on the small bedside cabinet, he bent over to rest a kiss on her forehead. Without so much as a flicker, her eyes stayed fixed on the ceiling.

'Here's your radio Abi,' he whispered. 'I've put fresh batteries in it so you can take it outside when you feel better. You're going to be fine sweetheart. I promise. All you need is a little rest and you'll be right as rain.'

Gemma stood over them. 'She's an angel isn't she? Come on now. Let her rest. Look at those dark circles under your eyes. You could use a decent sleep yourself.'

Too tired to resist. Jonathan allowed Gemma to coax him away. The moment he turned from the bed after one last despairing look at his daughter, Gemma quickly and discreetly tapped Abigail sharply on the brow. Gemma stared at her niece, suspicion burning in her narrowed eyes. Nothing. Abigail didn't flinch.

Abigail continued to focus on the white light blazing overhead long after the big blurry faces had melted away. Her vision pulsed and swirled in kaleidoscopic blobs of shifting hues while the scrunching snarl continued to chew up her headspace.

The radio sat at her side. Shiny, new and ...
Silent...

*

The rain spattered in great slow motion globs, exploding against the tarmac in a glittery dance of watery bombardments. Wave after wave. Jittery puddles, pounded and strafed. Thousands and thousands and thousands of raindrop missiles... A never ending barrage laying siege to the oil black ground and the cold damp air... The fizzing hiss and gurgle of the downpour flooded the storm drain in a wet, noisy tumult...

Until the screech came.

Slow and distant at first. Resonating somewhere beyond the veil of rain. Growing louder and louder until... a mighty thud... cut the noise and replaced it with an awful silence...

Until the scream came.

A brief song of agony. Of someone knowing they have reached their end. And the flood washed a thin tendril of red towards the drain. Then the redness invaded everything. Even the rain. Blood drops, drips and drains...

Her voice...

'I love...? One love...? I love...? One love...?'

*

Jonathan watched the steam rise from the plate Gemma laid in front of him. Roast potatoes, peas, carrots and a slab of meat. Tom, seated on the opposite side of the dining table, received an identical plate. Gemma plonked herself down between the two of them with her own generous helping.

'This is nice isn't it? Sitting down to a good meal with my two favourite men,' she smiled. 'We should do this more often. Plenty of gravy for everyone so help yourselves and dig in.'

'Thank you,' said Tom, taking the gravy boat and drowning his meat in a thick brown slurry.

Jonathan wasn't hungry. Instead, he poured what was left of the Merlot into his glass. He still couldn't quite figure out how Gemma had managed to invite herself back to Balemouth with him. His powers of dissuasion were clearly on the wane. He watched the last drip leave the bottle to ripple the surface of the little red pond. He found himself transfixed by Tom's mouth as it worked on a piece of beef too pink for Jonathan's liking.

'What's that on your lip?'

Tom stopped chewing and returned his father's bleary stare.

'A piercing.'

'*Another* piercing,' Jonathan corrected.

'Yes. *Another* piercing,' Tom confirmed.

'Looks smart. Suits you,' chirped Gemma.

'Thank you.'

'There's nothing smart about self-mutilation Gemma.'

Tom put his cutlery down and folded his arms. 'Here it comes.'

'And look at the state of your jacket. Looks like it's been attacked by a giant cheese grater. Could it be any tattier?'

'It's supposed to look like that! It's distressed!'

'I'm not bloody surprised. I'm distressed just looking at it.'

'I mean it's distressed leather. It's fashionable. Not that you'd know anything about that,' Tom railed.

'Oh, Jonathan he's fifteen. It's what they do. Rebellion,' said Gemma.

'Rebellion, huh? That won't wash when he starts looking for a job. Like it or not, if you want a job in this day and age, you have to conform. Rebels need not apply. No-one wants to employ a pincushion.'

'I don't need a job. I've got the band,' said Tom, watching his dad raise the wine to his scornful mouth.

'Have you any idea how many other rubbish teenage bands are out there? All dreaming the same ridiculous dream? For God's sake man, give it up. It's not going to happen.'

'How do you know? You've never bothered to listen to us play!'

'Play? You don't play your instruments. You bludgeon them!' slurred Jonathan.

Tom scowled, lifted his plate and headed upstairs to eat his dinner in peace. Jonathan offered a little *bye-bye* wave to the empty doorway.

'What?' he asked, noticing Gemma shaking her head and frowning at him. Dropping her napkin next to her plate, she left the table to follow her nephew.

She knocked briskly on his bedroom door. 'Tom? May I come in?'

'I s'pose.'

She entered to find him busily eating at his computer desk. Gemma perched herself on the edge of his crumpled bed. Her eyes roved across the disturbing walls with their galleries of flayed demonic entities and young women in imminent danger of being devoured by equally satanic ogres. That's if they didn't die of exposure first, clothed as they were in some type of medieval lingerie; all iron bras and steel knickers.

The floor was an entirely different kind of hell. Stricken socks and boxer shorts seeking rescue from an ocean of crumpled paper, tissues, fluff and hair. *Has this carpet ever been vacuumed?* It would take an industrial strength vacuum to tackle this sea of teenage detritus...

'I like your room. It's nice... cosy,' she offered, scrabbling for some kind of compliment.

'S'okay,' he mumbled.

'Don't take any notice of your dad. He's tired. And I suspect, between you and me, he may be a mite drunk,' she smiled, patting Tom on the knee.

'But he's forever having a go at me. Why can't he just leave me alone?'

'I know, I know. He's always been a bit, shall we say, quick to criticise and slow to praise. But I think we should give him the benefit of the doubt for the moment. He's worried about your sister. You must be upset about Abigail as well, aren't you?'

Tom swallowed, glanced at his aunt and nodded.

'Yes of course you are. We all are. But I imagine you more than anyone. Brother and sisters. That's a bond that can never be broken. You must be very close to your sister.' Gemma waited for Tom to respond. He offered another nod. 'It's okay I'm not expecting you to suddenly open up and be all slushy or anything like that. Sometimes it's better to keep our thoughts to ourselves.'

Tom shifted in his seat feeling decidedly awkward.

'Do you and Abigail talk to each other? Confide in each other?' she persisted.

'Not much.'

'Has she ever talked to you about your mum's accident?' Tom shook his head. 'Really? Nothing at all? Have you ever asked her about it?'

'No,' Tom squirmed, now deeply uncomfortable.

'Why not?'

'I don't want to upset her.'

'I see. That's very considerate of you. Still, I'm a bit surprised she hasn't said *anything* to you. I am right? She was *there* wasn't she? When it happened?'

Tom conceded with a nod.

'Then the whole thing seems very odd to me. Surely any normal person would want to share their feelings with someone? Someone they can trust?' mused Gemma. 'I can understand why she wouldn't want to open up to Jonathan. I realise kids are always wary when it comes to telling their parents anything for fear of landing themselves in trouble. But I thought she might be able to trust her own brother with her secrets. She can trust you can't she?'

'Of course she can trust me. She's told me secrets before and I've never told anyone else. But I don't get it? What makes you think she's keeping a secret about Mum's accident?'

'Nothing,' said Gemma, surprised to hear what by Tom's standards, was a full-blown speech. 'I think I'm trying in my own silly way to say that you can talk to me Tom. About anything. Whenever something's bothering you - your dad for example - and you need an ear to bend, you can talk to me. I'm here for you. You're my nephew, my family and I love you.' She leaned forward to rest a hand against his face. Tom blushed warmly to her touch. 'It must be hard trying to say anything to your dad at the moment. I know how stubborn he can be. Is he really always having a go about your appearance?'

'All the time! What's it to do with him what I wear or what I look like?'

'Exactly. Who needs fashion advice from a man who wears shirts like that eh?' she joked finally raising a smile from Tom. 'You leave Jonathan to me. I'll sort him out.' She stuffed a twenty pound note into his hand. 'Your left ear looks a bit bare. Room for another stud I think.'

Tom broke into a grin. 'Thanks!'

Gemma left the room with a parting wink.

Jonathan downed the last of the wine. He stared at his dinner, the steam having long since departed. He jabbed his fork into a soft carrot and let it stand there until gravity worked its magic and slowly pulled the fork against the side of the plate with a soft clink.

Gravity.

He looked at his thickening belly and squeezed. He leaned forward to meet his reflection on the glass table top. He poked his jowls.

Gravity. And age. And wine. A recipe for... For what?

His mind gave up and cursed the empty bottle. Hearing footsteps padding down the stairs he quickly swapped his empty glass for Gemma's plentiful supply.

'Why are you so hard on him?' she asked after taking her seat to cut a demure bite of pink flesh.

Jonathan pinched the bridge of his nose trying to gather his swimming thoughts. 'Because he worries me,' he said eventually.

'He worries you?'

'Yes. He worries me. He's pinning everything on that band of his. His whole future. Everything. What he fails to grasp, no matter how often I tell him, is how hard things are out there. He's a dreamer. And more often than not, dreams tend to be shattered Gemma. But he won't listen. Sylvia knew how to handle him. She always got the balance right. I'm nowhere near as good at this parenting business as she was.'

Gemma placed a sympathetic hand over his. 'Stop punishing yourself. Things have been fiercely difficult. For all of us. Tom's fifteen. He still has so much time to waste on dreams. We don't have that luxury. We don't have time to wait and hope that things will change for the better. Not anymore. Remember, your future matters just as much as his. You need to grab it now before it slips away.'

'I don't want to think about the future,' said Jonathan, tiredly.

'Why don't you sell that silly little shop? Go back to what you really love, Jonathan. Start teaching people about the stars again.'

Jonathan slipped his hand from under her perfectly manicured, shocking pink nails. 'Sell the shop? I can't do that. Sylvia loved that shop. I won't. How can you...? I mean I can't let her... I can't let it go. She'd never forgive me.'

Noting the smudge of pink lipstick on the rim of his glass, Gemma studied him for a moment. His food remained untouched. She glanced over his shoulder to the haphazard collection of pictures and magnets covering the fridge. Pictures of Sylvia, Jonathan and the kids. A display of familial contentment. No room for anyone else.

'Have the police made any progress recently?' she asked, eyes fixed on a snapshot of her sister with little mini versions of Abigail and Tom dressed in ghoulish fancy dress ready to go trick or treating.

'God no. I haven't heard from them in months.'

'And Abigail still can't remember anything? Surely she must know something of use? She must have seen *something*?' Gemma persisted, dissecting another sliver of meat.

'No. She saw the car speed off. That's it. Too fast to read the registration or see what type of car it was. It was chucking it down with rain and understandably, her immediate concern was with her dying mother. You already know all this Gemma. What makes you think she'll suddenly have something new to tell us after all this time?'

'Shock does funny things to people's memories. She may have details tucked away deep inside, details that could be revealed with the right persuasion. Have you considered hypnotherapy?'

'Why on earth would I want to make her relive that nightmare all over again?'

'I understand she's had a traumatic experience,' said Gemma, chewing firmly. 'And everyone quite rightly, has given her all the love, support and attention she could possibly wish for. However, I'm worried that we've all become so used to treating her like a china doll that we're scared to push her. Perhaps when she's better, she ought to be spoken to by someone with a firmer hand. A professional. We deserve to know the truth Jonathan. *I* deserve to know exactly what happened to my sister. Am I wrong?'

'Gemma, she watched her mother *die*. Right in front of her. Can you imagine what that must have been like? Now, if she knows something more, which I doubt, then she'll tell us when she's fit and ready. I won't allow anyone to force her. She's been through enough.'

'You're absolutely right. We'll discuss it later. When she's better. I take it you've finished eating?'

Feeling a spasm in his guts Jonathan pushed his plate out of harm's way. 'Sorry, I can't manage it. My stomach's full of wine.'

Gemma patted the back of his hand. 'Not to worry. I'll put it back in the oven. You'll be hungry later.' She swept up his dinner, fed it into the cooker and, after slapping the door shut, cast a critical eye over the kitchen. 'Look at this place. It's a mess.'

Jonathan craned his neck trying to see what the problem was. 'There's nothing wrong with the place.'

Gemma ran a finger over the top of the fridge and invited Jonathan to study the result. 'Look at this dust! And look at your hob. Thick with grease. The oven looks like it hasn't seen a scouring pad since it left the factory. The worktops are filthy. The toaster is sticky. How did you manage that? Crumbs all over the floor. I'm surprised you don't have mice.'

'Looks fine to me.'

'Typical. You men are never happier than when you're wallowing up to your necks in dirt. Well I won't allow it. I shall have to stay and help out for a few days.'

'That's really not necessary Gemma. We don't have a spare room for a start.'

But Gemma had already dressed for battle. Apron tied round her waist and rubber-gloved hands poised and ready to plunge into the hot suds filling the sink. 'I'll stay in Abigail's room until she comes home.' Seeing Jonathan open his mouth ready to protest she silenced him with one raised yellow finger. 'No arguments. And no need to thank me. We're family. And families must stick together.'

Too weary to argue, Jonathan slumped back in his seat rubbing his aching head.

Abigail's bedroom was small. Poky. Uncomfortably so. But tidy. Surprisingly so. Gemma had fully expected to find the usual teenage adornments and mess but compared to her brother's room, Abigail's was a model of restraint. No pictures on the walls. The carpet looked clean. Very little clutter. And mercifully it didn't have that fusty odour that lingered in Tom's. Bit stuffy though...

She opened the window to let the warm evening air in. The sun gilded the room in gold. From the single shelf displaying a few odds and ends, Gemma picked up the photo of Abigail and Sylvia and examined their happy, self-satisfied faces. Unmoved, she replaced the picture and set her small floral patterned suitcase down on the bed. So far so good. Jonathan and Tom were proving to be putty in her hands.

She opened the small chest of drawers and rummaged through from top to bottom. Brightly coloured T-shirts, pullovers, socks, thick tights, underwear... Nothing but clothes... Disappointing. Abigail's secrets were in this room somewhere. She could sense it. She tugged open the door of the modest built-in wardrobe and slowly flicked through the outfits hanging inside. The girl certainly had an odd dress sense. Far too gaudy for a start. She checked the pockets of a pair of dungarees and searched the motley collection of footwear on the floor, tipping up each shoe. Her hands worked deep into a pair of boots. Nothing... She shut the wardrobe and scanned the room. One last place to check.

Gemma's knees clicked under the strain as she crouched on all fours to peer beneath the bed. Ha! She smiled at the rectangular silhouette almost lost in the shadows, tucked tight up against the skirting boards. She worked her stout frame deeper under the bed grunting and puffing until finally, she grasped the edge of the box and slid it out into the light. Joints creaking, she hoisted herself up, nestled her ample backside on the bed and placed the prize on her lap. The box once contained the boots she'd found in the wardrobe. She lifted the sturdy cardboard lid and uncovered a little treasure trove. The largest item in the box was an unopened gift, wrapped in bright yellow and silver paper, with a matching tag bearing the message: *'Happy 16th Birthday Abi! Your life is ready to sparkle! Love Mum xx.'*

Gemma placed the gift on the pillow and removed a thick wad of photos. Artful pictures of elaborate church doors. Close-up details of handles, tiles and weathered wood. Stained glass. Small boats. Rusting and beached. Cracked walls and gnarled tree bark. A portfolio of saturated colours, pleasing textures and intricate patterns. A batch of family pictures followed. Abigail's life in shorthand. As a baby. As a toddler. Schoolchild. Adolescent. A teenager on the cusp of womanhood. Always in full colour. Sylvia appeared in them more often than not or occasionally Jonathan, depending on which parent was behind the camera. Sometimes a sullen little Tom would be standing next to his older sister pulling a moody face, making it clear he didn't want to have his picture taken.

These were happy memories of a happy family life. And they left Gemma cold. She didn't appear in a single shot. Not that this came as a surprise. She rarely visited the Squall household since she left this stifling wee town a dozen years ago. Not through lack of opportunity. Sylvia had invited her often enough. Every Christmas. Every Summer. Every milestone birthday. Each invitation politely refused, usually with the aid of a little white lie: 'Sorry, I can't. I'm volunteering at the winter soup kitchen... Sorry, I can't. I'm having the kitchen refitted... Sorry, I can't. I've been invited to give a speech at the Bowling Club Gala Dinner.' Each fib delivered without an iota of guilt because she knew Sylvia had an ulterior motive. These invites were merely an excuse for Sylvia to rub her perfect little family with their perfect little lives and their perfect little home right in Gemma's face.

Sylvia had always been a fine actress. She would have been quite at home on stage or screen. Her finest role was that of the caring, loving sister; a role she played to perfection after Gemma's childless marriage disintegrated. Yet somehow her sympathy rang hollow and Gemma could see behind the tender facade that she was secretly gloating. Sylvia relished playing the antithesis to her growing list of failures. No husband. No children. No perfect pictures.

Putting the photographs aside she delved deeper still. A shiny piece of quartz picked from the beach...A perfect clam shell... A piece of green, sea-smoothed glass... A cheap plastic ring... Useless, pointless objects. Symptomatic of a head full of whimsy. Exactly like her mother. And underneath it all... A small black book. Gemma's eyes widened.

Bingo!

She ran a finger over the gold lettering on the cover: *MY DIARY.*

Gemma riffled through the pages until she arrived at the last entry. Immediately below the date, a cutting, snipped from the *Balemouth Courier*, had been neatly glued to the page:

> TRAGEDY ON A835
>
> *Police are appealing for witnesses in relation to a fatal hit and run incident. In the early hours of Wednesday, August 16th, local shopkeeper Sylvia Squall was killed when a vehicle struck her outside McGregor & Sons Wholesale Market on the A835 just south of Strathcanaird. Mrs Squall was rushed to Raigmore Hospital, Inverness where she was pronounced dead on arrival. Anyone with any information should contact DC Ian Orlay of Police Scotland via 101.*

Beneath the cutting Abigail had written the final two words committed to her diary...

She's gone.

CHAPTER TEN

AERIAL

The nurse was busy. Henryk waited patiently and politely stepped aside for those with a more urgent need to see her. The bunch of flowers in his hands, a vivid spray of colour against the institutional magnolia dominating the walls. The wait proved to be a blessing, giving him ample time to rehearse what he wanted to say. It also gave him a chance to cool down. Compared to the fitful heat outside, the air-conditioned hospital was gloriously cool. The hottest summer on record they said. Records tumbling with each passing day. In contrast, last summer was one of the wettest since records began. Henryk wondered why anyone still bothered to listen to those duffers who stubbornly refused to accept global warming was responsible for these meteorological mood swings.

He didn't mind the sun. He tanned easily. And people bought more cakes, buns and ice cream when the sun was out. Takings at the bakery were up twenty-three percent on last summer according to his dad. A sadness fell over him as he imagined his dad's reaction to the news he would inevitably have to give him one day. Henryk had no desire to take on the business after the old man retired. He much preferred fixing things to baking things. Machines were infinitely more fascinating than cream-filled éclairs.

'One day son, all this will be yours,' he remembered his dad laughing as he opened his arms to encompass the shop. 'This is only the start of our empire! Perhaps we could open other shops. Yes! A franchise! Between us we can spread the name Zurawski across the UK like so much jam! Yes. Hard work and Polish grit. Me and you my boy!'

Henryk smiled feeling a tingle where the old man had slapped his back. The smile slipped. Yes, he would have to tell him soon. Once he'd plucked up the courage. Machines not scones. Soldering irons not piping bags. Oil and grease, not butter and...

'Can I help you?'

'Sorry, yes,' said Henryk startled and flustered to find the nurse suddenly at his side. 'I'm looking for Abigail Squall?'

'Oh yes. Poor girl. Yes. Follow me.'

The nurse led Henryk away from the hubbub of concerned relatives and porters ferrying wheelchairs in every direction, through a long corridor and into the Intensive Care Unit. They entered a quiet side room to find Abigail lying rigidly on her back. Her unflinching gaze remained locked on one of the ceiling tiles directly above. Henryk approached the bed, shocked at how red and inflamed her eyes were.

'Is she okay?'

'She's sedated. That's why she looks a bit zonked. The neurologist is still trying to work out exactly what's wrong with her but I'm sure she'll be fine. Won't you sweetheart?' the nurse soothed turning to check the state of the saline drip. Happy all was well, she reached across to administer a lubricating drop into each of Abigail's eyes. The patient blinked the drops away and the stare settled once more. 'Those flowers are lovely. I'll go and put them in some water shall I?' The nurse gathered the blooms and left the room before he could utter his thanks.

Henryk took a seat by the bedside. He considered holding her hand but, worried the act might be misconstrued, decided to play safe. He didn't want her to wake up and think he was taking advantage in any way. He studied Abigail's face closely. Even with all those alarming wires and dots stuck to her head she looked beautiful. He wished he had the guts to tell her so. To tell her how much he loved her face, her hair, her freckles, her voice, the way she moved... everything. And her smile! A smile that made his heart buckle every time he saw it. But there was no hint of a smile now. Her mouth twitched almost imperceptibly once in a while but otherwise stayed set and straight. Why did she have this effect on him? He must have seen thousands, maybe tens of thousands of faces in his lifetime so what was it about this very specific composition of parts that made the whole so beguiling? What was so special about this particular arrangement of eyes, nose, lips, brows and that small mole above her mouth that cast such a spell over him? See? He only had to look at her and his brain rambled on like some tanked up jakey. And now, damn it, he'd completely forgotten what he was going to say.

'Hey Abigail,' he offered eventually. She didn't move. Not a flicker. 'I brought you some flowers. The nurse is going to put them in some water for you. I bought them from Helen and Robert. Shop local, not global, right?' he beamed. 'They send their best wishes by the way. I was going to bring you some fruit, you know? Grapes and stuff. That's what people normally bring to hospitals isn't it? But I wasn't sure if you like fruit. Obviously I know you work in a grocery but just because you sell fruit doesn't mean to say you have to *like* fruit. I work in a bakery but that doesn't mean I'm contractually obliged to like bread, does it? As it happens I do like bread. And cakes. Well, not all types of cake. Or pastries. I don't like macaroons. Way too sweet... Shut up Henryk! Idiot. What are you gabbing on about?'

Cupping his burning face in his hands Henryk sank back in his chair mortified. 'Sorry Abigail. I'm a bit nervous. Why do I always feel like this around you? I can't speak properly. I can't think straight. Even my legs go weird. And look...' he held out a hand, open, flat and trembling uncontrollably, 'I'm actually shaking! It's ridiculous! I'm not normally like this, believe me. Anyway I hope you like the flowers. I have no idea what any of them are to be honest. I wasn't sure which is your favourite so I bought one of each. One of them looks like some sort of giant daisy. Maybe when you're better you'll be able to tell me which one you like best. Then I'll know for next time. Not that there'll be a next time. With you in hospital I mean. Obviously I'd like to buy you flowers again but not because you're ill. Not because you've had a bang on the head. But because you deserve them. Actually you deserve a lot more than flowers. You certainly didn't deserve this. Anyway, you'll be well again soon and that'll be it. No more hospit...' Henryk slapped a palm to his forehead. 'Jeez man! You're babbling again. Button it!'

He sat silently for a while listening to the stuttered rhythm of Abigail's breathing. A small frown troubled her forehead. She looked so vulnerable lying there, like she'd had the life torn out of her. And she was normally so full of life. Henryk couldn't bear seeing her like this. He couldn't bear not being able to fix things. He heard a machine beep softly somewhere over his shoulder. Machines he could fix. Not a problem. But looking at Abigail, broken and lost, he felt so helpless.

He noticed his handiwork on the bedside table. 'I fixed your radio,' he said, as if trying to prove he wasn't completely useless. 'It wasn't too difficult to do. A bit fiddly with the capacitors but it was fun. I enjoyed it. It was your dad's idea. He said you loved that radio. He thought it would make a good birthday present. It used to be your granddad's didn't it? Your dad gave me some money. I honestly didn't expect it but he insisted. Sixty pounds! Way too much. So I was thinking, when you get better, maybe I could take you...'

'There we go!' The nurse breezed back into the room with the flowers crammed into a vase. 'Sorry it took a while. Had to help one of the newbies with an IV.' She placed the flowers next to the radio tweaking the stems and blooms until she was happy they looked their best. 'These really are lovely. Are you her boyfriend?'

'Yes. No! Sorry. I mean I'm her friend. Just a friend. I work in a bakery.' Henryk's face burned a whole new shade of humiliation. Why in God's name had he felt the need to tell the nurse where he worked?

'Oh, that's nice. How come you're not fat? If I worked in a bakery I'd be the size of a whale. No will power you see? All those cakes and tarts wouldn't stand a chance,' she grinned.

'I'd better go. Get well soon Abigail,' said Henryk rising quickly from his chair.

'See you next time. Remember, I'm quite partial to a flapjack,' the nurse winked.

'Okay. Thank you. Bye,' Henryk nodded bashfully and left.

The nurse tucked Abigail's sheets in tight.

'He seems sweet. Bit gawky. But sweet. See what he brought you?' She lifted the flowers over the bed to give Abigail a better view.

Devoured as it was by the scorching turmoil inside Abigail's head, the nurse's voice failed to register. Abigail became aware of a psychedelic smear moving in front of her eyes. Vicious reds, stabbing yellows, bruising blues...

So loud...

So painfully loud...

Colours and noise...

It felt as though her frantic brain was trying to pickaxe an escape route through the back of her eyes. Another swell of radio clatter rose up like a massive white hot lava bubble, primed to explode into a brutal geyser of...

<DIED TODAY IN HER BEVERLEY HILLS HOME><*STAR SIGNS AND BOTTLENECKS, LIPSTICK STAINS AND SHIPWRECKS*><MORE THAN JUST A CHOCOLATE BAR – IT'S TWO CHOCOLATE BARS IN ONE WRAPPER!><*LET ME BE, LET ME BE, LET ME BE YOUR BEDTIME TOY!*>

'Shut up, shut up, shut up.'

Hearing Abigail muttering feverishly, the nurse stopped fussing with the flowers and listened.

'Shut up, shut up, shut up.'

She rested a palm against the deepening frown on Abigail's brow. Hot. Worryingly so.

'Sweetheart you look exhausted. You must try and get some sleep,' she hushed, placing a cold compress over her patient's forehead. In the softest of whispers Abigail began to sing.

'Oh Bobby, Bobby, he loves his rock and roll, look at him go. Bobby, Bobby, he loves his rock and roll...'

The nurse carefully lifted Abigail's head, plumped her pillow and eased her back down. 'We all love a bit of rock and roll sweetheart, but what you really need now is some rest. I'll come back to check on you soon.' The nurse gently closed the door and left what appeared to her, to be a nice quiet room.

<HOT GRIP MY PISTOL WHIP, NON-SLIP, ONE LAST TRIP, LET ME BE YOUR...>

'Shut up Tony. Shut up. Shut up. Shut up.'

Abigail gathered her fists and punched her ears hoping to silence them all with a knock out blow. When that failed she twisted and pulled at the lobes until she came close to tearing the skin. But nothing could prevent another balloon from swelling inside her headspace. Pumped full of radio noise, it strained and grew and stretched until...

<I GOT THE MONDAY BLUES AND THE TUESDAY REDS>
<ENGLAND IN COMMANDING POSITION AS THEY HEAD FOR LUNCH WITH 267 FOR 3><FROM THE MORTAL COIL TO THE BARREN SOIL><A BIG HELLO TO JASON ISAACS><LET ME BE YOUR BEDTIME TOY...>

Grimacing with each fresh, merciless detonation, Abigail pulled herself upright. The pain ratcheted up to a whole new level, forcing tears into her eyes. Turning her head, she saw the gaudy splash of colour fizzing from the flowers on the bedside table. She squinted, trying to make sense of the saturated hues and shifting daubs. Her sight spasmed and pulsed but there, a fixed point amidst the distortion, she recognised a familiar shape. Her precious radio.

She reached a tremulous hand towards its shiny dials and buttons and switched it on. Nothing happened. She wasn't sure why this had come as a surprise or why she'd felt compelled to even try. What made her think she'd be able to hear it above everything else? What made her think the radio would do anything other than add to the pain and the noise? Then again, she was desperate and there was no-one and nothing else to turn to. But there was something. Something deep in the unremitting din. A note of encouragement... She gripped the aerial and pulled it to its full extent.

~ *Abigail Squall Radio at your service! Broadcasting common sense and plain thinking to a world gone pure off its nut!* ~

Stunned, Abigail sat bolt upright. This new voice had hacked through and killed all the other signals stone dead!

~ *No, you're not dreaming. No, you're not delusional. Or mad. No more than usual anyway. This is Abigail Squall Radio taking full command of the airwaves and rendering all others in stupefied silence! No! Don't let go of...* ~

The radio voice vanished the instant Abigail let go of the aerial. Overwhelmed by the torrent of signals splashing back to claim her headspace, she quickly grasped the aerial again. And the sluice gate slammed shut.

~ *Don't let go of my aerial again!* – The radio voice pleaded. ~ *It's the only way I can make myself heard. Think of the aerial as your lifeline. And you don't ever want to let go of your lifeline.* ~

There was something about that voice. Something familiar. Frayed at the edges by a lifetime of smoking, it had a distinctly mischievous quality.

'I know that voice,' said Abigail. 'Who are you?'

~ *I recommend you resist the urge to converse out loud with me. We don't want everyone to think you've got a ticket to ride on the special bus, now do we? And by the way - what in the name of all that's small and furry was the ear punching and lobe twisting about? Think of me as your own personal DJ. Think loud! Think clear! As long as you hold the aerial good and tight I'll hear you Pookie.* ~

Pookie...?

Only one person ever called her Pookie...

'Granddad? Is that you?'

~ *Welcome to the Drive Time Show, Pookie! Any requests?* ~

Abigail's mouth gaped in astonishment. Staring at the radio's speaker, she burst into overjoyed laughter. *Granddad!* A slew of memories jumped forward. Visits to her grandparents' house. Being spoilt rotten by Sandy Squall, the smileyest man she ever knew. She could picture him now. Bald. A big, grey Hemingway beard. Hands like shovels wrapping her in hugs and hoisting her high in the air. High enough for her to touch the ceiling. Safe hands. She remembered the smell of his white woolly jumper. A comforting mix of cigar smoke, cheap aftershave and wood. Granddad was a carpenter. He made some of her favourite toys. All in all, he gave the impression of Santa after a semi-successful stint at Weight Watchers. Abigail was seven the very last time she saw him. That was when the smoking finally caught up with Granddad and asked for the bill...

'But...?' she began, the question hesitant. 'You're dead, Granddad. How can you...?'

~ *No amount of dying is going to stop me from helping my Pookie when she's most in need!* ~

Abigail hugged the radio tightly. 'Is Gran with you?'

~ *Oh no* ~ Granddad's voice dropped an octave. ~ *She broadcasts on Radio Hellfire, 666 Medium Wave. You think you know someone.* ~

'Why? What happened to Gran?' Abigail had fewer memories of Maisie Squall, a tall refined looking woman with a stern face. Maisie and Sandy divorced the year before he passed, but Maisie only managed to outlive her ex-husband by eighteen months. Another Squall killed by smoke.

~ *Let's just say that even old Beelzebub himself has described her behaviour as unacceptable. Depraved woman.* ~

And then another question entered Abigail's head. Her fingers clenched around the aerial and her heart tightened with hope. Could it be possible? Her parched throat struggled to deliver the words.

'What about...? What about...?' But her voice failed.

~ *Your mother?* ~

'Yes.'

~ *She virtually runs this station!* ~

Abigail's soul soared. Taking a deep breath, she tried to calm herself in order to ask the most important question of all.

'Can I speak to her?'

~ *All in good time. Right now we need to get you out of here.* ~

'But shouldn't I stay? The doctors might be able to fix me.'

~ *Never mind that phalanx of bloated goat scrota! They have no intention of actually helping you Pookie. They've given up on you. Haven't got a clue. Not a Scooby Doo. Blind leading the blind. They think you're insane. A Grade-A fruit loop. Beyond help. Lost cause. Hopeless case. Oh sure, they think you're a* fascinating *case. Which is why they want to do some tests. And you know what that means don't you? It means they want to shave your head and write CUT HERE across your napper with a big felt tip pen. And once they've finished drawing that dotted line, that's when they'll power up the Black and Decker, shear off the top of your cranium and ram electrodes into your brain. Not that you'll feel anything because they'll have pumped you so full of chemicals your blood group will read like the periodic table. And they won't stop there, oh no. You don't even want to begin to imagine what will be going through their minds when they snap on the rubber gloves and start poking and prodding your squishy bits. So I suggest you seize the initiative lass! Otherwise you will be doomed to spend the rest of your days sat in the corner of a mental institution, dribbling inanely down the front of your deeply unflattering beige smock. So... Shall we go?* ~

Abigail, more than a little alarmed by the gruesome tableau painted so vividly by Granddad, inspected her gown closely. Not beige, more an anaemic olive. The colour of upset stomachs and cheese mould.

'When shall we go? Now?'

~ *When it gets dark. Meantime, get some rest. Keep a hold of the aerial and I'll wake you when its time. Okay?* ~

'Okay,' Abigail yawned settling down with the radio in her arms.

~ *Sleep tight.* ~

And sleep she did...

*

... Until Granddad gently roused her with a few bars of *Eine Kleine Nachtmusik*.

~ *Wake up sleepyhead. Let's get you out of here.* ~

Abigail sleepily swung her legs from under the sheets and placed her feet on the smoothly cold floor. She felt something tug at her scalp. Keeping the radio tucked under the crook of her arm with one hand curled around the aerial, she peeled away the sticky sensors. The sky beyond the window had lost all trace of daylight.

'How long have I been sleeping?'

~ A few hours. Sorry I couldn't let you have longer but time is of the essence. Ooh, that looks sore! Be careful with that thing Pookie...~

Gritting her teeth, Abigail gingerly withdrew the intravenous drip from her forearm. A bead of blood escaped from the puncture wound left by the needle.

'Where are my clothes?' she asked stripping away the tape and catheter.

~ Don't know. Under the bed? ~

Abigail dropped to her knees and peered underneath. 'My boots are there but nothing else.'

~ Cabinet? Cupboard? ~

Fingers in contact with the aerial at all times Abigail scoured the room, flinging open doors and drawers.

'No! I bet Dad's taken them home to be washed. I can't go out in this!' she wailed trying to tie the cords of her flimsy gown tighter. 'This thing opens up at the back. People will see my behind!'

~ I see your point. Two full moons on one night could attract all kinds of unwanted attention. Don't worry. We'll find something along the way. ~

'That's easy for you to say. Wait a second...' She hesitated, braced herself, then quickly placing the radio on a chair she gripped the bedclothes. The room quivered under the blazing din of transmissions crackling into every synapse. Headspace reaching boiling point, she yanked the sheet free from the bed and wrapped it toga-like around her body. Modesty preserved she snatched the aerial and the noise cooled to zero.

She checked her reflection in the window.

~ I hear high street sheet chic is all the rage this season... And that's not an easy thing for me to say. ~

'It'll have to do for now.'

~ Then let's go. ~

Boots on, Abigail gathered the radio under her arm, crossed to the door and checked the corridor. No movement other than a single moth determinedly attacking one of the strip lights.

~ *I've never understood why moths do that.* ~ Granddad's voice whispered through the radio. ~ *It's not that I expect them to be winning Nobel Prizes for advancing the fields of physics or medicine. Or for sweeping aside the iniquities of neoliberalism with a failsafe, egalitarian, global economic strategy, guaranteed to eradicate poverty and hunger within a generation. I understand their IQs are measured in decimal places. But really? How bloody stupid do you have to be? They're bloody nocturnal for a start. If they love bright light so much why don't they come out during the day and fly for the...* ~

'The coast's clear,' Abigail interrupted, still too blearily exhausted to ponder the folly of the moth. She eased carefully into the passage and hurried onwards through a ward of snores and mutterings. At the end of another corridor she came across a nurse sitting at his station, his nose buried in a TV guide. Abigail swung left and tried to slink away but the nurse looked up when someone suddenly exited Radiology.

~ *Interesting. Notice what he's wearing?* ~ asked Granddad as Abigail crouched deeper into the shadows behind a trolley loaded with bedpans and sick bowls. She watched the tall, dreadlocked radiographer stride past.

'You mean his apron?' Abigail whispered.

~ *Exactly. His lead-lined apron. Ideal for blocking radiation and, I don't doubt, ideal for blocking other harmful transmissions. Catch my drift?* ~

The radiographer greeted the nurse with a wide smile and a peck on the cheek. They exchanged a few jovial words after which the radiographer headed off to the men's room. Abigail seized her opportunity and darted towards the X-ray room. A quick peek through the window revealed no-one else inside. She entered swiftly and headed for the small control booth occupying a corner on the opposite side of the room. Once inside, she stretched behind the operating console to browse the handful of protective aprons hanging from their pegs. Abigail nabbed one.

'Hello? Is it okay if I sit up yet?'

The voice sounded small and muffled but it was enough for Abigail's heart to slam hard on the brakes. Eyes wide with panic she peered though the control booth's window. Beyond the glass, surrounded by shelves and benches hosting a clutter of smaller but no less sinister looking pieces of tech, the menacing hulk of the X-ray machine dominated the room. But there was no sign of movement anywhere.

'Hello? My thumb's gone numb. Is that normal?'

And then she noticed them. A pair of elderly legs and feet, the colour of old paper, lying on the table, frail and vulnerable under the machine's intimidating scrutiny.

Abigail quickly left the booth and gently patted the old man on the arm as she passed.

'Everything's fine. I just need you to keep your eyes closed and lie still just a wee bit longer,' she said.

'Thank you Doctor.'

Abigail jogged to the door. Satisfied the corridor was deserted she left the old man obediently following her instructions.

She dashed to the nearest fire exit, pushed it open and hurried down the stairwell. Another fire door waited at the foot of the stairs. She slammed the crossbar down and left the building. Running on through the hospital car park, Abigail glanced over her shoulder. She half expected the State to have mobilised every agency at its disposal to secure her recapture: MI5, MI6, NCA, GCHQ, SAS, RAF, PC Godwin... But no-one gave chase. No alarms were sounding, no swooping searchlights, no snarling dogs or circling helicopters... Nothing but a herd of sleeping cars and whispering trees.

Taking cover in the shrubbery bordering the car park she allowed herself a moment to enjoy her first lungful of fresh air in what felt like an eternity. The soft breath of a breeze, still warm from the day's unrelenting sun, caressed her face and hair. She inhaled deeply.

~ *No time to hang around Pookie. Plenty of time to savour the sweet taste of freedom later. Now, why don't we give that lead apron a try?* ~

'Okay.' Abigail placed the radio on the ground. The broadcasting world took full advantage, instantly cramming her headspace:

<AND NOW FOR THE SHIPPING FORECAST...>

'Shut up! I'm not at sea!'

<EMPTINESS, HOW DO I ESCAPE THIS EMP-TEEEEE-Ness?>

'Three cream buns and a chocolate teacake should do it. Next stupid question!'

<GET RID OF TROUBLESOME GREY WITH COLOUR-ME-YOUNG!><*RAIN RAIN RAAAAIIIN, CAN'T STOP THE RAAAAIIIN FROM FALLIN'...*>

'Shut up! I'm not going grey and it isn't bloody raining!' Abigail wrapped the lead apron around her head fashioning it into something akin to a makeshift turban. It worked. To a point. Reducing the pandemonium to a gently simmering background chatter. As she bent to collect the radio her sheet slipped off. Shrubs and twigs snagged her hospital gown allowing the breeze to tickle her exposed backside. Flustered, Abigail gathered the sheet and wrapped herself from the shoulders to the knees before securing it with a tight knot at the waist. Picking up the radio she crouched low and scanned the hospital windows to make sure her embarrassing wardrobe malfunction hadn't been spotted.

~ *That was close! Exposed yourself any longer and NASA might've launched a lunar lander just for you!* ~ Granddad chuckled.

'It's not funny! I can't go round like this. Look at me! I look like a demented guru.'

~ *In that case, if anyone asks, tell them you're on a mission from God. Then invite them to join you on your holy quest. Tell them that in order to reach salvation, they will have to forgo all earthly temptations including alcohol, chocolate, Game of Thrones and Facebook. After that I guarantee they will gladly stick their heads inside a nest of angry wasps just to get away from you.* ~

'Stop laughing. This is serious!' Abigail protested, trying hard not to laugh herself.

~ *Sorry Pookie. You're right. How's the apron? Does it work?* ~

Abigail pressed the X-ray proof turban tighter to her scalp. 'It helps. A bit. Useful as a backup I suppose, if I have to let go of you. But what am I going to do now?' She looked beyond the hospital complex towards a sprawling, unfamiliar cityscape dominated at its heart by a castle illuminated in gold. 'Where am I anyway?'

~ *Inverness. You've been here before haven't you?* ~

Yes, she had. Several times. Not enough to know it intimately. Jonathan used to work at the university and Sylvia would bring her here on the occasional shopping trip, or to visit Aunt Gemma after she moved away from Balemouth. But they'd always left before nightfall. This was the nearest major conurbation to Balemouth and the hustle and rush of the place always made her hanker for the space and calm of her little seaside home.

'I don't think I should be doing this. Maybe I should go back.' said Abigail, staring at the open fire exit and feeling suddenly very vulnerable.

~ *No Pookie. Back there lies ever strengthening doses of brain-scramblers followed by a lobotomy for dessert. Surely you've seen One Flew Over The Cuckoo's Nest?* ~

'But I seriously won't get very far looking like this. What do I do Granddad?'

~ *I suggest you seek help from the Salvation Army.* ~

'Be serious Granddad!'

~ *I am being serious. If not the Salvation Army, then Cancer Research or Help The Aged or the British Heart Foundation or Oxfam or Barnardo's. You with me yet?* ~

'You want me to find a charity shop?'

~ *Bullseye!* ~

'But now? In the middle of the night? Why? They'll be shut. And besides, I haven't any money. And even if I did, and even if they were open, they'd never serve me. Not looking like this!'

~ *Pookie, deep breath. Calm... That's it. You're in control now. Remember that. Deep breath. There you go... Okay. Right, as of this moment* you *are the charity case. So trust me, in your current predicament a closed charity shop is precisely what you need.* ~

Abigail spent a little over half an hour carefully nipping in and out of the shadows, avoiding any sign of movement; vehicular or pedestrian. Not that the streets offered up any significant activity to speak of at such a late hour. Abigail encountered more foxes and rodents than people.

Closing in on the River Ness she came across a branch of Oxfam. And Granddad could not resist an ~ *I told you so!* ~ at the sight of the bulging bags clogging up the doorway. Abigail wasted no time. She split open the bin liners and carrier bags until a pool of clothes, books, shoes and CDs spilled around her feet. Picking through the mound of pullovers, skirts, t-shirts, blouses and trousers, she stuffed the more promising items along with the radio into an empty bag and ran off.

The apron began to slip from her head as she ducked down a side road:

<LONDON FTSE DOWN 17 POINTS AT THE CLOSE><*SMOTHER ME IN HONEY COATED KISSES*><HAVE SACKED THEIR MANAGER AFTER ONLY EIGHT GAMES IN CHARGE><*DOO DE DOO DE BIDDLY BOP*><NO WIN NO FEE SO WHAT HAVE YOU GOT TO LOSE?><*YOU'RE THE ITCHY ITCH I CAN NEVER SCRATCHY SCRATCH...*>

The improvised headgear unravelled further. Her headspace buzzed and thrummed while her legs, unused to the exertion, burned in protest. A blister began to plague her foot as she turned another corner and hauled the heavy, awkward bag down a narrow alley. The alley ran behind a row of sleepy houses with postage stamp gardens and on to a footpath of baked earth. Between banks of whin and broom she skirted a broad stagnant pond, its oily surface burnished by the moonlight, before the path opened out onto a large expanse of overgrown wasteland. A tall, poorly maintained fence crowned with barbed wire, encircled the whole area. It looked like a brownfield site earmarked for development which in the meantime had become a fly-tippers paradise. Abigail peered through the latticework. A healthy crop of rusty paint cans had taken root beside a mouldy mattress, its springs and innards bulging out through a great split in its belly. A short distance to the left, a limbless mannequin perched on a mouldering sofa, stared blankly at a stack of tyres while a fox sniffed around the remains of a dead fridge then trotted off deeper into shadows to inspect the burnt-out shell of a Mini.

Abigail followed the perimeter until she came across a ragged hole in the fence. Prising the edges apart she squeezed through and headed straight for the abandoned car. The fox sped off into the darkness. She clambered inside, took off her sheet and used it to cover what remained of the back seat. For the first time since fleeing the hospital she felt safe. Safe enough to change her outfit. Pulling off her boots and throwing off her gown, she plunged her hands into the bag of clothes, quickly sifting through the donations. The lead apron slipped completely from her head. Unhindered, the noise pounced, searing its way into every fold and furrow of her brain:

<OBSERVATION MESSAGE FOR ALL UNITS: WHITE FEMALE RECENTLY MADE OFF FROM RAIGMORE

HOSPITAL. MENTAL HEALTH ISSUES. 17 YEARS OLD. SLIM BUILD. SHORT BLONDE HAIR WEARING GREEN HOSPITAL GOWN><*LET ME BE YOUR BEDTIME TOY, LET ME BE YOUR BEDTIME TOY, LET ME BE...*>

Three pairs of trousers were rejected before she settled on a pair of jeans that were a couple of inches too long but otherwise a decent fit. She turned them up at the ankles and set about selecting a top while the noise made her eyes bounce...

<*LET ME BE YOUR BEDTIME TOY, YOUR BEDTIME TOY, AND I'LL BRING YOU BEDTIME JOY, BEDTIME JOY...*>

Abigail buttoned up a garish pink shirt, tugged on a woollen tank top and hid her blonde shock under a stripy red and black beanie hat. And, to complete the new look, Lady Luck offered up a brand new pair of *Star Wars* socks. R2-D2 and C-3PO were perhaps a tad too big for her blistered feet but, once she'd put her boots back on, her toes were thankful for the extra comfort the Force provided. Hands free at last she held the radio close, secured the lead apron over her head and bedded down on the carpet of unwanted fashion disasters.

~ *Comfortable?* ~

'I think so.'

~ *Good. Now don't you fret. We'll have you back home, back to normal and back up to your usual mischief in no time. Meanwhile, let's see if we can give you a solid night's sleep. You've earned it. Goodnight Pookie.* ~

'Goodnight Granddad.'

Abigail fell asleep. Her fingers loosened their grip on the aerial and the apron gradually unwound from her head. A gently burbling stream of fragmented news bulletins and scattered pop choruses flowed on inside her exhausted head.

*

The stream settled into a steady hiss.

Heavy rain.

A screech. Violent. Sudden. A car trying to stop.

Fails.

The dull thud of metal striking the unwary.

And a scream.

Folding into the steady hiss.
And on the ground.
The red and the clear.
The fast and the slow.
Blood in rain water.
Flowing into the hole and the dark.
'I love...? One love...? I love...? One love...?'
The only words left to say.
Over the fading engine...
There was a number...
The killer had a number.
Black on yellow.
What was it?
What *was* it?...

*

... Thud.
~ *Stop that! You'll hurt yourself!* ~
...Thud.
~ *Abigail! Stop it!* ~

Abigail woke sharply. She blinked, and the lingering images of blood and rain were wiped clean. Her hand hurt. The fingers gripped the aerial so hard her knuckles had blanched bone white. But it wasn't enough to quell the bickering interference of music and voices scratching away at the back of her mind. She tightened her grasp until the skin stretched so taut it threatened to tear.

'Make it stop. Please make this noise stop.'

~ *We will Pookie. But banging your head against the nearest available hard surface is not the most practical approach to solving this problem.* ~

Abigail rubbed the dull ache playing at the side of her head. A little shower of rust rained from her hat.

'I was banging my head?' she asked.

~ *Like a deranged woodpecker. You must've been having a nightmare. And you kept letting go of me. I can't help you if you keep letting go of me.* ~

'Sorry Granddad. I'm not sure anyone can help me. I don't know what to do. I'm so tired. I don't think I can carry on.'

~ *Now listen here you, I will not tolerate that kind of defeatist talk. Not from my Pookie. You never gave up on anything. Not without a fight. Even if you had to resort to the occasional, shall we say, slightly underhand method to achieve what you wanted. Remember the Rubik's Cube I bought for your sixth birthday? You spent ages trying to solve that puzzle but you could only ever manage to complete one side. Remember? Used to drive you mad. So what did you do? Did you give up? No! You peeled off all the coloured stickers then stuck them back on in the right order. Now, there are those that might call that cheating but not me. I call it unorthodox problem solving.* ~

Abigail smiled remembering the moment she handed the completed puzzle to her dad who hadn't witnessed the "unorthodox problem solving". Jonathan, impressed with his little girl's cleverness, hoisted her high on his shoulders. High enough to let her nab a Jaffa cake from the kitchen cupboard as a reward.

'But I genuinely don't know what to do Granddad,' she said, her voice heavy with despair. 'I haven't got a clue where to start. I don't know how to make this noise stop.'

~ *Attack the source of the problem Pookie. The root cause. Then it will stop. It's the only way.* ~

'What do you mean? Attack what source?' asked Abigail. She peered outside. The sun had plucked itself free of the horizon and into a curtain of cloudless blue. Another long hot day in the making.

~ *You must destroy it. Pull it down. Then the noise will stop. And that comes with a Granddad Squall, satisfaction or your money back, guarantee.* ~

A hot air balloon, the colour and shape of a great avocado, drifted leisurely above the city jumble. A short sharp blast of the burners lifted the basket clear of a church spire waiting to pop the pear and spray the rooftops in guacamole.

'The transmitter? Are you talking about pulling down the transmitter? I can't possibly do that by myself.'

~ *Don't fret, we'll find help. But first things first, we need to get out of this town and head for home. They're looking for you. And they're getting warmer.* ~

Bang on cue Abigail spotted a police car pull out of the housing estate to cruise alongside the fence on the far side of the wasteland. She lowered herself out of sight.

~ *And please don't think I'm being critical in any way when I say this, but don't you think you could've chosen something a wee bit less stark staring mental to wear by any chance?* ~ asked the radio.

Now seen in harsh unforgiving daylight Abigail had to concede her outfit did look completely insane. The thighs of her denims were embroidered with big swirling daisies, the flower heads nicely augmented with bursts of golden beads. The jeans took no prisoners in their clash with the eye-throbbing pink shirt but neither could match the itchy wool tank top for sheer hideousness. The thing was adorned from collar to hem with snowflakes and Christmas puds, all surrounding a jolly looking Rudolph. The reindeer's nose protruded from the middle of Abigail's chest in a big red pompom.

~ *Whoever designed that top should be marched to The Hague and tried for crimes against humanity.* ~

'But I needed something warm and nothing else fitted!' Abigail protested, still staring in horror at the festive aberration. A quick rifle through the items scattered over the scorched floor confirmed her lack of options.

~ *Don't worry. You've graduated from demented guru to Santa's nutty little helper. Either way people will give you the widest possible berth so you'll be fine. Now, I'm no mechanic so please feel free to get a second opinion, but I am fairly convinced this car is not roadworthy. And as we are fifty-six miles from home I propose we find some other means of transport.* ~

'But how am I supposed to catch a bus or anything? I don't have any money.'

~ *Better start walking then hadn't we?* ~

'Thanks Granddad.'

~ *You're very welcome.* ~

Abigail dared to peek outside. The police car had gone. Leaving the torched Mini's rusting, wheelless, engineless carcass behind, she hurried for the gap in the fence.

CHAPTER ELEVEN

STATIC

Home time.
The school grounds hummed to a soundtrack of children laughing, playing, gossiping, running...

Tom leaned by the gates trying not to draw attention from the river of blazers and shoulder bags flowing by. A forlorn hope. His studded ears and leather jacket with its gruesome spattering of heavy metal logos attracted every single face. Their expressions ranging from the mildly dubious to outright derision supplemented with an occasional thumbs up. He even received a: *'Liking the look big man. Nice one'.*

Tom ignored them all. Insults and compliments. Instead he gave his full attention to a lad, perhaps a year younger than himself, standing in the middle of the playground bullying a much smaller boy into handing over a few coins. This was Stevie Morton, the youngest of the Morton tribe. Youngest and the least intimidating unless, like this poor sop, you were half his size. Stevie trousered his earnings and sent the boy on his way with a kick up the bum. Snivelling back tears the boy half running, half walking, brushed past Tom on his way out.

Tom took out his phone, scrolled through his Contacts and stopped when he reached SUSANNAH. The new school year provided a rich harvest of unwitting victims and Stevie, eager to exploit this fresh bounty to the full, strolled up behind an acne ridden newbie. With his fingers closing in on the boy's collar, Stevie suddenly let his prey off the hook and fumbled through his pockets instead. He pulled out a phone and pressed it to his ear:

'Ullo?... Ullo...?'

Tom ended the call without a word. He smiled and watched Stevie scowling at the display in his hand. Finding himself alone in the playground, the wannabe gangster pocketed the phone and headed for the gates. Tom tucked himself safely behind a tree. He heard Stevie's lolloping gait scuff by and continue up the hill. He waited a few moments allowing a discreet gap to open up then, with his heart upping tempo, he stepped out and followed the thief.

It didn't take long for Stevie's troublemaking instincts to kick in. Less than a hundred yards from the school he decided to invade a play park and made straight for the slide. Shoving a chubby girl on to her backside he claimed the ladder for himself. Up he climbed thoroughly enjoying the fear his presence had instilled below. One by one the previously carefree kids began to desert the swings, see-saws and monkey bars. The merry-go-round slowly revolved to a squeaky halt.

Stevie reached the summit, plonked his posterior on the steel, folded his arms and slid down, his face set in the same trademark Morton scowl throughout the descent. He got up and stomped back to the ladder, yanking another none-too-bright youngster who'd dared presume it was his turn, clean away from the slide as he did so. Stevie climbed again to repeat the whole joyless ride.

After watching him climb the ladder for a fourth time Tom decided to move in. Stevie slid to the bottom but before he could set off for another go, Tom shoved him against the sun-hot metal and knelt hard on his chest.

The thug wheezed and squirmed. 'Get off me ya spaz!'

One hand clutching Stevie's throat, Tom balled the other into a fist and let it hover with intent over his face.

'Gimme that phone,' demanded Tom, trying to lace his voice with what he hoped was a convincing dose of menace. It worked. Stevie's bravado melted into shameless terror. His nervy fingers searched every pocket until they eventually located the phone. Tom snatched the device, tucked it safely away then raised his fist again.

'Now give me twenty quid!'

Stevie scrabbled through his pockets. 'I've only got a tenner... And one pound fifty-two in change,' he wailed at the paltry sum he'd managed to collect. His eyes quivered when Tom's fist rose higher. 'Honest! Take it!'

Tom took the cash. The kids cheered and applauded. One brave soul yelled; 'Go on! Hit him!'

The vocal support suddenly ended the moment two other lads, both in their late teens entered the arena. Jamie and Ben Morton. Fists clenching. Mouths twitching. Pace quickening. Scowls locked and loaded. Tom didn't like the odds and sprinted off as fast as his chunky, multi-strapped boots would allow.

'I'm gonnae cut you!' he heard Stevie yell, apparently back in full Mr Tough Guy mode thanks to the arrival of his brothers. Tom skidded a sharp left out of the play park and charged downhill towards the school sports fields. He could hear the Mortons chasing. Whatever they lacked in social grace they more than made up for in raw speed. And he didn't doubt for a second that at least one of them had a blade.

Tom raced straight across the football pitch raising the ire of the referee and of all twenty-two girls preparing to kick off. A quick glance over his shoulder showed the Mortons, despite having to dodge a sliding tackle or two, were still closing the gap. Jamie tucked a hand inside his hoodie.

Sweat dripping from his boiling face Tom left the sports fields, sprinted over a small wooden bridge spanning the old mill-house lade and onto a footpath which led him into Balemouth's oldest quarter; a cobbled maze of whitewashed fishermen's cottages and sandstone bungalows. Lactic acid burning his calves and a stitch jabbing deeper and deeper into his side, his pace began to flag with every punishing stride. Unlike the Mortons... still closing in like three relentless Terminators in cheap tracksuits.

Tom veered sharply right. He spotted a postbox ahead. Taking out both his own and Susannah's phone he slotted them into the mouth of the red pillar as he staggered by, a fraction before the Mortons appeared. Lungs shrivelling, he hauled himself into an alleyway and managed to stumble a few more yards before his faltering legs finally convinced him he had absolutely no chance of outrunning the footsteps now clattering up behind.

All or nothing...

Unleashing a crazed war cry Tom stopped, turned and launched at his pursuers with everything he had left in the tank. For a moment, the sight of this screaming kamikaze headbanger ramming into them at full pelt, caught the Mortons off guard. Tom managed to land a fist into Jamie's face and a boot into Ben's groin before the downpour of knuckles and heels completely overwhelmed him. Tom curled himself on the ground doing his best to shield his face from the fury while busy hands turned out his pockets, taking money, mints, tissues...

He heard a small flicking noise.

The blows ceased.

Cupping his traumatised manhood in both hands, Ben slumped to his knees whimpering in agony. 'OOOooohh... AAhheeeee...'

'Do it Jamie. Cut him. Make him bleed,' goaded Stevie.

Tom allowed a sliver of daylight to sneak though his fingers. Enough to see Jamie crouch over him. A drop of blood fell from Jamie's nose... and landed on the small butterfly knife in his hand.

'Where's Stevie's phone? Where's ma brother's phone ya freak? Tell me where his phone is or I'll shank ye!' he snarled, moving the blade to within an inch of Tom's battered face.

'What you waiting for? Slice him. Open his skin,' Stevie hissed.

'Do, do... do it J-Jamie,' Ben stammered breathlessly.

Jamie's fingers stiffened around the knife's handle. 'Looks like you've got some stuff stuck in your ear. D'you want me to cut them oot for ye?' he said, sliding the tip under one of Tom's earrings.

Despite the sweat stinging his eyes, Tom glared defiantly back at him.

'Hey! Get off him!'

Startled by the booming command, Tom broke his stare and turned to see a bulky, bald headed man with an even bulkier mastiff walking through the alley. The dog walker's mighty biceps bulged, straining under the huge effort required to rein in the beast tugging fiercely at its studded, industrial strength leash. Saliva drooled from a mouth crammed with meat shredding, bone splintering teeth. Somewhere behind that man-eating grimace, a growl rumbled forth, filling the alley with murderous intent. Then it barked. The kind of bowel loosening bark that meant serious business. Serious *biting* business. The Mortons fled. The dog walker and his demonic pet chased them out through the alley and into the street beyond.

Tom heaved his pulverised carcass against the wall. He tasted blood. He dabbed his mouth and pulled away his fingers to see the tips stained red. With the adrenaline ebbing, every ache and pain queued up to introduce themselves. Kidneys, spine, shins, hips, stomach, hands, neck... The full anatomy of agony.

Anatomy Of Agony...! That's a bangin' name for a song!... He nodded to himself. With a title like that, the song would need a proper earthquake of a bassline... *Anatomy Of Agony* from the album: *Pathology Of Pain... Brilliant*! - thought Tom. He made a mental note to tell the band later. Nothing like a good thorough beating to provide some much needed inspiration. He started to laugh at the absurdity of it all but quickly stopped when his ribs failed to see the funny side.

The dog walker returned with his hell hound. Judging by the lack of blood smeared on the dog's chops the Mortons appeared to have escaped unharmed.

'You all right son?' he asked. On hearing its master's concerned tone the dog instantly dropped its intention to maul Tom's face into a pound of quality mince and sat on its haunches panting happily. 'Shall I call the police? Those neds need to be stopped and sorted out.'

'No, no, I'm fine,' Tom croaked.

Helping Tom to his feet the dog walker sucked in a breath and winced at the sight of his bruises. 'You don't look fine to me. I think we should get you to a doctor.'

'Honest. I'm good. Looks worse than it is. Thanks a lot for helping me out.'

'No problem son. Where you heading?'

'Home.'

'You want a lift?' the dog walker asked. 'I live just round the corner. Though I really do think we should get someone to take a look at you.'

Tom waved a dismissive hand. 'Thanks. Really. I'll be fine. Just a bit bruised.'

The dog walker remained unconvinced but decided not to push it. 'Right you are. Well, take it easy. I doubt those gutless idiots will be back here any time soon but watch your back just in case, eh?'

'Will do,' Tom assured him.

With a small tug on the lead the dog walker continued on his way. 'So much for a nice relaxing walk, eh Petunia?'

The notice on the postbox stated that the last collection would be at 5:30pm. And bang on cue a Royal Mail van pulled up kerbside. The postman stepped out, opened the rear of his van and took out a mail sack.

'Excuse me?'

'Jeeeesuus, pal!' the postman railed at the youngster, dressed like a mangled crow, who'd suddenly appeared at his side. 'I nearly shat myself there! You shouldn't creep up on people like that! What the hell happened to you? You've got a face like a butcher's shop window.'

'I fell. And I've accidently dropped my mobile phone, sorry, both my mobile phones in the postbox. Any chance you could get them back for me please?'

The postman's eyes narrowed in distrust. '*Both* your mobile phones? You're telling me you've somehow managed to *accidently* drop *two* phones in there?'

'That's right.'

'You havin' a laugh? I can just about imagine how you might possibly, maybe, lose one phone in there. But two? That takes a certain amount of skill.'

Tom shrugged. 'What can I say? I was posting a letter. They were both in my hand at the time. I let go. I'm an eejit. Sorry.'

'Okay, whatever.' The postman sidestepped Tom to unlock the postbox. He sifted through the contents, bagging the mail until sure enough, the phones were located. Eyes narrowing yet further he handed them to Tom.

'Thanks.'

'Nae bother,' the postman frowned, watching Tom limp away. With a shake of his incredulous head he dismissed the whole bizarre episode, locked the postbox, threw the sack in the van and drove off.

After a long, excruciating walk spent continuously recalibrating his pain threshold while constantly looking over his shoulder, Tom finally made it home. The sight of the police car parked outside triggered every internal alarm bell in his belfry. Had the dog walker called the police after all? No, not possible, he had no idea who Tom was let alone where he lived. Had one of the play park kids recognised him and reported Tom for robbing Stevie? No, ironic as that would be it seemed a little far-fetched. The footballers? The referee? The postman? No, no and no. Only one way to find out. He braced himself and stepped inside.

Quietly closing the door behind him he heard voices emanating from the open door of the lounge. Tom crept a few paces along the hall. Opting to remain out of sight, he watched the action unfold through the slit separating the lounge door from the jamb. Pocketbook open on his lap, a young constable occupied the armchair opposite the sofa where Jonathan and Aunt Gemma were seated. Jonathan clutched his despairing head in his hands. Gemma laid a comforting hand on his back.

'I don't believe this. Can things get any worse?' Jonathan aimed the question at the policeman.

'We're doing everything we can sir. Enquiries are ongoing. Every officer has been given her description. I'm sure she'll...'

'Don't you dare say that!' Jonathan snapped, cutting the constable short. 'You can't be sure she'll turn up safe and sound. She's been out all night in nothing but a hospital gown. She'll be freezing. She'll be confused. She's vulnerable. What if someone...?'

Gemma squeezed his shoulder. 'Jonathan the police will find her. You have to trust them. They know what they're doing.'

Jonathan glowered at the policeman. 'Do you? Do you really know what you're doing? My toothbrush is older than you.'

Unfazed by the insult the policeman edged forward in his seat. 'Sir, I'm just trying to...'

'Yes you are trying. You are very trying.' Jonathan grumbled.

'Jonathan!' Gemma squeezed harder. 'There's really no need for that attitude. It isn't helpful. Let the man do his job.'

Jonathan took a deep breath, shut his eyes and pinched the bridge of his nose. He needed a drink. 'Sorry,' he said, looking back at the policeman. 'I'm feeling a mite stressed.'

'Understandable sir. But I believe I can put your mind to rest on one point at least. It would appear she's managed to swap the hospital gown for a warmer change of clothes.'

'Really? How did she manage that?' asked Gemma.

'Our colleagues in Inverness received a call from a taxi driver who claims he passed a female wearing a white sheet and a strange looking hat hanging around the doorway of a charity shop last night. He described her as looking like some kind of weird Buddhist monk. Seems she helped herself to a bag of clothes and ran off. Unfortunately, the driver didn't bother reporting the incident until after his shift.'

'Unbelievable! Why didn't he report it straight away? Didn't he think it suspicious to see a young girl stealing charity donations in the middle of the night?' asked Jonathan, shaking his head in disbelief.

'He didn't think it warranted the police. Hardly crime of the century is it? – his words, not mine. It wasn't until he heard the local radio news mention a girl who'd absconded from the hospital taking her bed sheet with her, that he put two and two together and picked up the phone.'

'We will of course replace those charity donations officer. And the sheet,' assured Gemma, feeling the need to make amends.

'I don't think that'll be necessary madam. But there is more. We had a report early this afternoon from the same Oxfam store. Apparently a young woman dressed in what they described as "bizarre clothes" stole a collection tin from the counter while the staff weren't looking. They checked their CCTV which shows the female taking the tin but strangely, it also shows the same female returning a short while later to put the tin back again while no-one's looking.'

Gemma clutched her face mortified. 'Oh no! No! That's awful. Not Abigail surely?'

'That's what we're attempting to ascertain.'

Jonathan held up a hand, confused. 'Wait. How did they know it was missing at all if no-one saw it being taken or returned?'

'Because the volunteer running the shop was adamant the tin was almost full at the beginning of the day. She was planning to bank the takings at some point this afternoon but when she went to do so, she found the tin empty. That's when she decided to check the CCTV and found the culprit caught on camera. However, when I say the tin was empty, that's not strictly true.' The officer removed a folded piece of paper from his pocketbook before continuing, 'They did find a note inside. And a pen. Inverness faxed me a copy of the note. Do you recognise this handwriting sir?' He unfolded the sheet of paper and handed it to Jonathan.

The note read:

> *Sorry for the inconvenience. I owe you £42.50.*
> *I need the money to get home.*
> *I will pay you back when I get better.*
> *I will also give you a bag of my own clothes which are much better than the ones I took.*
> *But first I need to pull it down.*
> *I also took a pen and this bit of paper which I am returning to you now.*

Jonathan handed the note back. 'That's Abigail's writing.'

The policeman handed him another sheet of A4 featuring an image printed from the shop's CCTV footage. 'I know the quality's not great but could this be Abigail sir?'

Jonathan studied the individual in the shop's doorway. Dark hat, jeans, pink shirt, fussy tank top... *Was that a reindeer?*... Charity tin in hand. Her face partially obscured but enough on show to leave no doubt.

'Yes, that's Abigail,' he confirmed.

Gemma took the picture and looked aghast. 'What *is* she wearing?'

'It's a Christmas jumper,' the policeman answered.

'A Christmas jumper?' Gemma repeated handing the picture back to the officer. 'But it's the middle of summer.'

'As good a time as any to clear out the wardrobe I suppose. And who can blame them for getting rid of that monstrosity,' the policeman smiled trying to lighten the mood but Jonathan's expression showed he was in no mood for levity. 'Anyway, if nothing else it certainly catches the eye, so hopefully it'll make her easier to find.'

'We will of course refund the shop's money and top it up with a further donation. Please give them our heartfelt apologies,' Gemma insisted, clearly embarrassed.

The policeman dismissed the notion with a flick of his hand. 'That's very kind madam but I really wouldn't worry. The missing cash is way down our list of priorities.'

Gemma clipped her purse shut. 'So Abigail's trying to make her way home.'

'It would seem so. Unless she left the note to try and throw us off track. Her description has been circulated to all staff at the Inverness train and bus stations and officers are still there trawling through their CCTV systems to see if she's already passed through, which might take them a while. Mr Squall, on her note she states; "I need to pull it down" - Do you have any idea what she means by that? Pull what down?'

'I haven't the foggiest,' admitted Jonathan. 'In her mental state... who knows?'

'Not a problem. Do you know of any favourite places she likes to visit around here? Places where she likes to escape to when she feels stressed or needs to be alone?'

'Secret hidey-holes you mean?' said Gemma.

'Exactly.'

Jonathan leaned forward. 'Why don't you keep it simple and look *everywhere?*'

'We are sir but it will speed things up if we had a list of priority areas to search first.'

'It might speed things up if you stopped sitting in that chair and started looking for her yourself,' said Jonathan.

Gemma pulled him back. 'Please excuse Jonathan, he's upset and if truth be told, a little tipsy. He doesn't mean to be curt.'

Jonathan turned to his sister-in-law in disbelief. 'Are you actually apologising on my behalf?'

'I'm merely pointing out how upset you are.'

Hearing the floorboards creak in the hall behind him Jonathan leapt to his feet. 'Abi!' The hope died from his eyes when Tom entered the lounge.

'Pleased to see me as usual eh, Dad?' said Tom.

Jonathan's face darkened when he saw the blood and bruises on his son's face. 'What the hell have you been up to?'

'I fell.'

'You fell? You fell several times against the same fist I take it!'

Gemma hurried over and took Tom's head in her hands. 'Oh my God! What happened?'

'He's been fighting,' said Jonathan.

'No I haven't. I fell. Why are the cops here?'

Jonathan pulled Tom away from Gemma. 'Why do you always insist on taking centre stage? Your sister's missing, could be badly hurt or worse but as long as we're all watching you, who cares eh Tom?'

'Tone it down Jonathan! He's just as worried about Abigail as we are. How was he to know she's run away?'

'Please Aunt Gemma, I'm fine.'

'Has Abigail contacted you? Have you seen her? If you know where she is you'd better tell me right now!' Jonathan demanded.

'No! I've no idea where she is. I didn't even know she was missing until I stepped in here.'

'You'd better not be lying to me.'

'I'm not lying!'

Father and son locked eyes. Jonathan blinked first. 'This is impossible,' he wailed. Jonathan stormed through the arch separating the lounge from the dining room and carried on into the back garden. He picked up an empty wine bottle from the patio table and hurled it against the shed. Exhausted, he slumped into a chair smothering his face in his hands.

Realising this would be an appropriate time to make a swift exit, the policeman rose to his feet. 'I can see you have your hands full here so I'd better leave you to it. We'll be in touch,' he added, smiling awkwardly at Gemma.

'Thank you officer.' Gemma showed him out. She watched him drive off then closed the front door. 'Tom! Come here.'

Tom duly appeared. Gemma ushered him into the downstairs toilet where she examined his battle scars, wincing and tutting at every wound she uncovered.

'Men. Honestly. You and your dad are a nightmare. Lucky I'm here to look after you both. Now, let's patch you up. Dear oh dear. What a mess. I hope she's worth it.' Gemma gave Tom a knowing smile before raiding the medicine cabinet for cotton balls, TCP, plasters and bandages.

Tom pulled out Susannah's phone. Happy to find the device unscathed, he took a closer look. It was, as she'd said, proper swish. He smiled. What a ridiculous question! The answer was patently obvious. She was worth every cut, every graze and every last bruise.

*

'Tell us who did it mate and we'll go get 'em. After all we are the Hell Spawn Avengers. It's what we do. We spawn. And we avenge.'

The band had convened in the Squalls' shed ostensibly for a rehearsal but so far Rick, Wizz, Kris and Susannah had spent most of the evening admiring Tom's impressive catalogue of injuries. Tom tried his best to deflect the fuss by ramping up the volume and thudding his bass in the hope the others would get the hint and join in, but he could only manage a few bars at a time before the crippling flashes of pain sparking from his bandaged wrist and split knuckles forced him to stop.

'Listen,' he said, 'I've got a brilliant idea for a new song. It's called Anatomy of...'

Wizz shut him up with a mighty whack on a cymbal. 'Never mind that now,' she said silencing the crash between her thumb and forefinger. 'Tell us who did that to you.'

'No-one did anything. I fell.'

Wizz carefully laid down her sticks on the snare, stepped away from her kit and stood directly in front of Tom. Arms folded she tapped an impatient foot until he deigned to meet her eye.

'I put my sticks down Tom. You do know what that means don't you?' she said.

'No, I'm not sure I do.'

'It means I'm listening Tom. It means I'm listening to you Tom. So, would you like to try again?'

'Try what again?' he asked genuinely confused.

'Try answering my question again, only this time without using the words; "*I fell.*" Capiche?'

'But I did. Fall, that is.'

Scrutinizing him in laser-guided detail, Wizz moved closer still. 'Are you sure about that Bass Boy? I mean it's certainly not difficult to imagine a scenario where a seemingly innocuous fall could result in the kind of injuries normally associated with a pile up on the M8. So let me give it a shot - It's another beautiful day so, like any young outdoor enthusiast, you decided to go for a ramble across the rugged beauty of Knockan Crag nature reserve. But lo! A randy bull recognised you for the shameless little heifer you are. Enticed by your come-to-bed eyes, he chased you all the way to the Glenfinnan Viaduct, where with nowhere left to run, you were confronted with a choice; let the bull pump your exhaust pipe with twenty inches of solid beef passion, or jump. And jump you did. Right on top of a truck delivering a consignment of landmines. The resulting explosion launched you skywards, several hundred feet into the blades of a search and rescue helicopter. Dazed, but hair neatly trimmed, you landed on the West Highland Mainline where the 5:15 to Dingwall travelling at 90 miles per hour bounced you down the tracks all the way to Brora were you woke up several hours later to find yourself having an epileptic fit inside the world's angriest cement mixer...'

Wizz edged nose to studded nose with Tom. 'Can you tell I don't believe you yet Bass Boy? I put my sticks down. Just sayin'.'

Tom's shoulders slumped. 'Please, can we not do this now? This is the one place where I get to chill. I get enough grief from my fascist dad and now my aunt's decided to stay for a few days and she's another brain ache. And is if that wasn't enough, the police are after my bloody sister because she's run away from the loony ward. So, can we please just practice?'

Susannah bounded from her seat to join Tom. 'Abigail's run away?'

'Tom, at some point we need to have a chat about sharing,' Wizz sighed. 'Meanwhile, that's all folks! Practice is cancelled!'

Kris having just donned his guitar to strum his first D of the session rolled his eyes. But Wizz was on a mission and made her intentions clear by yanking the jack from Tom's bass and powering down his amp before he could pluck another note.

'Wizz, wait. Why?' he sputtered.

'Look at you Tom. You're in no fit state to play. How can you concentrate when you're worried about your sister?'

'What else can I do? The music helps take my mind off things. Besides, Abi can look after herself.'

Rick accompanied Wizz and Susannah in the *let's-all-fold-arms-in-front-of-Tom* competition. 'You should be out there looking for her,' he said. 'If it were my sister I'd be out there morning, noon and night until I found her.'

'That's so sweet of you!' Susannah smiled.

'Pleasure sis'.'

'She could be anywhere. I wouldn't know where to start,' said Tom, exasperated. 'The police reckon she's left Inverness and she's heading back here. But like I said she's a bit loopy at the moment so who knows where she could be?'

'Precisely,' said Wizz unfolding her arms in order to hold Tom by the shoulders and thus making it impossible for him to look at anything but her. 'She could be anywhere. She could be in trouble. Which is why we're going to help. Back in the van people! There's a damsel in distress out there!'

With a theatrical sigh Kris placed his guitar back inside its battered, sticker festooned case. 'Rock Gods and seekers of the lost. That's us.'

Feeling somewhat perplexed by the whirlwind speed of events unfolding around him, Tom remained rooted to the spot while the others filed out. He snapped back into action when he saw Susannah pulling on her jacket with its brand new Hell Spawn Avengers logo, designed by Wizz, stencilled on the back. He quickly slipped her phone into her bag with a millisecond to spare before she turned to him.

'What are you up to?' she asked, eyeing him suspiciously.

'Nothing.'

Susannah checked her bag fully expecting to find something missing but instead, to her astonishment, she found a proper swish addition.

'Tom!' she beamed and looked up.

But he'd already left.

Gemma watched Wizz steer the battered old camper van, fully laden with a cargo of Hell Spawn Avengers, out of the driveway. 'That was a brief practice session. Where are they off to now?'

'Probably decided to go and mug an old lady,' came Jonathan's weary retort.

Gemma tugged the curtains together. She turned to face Jonathan, collapsed on the sofa like a felled tree; eyes closed, one arm resting on his belly while the other draped over the side.

'You are a picture of exhaustion Jonathan. I have an idea. Why don't we head out for a meal? Somewhere nice. My treat. It will do you the world of good to escape this house for a while. We could have a proper chat. Just the two of us.'

'Thank you no, I'm not in the mood. Besides, I'm not particularly good company at the moment.'

Gemma moved round the sofa and knelt behind Jonathan's head. Her knees emitted an alarming pop as they bent to the carpet. She looked at his hair; greying but no sign of baldness. His torso rose and fell with each tired breath. The hand dangling from the sofa brushed the rug where a half empty bottle of claret waited. He had strong hands. Clean. And powerful legs leading to narrow hips. His stomach was a little on the thick side but who was she to criticise in that department? Good broad shoulders. He had undone the top two buttons of his shirt, enough to allow a view of the dark sprigs of hair on his chest.

'Nonsense,' she said softly. 'You're always good company. So you're a wee bit uptight at the moment. Completely understandable given the circumstances. You just need to unwind a little. When was the last time you allowed yourself to relax?'

She placed her hands on his shoulders and started to massage the tight knots of muscle. Fingers and thumbs gently kneading at first before working deeper into the stress. Jonathan released a slow sigh. It felt good. When *was* the last time he allowed himself to relax?

'I can't remember.'

'That's my point. You're a good man. You're like me. Always putting others first. Always making sacrifices. But sometimes you have to spoil yourself or let someone else spoil you. Especially now, at our age. I think we've earned the right to put ourselves first. Does that feel nice?' she asked, sliding her thumbs under the cushion to massage the nape of his neck. A sturdy neck. And a well-defined jawline. No sign of his chin melting into his throat like so many men of his age.

'Mmmm...'

Emboldened by the contented purr tingling her fingertips, Gemma slowly spread her fingers under his collar allowing the tips to slide over the skin down towards his chest.

'And time moves so quickly,' she said in a near whisper, her glossy lips pursed close to his ear. 'Life swallows up the years without bothering to chew them. It gulps them down whole and before you know it, they're all gone. We mustn't let our years slip away, Jonathan. When opportunity knocks we need to open that door and to hell with what everyone else thinks... You have some serious knots here. It's difficult to work them from this angle. Why don't you sit up and take off your shirt?'

The one remaining sober cell buried deep in Jonathan's cerebellum whacked a massive gong. *Escape now!* His eyes sprung open. He sat up so quickly his head swam in a thick dizzying lather. When Gemma's hands attempted to position him back against the sofa, Jonathan leapt to his feet.

'What's the matter? Don't be silly. You can leave your shirt on. It was only a suggestion. I haven't finished yet. It will help relieve your stress, I promise,' Gemma persisted feeling the tingle fade from her fingers and elsewhere. 'Where are you going?'

Jonathan was halfway to the door. 'To look for my daughter.'

Gemma heaved herself from the floor, the strain producing a pop in both knees again. 'I'll come with you.'

Jonathan prevented her from gathering her coat and swiftly guided Gemma back to the sofa. 'No. You stay here and man the fort. Someone needs to be here in case Abigail returns or if the police try to get in touch. Okay?'

'But you're in no fit state to drive. Let me.' Gemma reached for the keys in his hand but Jonathan pocketed them in the nick of time.

'No. Gemma. Thank you. I'll be fine. I really need you to stay here. Will you do that for me?'

Gemma conceded with a disappointed nod and watched him hasten into hall and out of the house. She parted the curtain an inch, enough to see him climb inside the little delivery van and speed off. Her gaze drifted to the sky. The last smudge of daylight was fading fast. She tugged the curtains together.

'Little bitch.'

The Hell Spawn Avengers cruised through the centre of town and followed the curve of the promenade. A satisfying assault of Slipknot roared from the speakers while all eyes scoured the streets and pavements for Abigail. No luck so far. Even at this late hour, a surprising number of people were out and about. The pubs were calling time. Their clientele, having worked up an appetite by quenching their thirsts, now headed for the chip shop or the burger van.

Tom found himself fascinated by the huddle of bored teenagers gathered at the fountain. The same half dozen or so who hung around the same spot, at the same time, wearing the same gear, every single day. What was the attraction? It was a nice enough fountain. Not exactly the Trevi though was it? Would they still be hanging out there in ten years time; still wearing the same regulation hoodies and joggers, still not sure how to hold a cigarette properly, still intimidating pensioners with the same *wut-yoo-lookin-at?* attitude and still getting spazzed on cheap vodka and legal highs? Probably.

A passing patrol car received a middle finger salute from the rebel leader. This prompted some laughter, though much of it seemed to be of the nervy variety. Had Tom just witnessed the highlight of their day? Probably.

There was bugger all else for the young to do in this seaside Grannyville. No jobs unless you wanted to feed, entertain or accommodate tourists. And there didn't seem to be as many of those as there used to be. And who could blame them? For the price of a long weekend in Balemouth you could spend a full week in Greece or Spain. No contest. In truth two hours was all you needed to see everything Balemouth had to offer. The ruined castle was frankly no more than a glorified pile of fly-tipped rubble. The star exhibit in the museum was a German WWII shell which some myopic Luftwaffe pilot had dropped here when he mistook Loch Broom for the River Clyde. The beach, obviously, would always be the town's main draw. Very long, very sandy, very beachy. Beachy enough on sunny days like these to pull people in like bees to nectar. Again Tom failed to see the point. Why did so many people feel the need to sit on a gritty towel, smear greasy lotion all over their hairy bellies and flabby backs, and slowly baste themselves like so many oven-ready chickens?

Prospects for the young were indeed bleak. Which is why the majority opted to leave for the bigger, brighter lights to the south and east. But Tom considered himself lucky. He had the band. Hell Spawn Avengers. He had come to love that name. They were going places; record deals, headlining slots at Hammerfest, Bloodstock and Download festivals, groupies, TV appearances, world tours, private jets, groupies, platinum discs, cover stars for Decibel, Revolver and Kerrang, more groupies…

'What are you thinking?' Susannah had to yell the question into his ear canal to be heard above the music.

'Nothing much.'

'You looked a million miles away. You worried about Abigail?'

Tom felt a pang of guilt. Abigail. Yes. Why wasn't he thinking about his sister? His big sister. His only sister. A sister, potentially, in real danger.

'Aye,' he lied.

Susannah shuffled closer on the frayed leather seat at the rear of the van and took a hold of his hand. His heart instantly matched Slipknot's brutal b.p.m. 'Don't worry, we'll find her. She'll be okay, you wait and see.'

Wizz pulled the van into a petrol station forecourt and turned the volume down from volcanic eruption to Boeing 747 on take-off.

'Fuel stop. Anyone want anything?' she asked.

Kris heaved the side door open. 'I'm coming with you. Need to stretch my legs.'

Rick followed. 'You at the back!' he bellowed. 'Want anything?'

A strange quizzical frown wrinkled Rick's face when he spotted Tom's hand in Susannah's. Tom quickly freed it to scratch a sudden itch on his nose. 'Don't mind. Chocolate. Anything,' he answered, blushing.

'Sis'?' Rick continued still staring at Tom.

'Chonion,' grinned Susannah.

'Chonion,' Rick nodded and slid the door shut leaving the two of them alone. Tom watched his bandmates enter the shop. In the street beyond he recognised the van pulling up at the town's solitary set of traffic lights. The Green Grocery van. He could just make out his dad's face, bathed in red. No doubt listening to some very different music. Some mature cheddar from the Eighties or Nineties for sure. The lights changed to green and the little white van disappeared.

Susannah slipped her fingers back through his. She'd dyed her hair a vivid scarlet tipped with black, the fringe framing a pale heart-shaped face. She looked at him intently through depths of ocean blue.

'Are you sure you're okay?' Her words departed from a mouth painted maraschino cherry.

'I'm fine,' he said clearing his throat. He decided if she asked why he was trembling he'd claim he was cold. 'You?'

'I'm worried about you.' She manoeuvred herself so she could peer deeper into his eyes.

'Why?'

'Because of your bruises,' she said.

Tom had completely forgotten the pain. All he could feel was the touch of Susannah's hand and the warmth of her thigh pressing against his.

'It's nothing.'

'And Abigail. You must be really worried about her?'

'Like you said. We'll find her. She'll be okay.'

'Do you two get along?' asked Susannah. 'I mean are you and Abi close?'

A good question. Abigail was a whole other type of Squall. Her clothes. Her music. Her interests. Her personality. Even her diet. All wildly different to his. Were they close? They were brother and sister. Does it get any closer? Sure they used to fight like cats and dogs when they were small but Abi would always stick up for him and see off anyone who tried to bully her little brother at school. And whenever Dad moaned about his music Abigail would always step in and defend him with arguments about freedom of expression and the wonder of diversity or something else Tom would struggle to comprehend. And she invariably knew just what to give him for Christmas and birthdays. In short, she was always there when he needed her. Except now she wasn't... And that didn't feel right at all.

'I s'pose. She does her thing. I do mine,' he replied guardedly.

Susannah chuckled. A beautiful noise. 'You sound like Rick. He's my brother and I love him but sometimes I wish he would stop trying to be funny all the time. It's like he's scared of serious conversation? Do you two ever talk to each other about, you know, important stuff?'

'Important stuff?'

'Like about what happened to your mum?'

Sylvia's face flashed briefly in Tom's mind. A smile and a ruffle of his hair... A lump tightened at the back of his throat. 'She tries sometimes but I don't... I don't think I'm much help.'

Tom recalled the one and only occasion Abigail tried to talk to him about Sylvia. Alone in the shed, surrounded by Sylvia's tools and projects, Abi wanted to tell him how much she was missing Mum. She tried so hard to express the emptiness she felt inside but the words kept failing her. She wanted him to know she understood the pain he was suffering. She wanted him to know she was there to share in that gnawing void. But it was all so awkward. The conversation uncomfortably direct somehow. Like a needle picking at a scab. Events still too raw. He couldn't bear to look at the tears forming in her eyes so kept staring at the floor, the ceiling, the door, anywhere but his sister. And then, when she came over looking for a hug, he walked away.

She never broached the subject again. But they knew. They both knew the pain the other held. Tom needed to keep his close. Away from prying eyes. It was something to be nurtured and not to be shared. It fuelled his anger for an unjust world. And he embraced that anger, the way the drowning man embraces the lifebelt. He'd never admitted this to himself until now. He blamed Susannah. It was the way she looked at him. Honest and pure.

'Abi must be tough,' she said, 'I know I couldn't have coped with everything she went through. I can't imagine actually seeing my mum die. I couldn't handle that. Still, she's lucky she has you to lean on.'

Susannah's lingering, sympathetic gaze stoked the guilt. He hadn't been there for Abigail at all. Too wrapped up in his own feelings to provide any kind of support to his sister. Nothing there for her to lean on. What kind of a brother was he?

'She is tough. Tougher than me.' Another confession for those perfect blue eyes.

'If you ever need to talk. About anything. You can talk to me. You do realise that don't you?' Susannah insisted, putting a hand to his face to prevent him looking away. 'Anytime. Just give me a call,' she smiled and waggled her newly recovered phone.

Unsure what to say, Tom offered her a sheepish smile. Susannah moved in on the smile and landed a soft, tingling kiss on his lips.

The van door slid open. A packet of crisps bounced off Susannah's head.

'Cheese and onion for the lady!' Kris yelled.

'Chonion! Thank you!' Susannah grabbed the bag and grinned at Tom. The stunning kiss had sent his spirits rocketing to the stratosphere. Life was very definitely on the up!

Rick studied the pair warily. 'What are you two up to?'

'Nothing,' crunched Susannah.

Kris tossed a chocolate bar to Tom. 'They didn't have any Double Deckers so I got you a Twix. I know you're partial to that chewy yet crunchy combo.'

Tom smiled dopily at the gold wrapper. His smile tasted of lipstick. *Did that really just happen?!*

'Music maestro!' yelled Wizz with a flourish before firing up the volume until the windows pulsed with Slipknot fury.

Susannah pulled Tom close, held her phone in front of them and captured a selfie.

CHAPTER TWELVE

ULTRA HIGH FREQUENCY

Abigail pressed herself deep into the shadowy recess of an old church doorway. A rickety camper van with a sore throat for an engine passed by. Music blaring angrily from within it sped on towards Castle Street. There was a logo on the side of the van but she couldn't quite catch what it said. *Hell...* something. *Hell Spam Avenue...?* Something like that. Made no sense. Then again nothing in her world made any sense right now. When the music evaporated to silence she peered out. Deserted. She hurried from the church, crossed the road and jogged into a narrow, dingy side street. No street lights. Perfect.

~ *Pookie, you really* must *change that outfit. You look like you lost a bet,* ~ quipped the voice from the radio.

'I know, I know.' Abigail slumped against a set of wheelie bins guarding the rear of Mama Conti's Pizzeria. The mouth-watering scents of hot cheese, tomato, garlic, basil and warm dough swirled thickly in the air. Abigail was *so* hungry. She hadn't eaten since Inverness; a stodgy egg and cress baguette from one of the many meat biased snack outlets at the bus station. The comedian behind the counter had nodded at her tank top and said, 'Strewth! You're keen aren't ye? Only a few months to go though eh, love?' To which Abigail simply looked at him blankly then launched into a chorus of - '*Jingle bells, jingle bells*! - at the top of her lungs before walking off to board the coach to Ullapool. Probably not the wisest of moves in the circumstances but what the heck? The sandwich along with the bus fare, blew a great big chunk out of the cash she'd *borrowed* from Oxfam.

Despite Granddad's; ~ *Needs must...* ~ and ~ *Desperate times require desperate measures...* ~ themed pep talks, Abigail could not help but feel guilty. She meant precisely what she'd said in her note. As soon as she was well and able, she would return and deposit no less than fifty pounds into the collection tin. The bus journey itself proved uneventful. No Special Forces, SWAT teams or crack Black Ops units lay in wait. And no further wisecracks from people hardly at the vanguard of cutting edge fashion themselves. The driver looked so bored he scarcely registered her existence.

Tucking her hat and the lead apron inside a discarded carrier bag, she sat the radio beside her on the back seat of the bus. Keeping hold of the aerial, she used the journey time to try and make her self less blindingly conspicuous. She tore off Rudolph's nose and turned the tank top inside out which had the effect of offering the world a more surrealistic yuletide scene as knitted by Picasso. She rolled up the sleeves of her shirt hiding as much of the eye-searing pink as she could then patiently picked away at her jeans, unstitching much of the embroidery and all of the beads.

At Ullapool she used the last of the money to catch a bus to Rhue where she set off at a brisk pace along the Wester Ross Coastal Trail for a thoroughly enjoyable six-mile trek for home. For over two hours she followed the stunning coastline northward, the sun casting ever lengthening shadows over the landscape and saturating all the shades of the sea as it arced for the horizon. Breezes of cool salt flowed in from her left to mingle with the aroma of warm hay rising from the fields to her right. Those scents transported her back to a summer day long since passed when she ambled for hours lost in thought through the very same fields, absently kicking the heads off dandelions, scattering their seeds and watching the milky sap ooze from their broken stems. The blood of a flower.

Not a single human being troubled her along the way. Instead, she had a whole David Attenborough box set of wildlife for company. Squadrons of sand martins dive bombing for midges. Grey seals sunning themselves on the rocks. Gulls, guillemots, geese, dozens of lolloping rabbits, a dormouse, a hare, and no less than three red deer. Until finally, as the sun bade farewell, the Great Inverness Oxfam Robber left the trail and descended towards the familiar string of lights fringing the bay below.

And now, here she was, beside a bin full of stuffed crusts and mozzarella smeared pizza boxes, without the vaguest notion as to what to do next. Other than eat. *So hungry...*

She peered up at the light above the pizzeria's back door. A flitting moth headbutted the lamp in ever increasing frustration.

~ *There's another one! What is the bloody issue with these moths? A more retarded creature on God's earth you will not find!* ~

By way of an experiment, Abigail opened the carrier bag, took out the apron and fashioned it into a rudimentary helmet. She stretched the beanie hat over the bowl-shaped apron, placed it on her head and let go of the aerial. The transmissions instantly flooded her headspace but the customised hat did succeed in muting the noise to an acceptable level. She wobbled her head from side to side, backwards and forwards, testing the fit. The beanie-apron-helmet stayed firmly in place. She removed it for a more accurate comparison...

<LET ME BE YOUR BEDTIME TOY, LET ME BE YOUR BEDTIME TOY, LET ME BE YOUR BEDTIME TOY...>

She swiftly gripped the aerial killing the pop trash.

'I really, really, *REALLY* hate that song!'

~ *Imagine then, if you will, taking your hatred and multiplying it by a factor of ten, then times that by fifty squillion billion trillion and you'd still be nowhere near hating that steaming vat of farmyard slurry as much as I do.* ~ said Granddad. ~ *What is going on with this modern music? It's as if Peters & Lee, Manfred Mann, Leo Sayer and the Goombay Dance Band never happened? To quote the Bee Gees; it's a tragedy.* ~

'Wow. I'd forgotten just how appalling your taste in music was.'

~ *Careful young lady. I have my entire collection right here at my fingertips. Any more cheek and I'll be treating those cloth ears of yours to an entire evening dedicated to Nana Mouskouri and Demis Roussos; the cream of Greek easy listening.* ~

'Cream of Greek cheese more like.'

~ *Philistine!* ~

The pizzeria's back door suddenly opened. Abigail scarpered into the darkness. She cut through Marr & Son's Boat Yard, ducking under a pair of fishing boats perched on cradles ready to have their hulls cleaned and coated, and on in to Church Lane. Then a sharp right into Quay Street where she took refuge in the bus shelter next to the Marina Hotel car park. She studied the timetable. No more buses tonight. No reason for anyone else to join her until at least 6:56. Not that she planned on hanging around to catch the Number 14 to Leckmelm. She only needed a moment or two to catch her breath.

On the other side of the lifeless street, beneath a lamp post casting a feeble cone of orange, a TV repair shop caught her attention. The store's windows displayed an array of screens all switched on and fully operational as if paying testament to the proprietor's efficacy. *All Makes, All Models* - boasted a sign above the door. Each television had been tuned to a different channel. One was showing a cartoon: a dog chasing a cat chasing a mouse. A wildlife documentary played on another. The biggest screen offered up a bloodthirsty zombie movie, while directly underneath, she saw yet more disturbing images: the promotional video for *Bedtime Toy*. Tony V's glow in the dark smile, lecherous eyes and silky moves doggedly pursued a harem of scantily clad dancers back and forth over an enormous four-poster bed swathed in satin. And on the television tucked in the bottom left corner of the window, a World War II documentary played out: black and white footage of allied troops advancing quickly through city ruins, explosions and bullets everywhere. Meanwhile, on a cute little portable occupying the topmost shelf, a car chase in full throttle: cops chasing robbers through a grainy Eighties New York backdrop.

~ *Looks like modern TV is just as rubbish as the music.* ~ scoffed Granddad. ~ *Bring back Bonanza! Bring back Little House On The Prairie! Bring back Take The High Road! Bring back...* ~

CRASH!!!

The window exploded in a shower of glittering glass. The robber's scarlet Mustang burst from the shop, sparked hard against kerb and veered towards the bus shelter, large-as-life. Abigail scurried under the bench. Tyres screeching, the robber flung the steering wheel hard back to the road missing the shelter by inches and smothering Abigail in a plume of dust and burning rubber. Blues and twos blaring, the cop car squealed in hot pursuit. Coughing and sputtering she watched the cars skid headlong into an alley, obliterating a stack of cardboard boxes piled up at the entrance for no good reason before they vanished out of sight...

Silence...

Abigail rubbed her bewildered eyes and, in a single blink, every mote of dust, every particle of rubber and every splinter of broken glass disappeared. She looked back to the TV shop. Behind the pristine window, the high octane drama of the car chase continued safely within the boundaries of the little portable television screen, as if nothing had happened.

'What...?'

CRASH!!!

A hail of bullets reduced the shop window to a fine filigree of spidery cracks. The pane gave way and slumped to the ground in a deluge of sparkling fragments. Allied soldiers rushed into the street and fanned out firing at an unseen enemy. In scratchy black and white they advanced rapidly, dodging the bombs mushrooming dirt and masonry high into the air. The bus shelter rattled under the battering downpour of broken bricks and chunks of hard clay earth. Rifle at the ready, an American GI approached with caution. Satisfied the girl cowering under the bench posed no threat, he lowered his weapon and held out a hand ready to pull her to safety.

BANG!!!

The blinding flash of a mortar shell consumed the street in a shroud of white smoke and grey dirt. Abigail's ears sang... One long, blade-sharp refrain... The soldier's mangled body lay by the kerb, black blood pooling from ragged wounds until the billowing cloud swallowed him up. Abigail shrank against the back of the shelter terrified. The dust slowly settled then dissipated completely. She peered nervously through the shelter's graffiti etched perspex... Not a trace of the body remained. The battle was over. All the combatants had vanished. No bullets. No bombs. No damage. Nothing. The street had been swept clean and returned to its pre-war self.

Silence...

The war documentary continued on its screen safely contained behind the undamaged shop front. Abigail clutched her radio tightly in both hands.

'What's happening Granddad?'

~ *This was inevitable I'm afraid, though I was hoping I could hold them off a bit longer.* ~ His voice had lost its usual humour and held instead, a grim determination.

'Hold what off a bit longer?'

~ *Sorry Pookie but the airwaves are a busy place. It's not just radio transmissions we're dealing with here. It would appear we now have television signals looking to gatecrash the party.* ~

'What can I do to stop them?'

~ *Concentrate. Try to ignore them. Remember, none of it is real.* ~

CRASH!!!

A cartoon mouse streaked through the shattered shop window, narrowly avoiding the swiping claws of a cartoon cat. Cat and mouse darted up the lamp post, across the rooftops and down a drainpipe. The frantic mouse spotted Abigail and scampered over the road to hide behind her back. The trembling rodent peeked over her shoulder. The cat closed in with a wicked smile. Then a deep, bone rattling growl filled the street. The cat froze. Dribbling rabidly from its meaty jowls, a massive cartoon bulldog leapt from the shop. A nametag dangled from its collar – *Mauler*. The dog bowled after the cat. Cat and dog bounded up the lamp post, across the rooftops and down the bulging drainpipe. The cat shot back into the shop, picked up the TV set they all escaped from, and whacked it over the dog's head. The dazed, cross-eyed dog teetered drunkenly on its hind paws while a halo of twittering canaries circled the huge lump rising from its head.

The victorious cat rubbed its paws and eyed the mouse with an evil lick of its lips. The saucer-eyed mouse cowered further behind Abigail. Slapping himself across the chops, Mauler recovered his senses and swallowed the annoying little flock of canaries in one gulp. Once more cat and dog flew up the lamp post, across the rooftops and down the drainpipe. The dog skidded to an abrupt halt when the cat leapt on to the bus shelter's roof. Seeing Abigail, Mauler decided to leave the cat alone and treat himself to a much tastier morsel. Fangs bared and snarling, he padded slowly forward...

'I'm finding it really hard to ignore them Granddad!' Abigail yelled as the beast's steel trap jaws slavered ever wider.

~ *Close your eyes and shake your head while I give my frequency output a tweak!* ~ the radio shouted.

Abigail clamped her eyes tight and shook her head until she felt sure she could feel her brain wobbling inside.

Silence...

She opened her eyes. The street was empty. Behind the shop window, the dog, the cat and the mouse continued their madcap chase within the safe confines of their twenty-two-inch screen.

CRASH!!!

Tony V and his troupe of dancing girls smashed through the shop window and pranced over the pavement to the jaunty trash pop of *Bedtime Toy*. The tightly choreographed dancers bounced, pirouetted and cart-wheeled in skimpy lingerie while the pastel-suited Tony V, all flailing limbs and shiny teeth sang:

Take me from your drawer,
Place me on your pillow,
Let me put a smile on your face,
It's just you and me now,
So let me show you how,

To make the night oh oh! So so! Right!!

Hold me, feel me, squeeze me babe,
Let me be your bedtime toy,
Touch me, love me, use me babe,
Let me bring you bedtime joy!

The dancers began to thrash each other with oversized pillows. Through a snowstorm of feathers Tony V, affecting his finest *come-and-get-me* leer, span up close and personal to Abigail.

You are the beauty, I am the beast,
You now you want me, you know you need me,
So what're you waiting for?
Press my button for a night full of lovin'...

~ Hit him! ~ Granddad growled. ~ *Please! Hit him hard while I try another adjustment. Go on. Rearrange his smug teeth!* ~

Abigail threw a punch at Tony V's sparkling veneers. The singer vanished instantly. The street returned to normal. Tony V and his company continued to perform their lurid routine behind the shop window, mercifully mute.

~ *He's the one Pookie! That prancing nancy boy started this. He flicked the switch and opened the floodgates. If you want to permanently remove that bloody awful tune of his and everything else from your head, then you must find a way to make him switch it off again. You could try asking him nicely or you could try extreme violence. Whichever you prefer.* ~

Abigail stepped from the bus shelter and glared at Tony V preening and pouting his way through the *Bedtime Toy* video.

'Extreme violence it is,' she said with a slow, deliberate nod.

CRASH!!!

Hordes of zombies burst through the shop window dripping flesh and gore all over the pavement. Arms outstretched, mouths gaping and groaning they sprinted towards her.

Abigail screamed.

~ Holy monkey jobbies! Sorry! Can't seem to find the right output configuration! Shut your eyes and shake your head! ~ yelled Granddad.

Eyes pressed shut, Abigail shook her head so hard she almost dislocated her neck.

The groaning and the shuffling ceased.

Eyes open. The street and the shop, quiet and empty. The zombies, caged within their television set, were happily disembowelling another unfortunate cheerleader.

~ Scary, ~ Granddad puffed. *~ But not as scary as waking up next to your gran after she'd been hitting the gin. Shall we go? ~*

Abigail hurried off before anything else attempted to flatten, shoot, eat or seduce her.

CHAPTER THIRTEEN

BROADCAST

W izz parked the camper van by the cemetery gates and turned the music way down in respect.

Rick peered across the tombstones coated in silver moonlight.

'Midnight. Full moon. Graveyard. A van full of teenagers. This is guaranteed to end in a bloodbath.'

'Shut up and eat your Snickers.'

'Why are we here?' asked Kris.

'Because we've looked everywhere else,' said Wizz still scowling at Rick. 'And Tom's right, this is an ideal place to hide. Quiet. Dark.'

'Do you really think she might be going to visit your mum?' asked Rick.

Tom nodded. 'It's possible. I mean who knows where Abi's head's at? Maybe she thinks Mum is the only one she can turn to right now.'

'Okay team. Torch apps on,' Wizz commanded unclipping her seatbelt. 'And please show respect to our sleeping friends at all times when you're out there,'.

'It's better if you guys wait here,' said Tom.

'How come?'

Susannah gripped his arm. 'We should come with you. It's a bit spooky on your own.'

'It's not spooky. It's just a field full of dead people.'

Wizz glared at Kris stupefied by his insensitivity: *His mum's in there!* – she mouthed. But Kris failed to get the message and blankly shrugged his shoulders.

'No, seriously guys, it's best I go on my own. If she is here, and she sees a whole bunch of people coming for her, she'll just run off. Who wouldn't?'

'Good thinking Tom. We'll stay here.'

Wizz transferred her disdain to the singer. 'So how much did you get for your backbone on Ebay, Rick?'

Tom slid the door open and stepped into the dark.

'If you get attacked by a zombie, give us a call so we can start advertising for a new bass player.'

'Thanks Kris. I'll bear that in mind.' Tom closed the door and left his friends safe and secure inside the trusty old van.

Passing through the gates he made his way between row after row of regimented stones and monuments. No need to use the torch app.

The moon provided ample light. He heard a bird rustling somewhere in the treetops overlooking the cemetery's crumbling border walls, their branches silhouetted against the sky like so many blood vessels. Susannah had a point. It was a spooky place to be alone. And no amount of sensible, logical reasoning could dissuade his primitive core from envisaging a whole horrorfest of fanged creatures hiding behind those headstones, each one of them waiting for the right moment to scurry forth and rip him messily apart.

He glanced back to the van. Lost now, behind a headless angel... *It's just a field full of dead people...* Kris had a disconcerting knack for blunt statement. His point was crude but undeniably true nonetheless. Tom was trespassing in a field belonging to the dead and gone. His eyes moistened with mounting frustration as he struggled to recall where she lay. So much easier to negotiate in daylight. At last he recognised the diminutive ivy covered shelter by the wall. A little place of refuge for those wishing to sit and contemplate. The main path split into a cross junction. He turned left. Three rows down. And close to the centre. He paused, taking a good look around. No movement. No Abigail-shaped silhouettes. The bordering inkblot of trees susurrated in a breeze still infused with the day's warmth. A gentle hush which did nothing to calm his thudding heart.

'Abigail?' he whispered.

No response.

Tom took out his phone and used its display to pick out the names on the headstones. And there it was. Behind the flowers they had laid only a few days ago, now wilting badly, unlike the steel rose which glinted proudly under the glow of his phone. He moved forward stepping on the grass trying hard not to envisage what remained several feet directly beneath. He knelt in front of the headstone.

Sylvia Squall

Taken too soon

"This is not goodbye..."

Goodbye... He stared coldly at the word. A splinter of anger needled its way through his chest. He'd never had the chance to say that word.

Abigail had. The anger dissolved into a strange mix of envy, bitterness and most strongly of all, guilt. He resented Abigail for being at Sylvia's side when she died. It felt somehow, like a final act of favouritism. It was a stupid, immature feeling and he hated himself for thinking it. His mother never showed any bias in her affections. She plainly loved them both in equal measure. But he should have been there too! Another set of eyes. Another pair of hands. He could have done something. Something Abigail didn't manage to do for whatever reason. Perhaps if he'd been there, he could have saved her. Persuaded her to park in a safer spot. Yelled a warning. Pushed her out of the way. Swapped places with her...

His trembling fingers reached for his mother's name... The moment he touched the cold permanence of the S, the grief, locked tightly away for over a year in a dark cell at the very epicentre of his being, surged forth. Defences breached, Tom's body quaked and shuddered against the irrepressible flood.

'Don't go,' he gasped. 'Please don't go.' The tears streaked and dripped from his cheeks. 'I miss you.' His bruises and cuts ached under the heavy weight of his sobs. Through water-fogged eyes he saw someone approach. But the all-consuming despair left no room for fear or alarm and soon enough, he recognised Susannah.

She knelt by his side, gathered him in her arms and without word, she let him weep until his pain ran dry.

*

Jonathan shook the bottle. One mouthful left. He tipped the wine into his mouth, allowing the liquid to grow warm on his tongue before he swallowed. Taking Polaris as his starting point he mapped out the sky. Jupiter certainly the most interesting feature. A bright, bold punctuation mark close to the horizon. Mars also visible but faint. They were planning to send a manned mission to that hazy speck. Astronauts were being trained to endure a three-year trip away from home... He imagined the stillness of Mars. The emptiness. All so appealing. Three years away from the drudgery, the responsibility, the noise and stresses of everyday life and, above all, three years away from the wretched guilt. The kids would be fine. They didn't need him. Given half a chance, he would volunteer to take that trip in an instant. Though he firmly suspected his inadequacies would follow him to the ends of the universe...

A tiny dot sailed slowly towards Orion's Belt. Way too high to be an aircraft. He wondered if the scientists aboard the International Space Station could see this insignificant little town amidst the clusters of big city lights peppering Northern Europe.

Back down to Earth.

Or rather the sea...

The lights from the promenade at his back threw ribbons of gold and ivory over a sheen of black. He'd taken his shoes and socks off to enjoy the sensation of damp sand between his toes. The lazy surf bathed his bare feet, retreated... then returned for another lick. So feeble they could hardly be classified as waves. The air so still. The surface of the sea smooth as glass. The polar opposite to the storm of emotions tearing at his insides. What would happen if he started walking into that deep blackness? Up to his knees. His waist. Chest. Neck. Until the water poured into his mouth. Into his lungs and stomach. What would happen if he simply allowed the sea to take him away and cleanse him of this unrelenting pain and guilt?

Stop being pathetic!

Jonathan threw his head back and sighed. The space station sailed on. Yes. Time to cut the self-pity crap and fix things. Time to start acting like a father.

Back to Jupiter...

... As close as you'll ever get to time travel ...

He remembered Abigail staring through the telescope lost in the wondrous beauty of Saturn.

... 'Do you think there's anyone up there looking down on us?' ...

And what else had she said?

... 'There must be *something* behind all this. Something *more* – do you not think so?' ...

She had been talking about God. About the possibility of an afterlife.

And he'd denied it. Why? How can anyone stare in to the cosmos, become lost in its enormity and not feel the weight of its power? The universe held an unfathomable number of secrets. So why deny even the remotest possibility? He had no time for religion or the idiocy they peddled. They had hijacked the concept of God and distilled it into a nonsensical soap opera. No, if God existed, it existed in the gaps between sub atomic particles. It resided in every nucleus, at the heart of every atom and cell, in the core of every sun, every planet. It formed the energy which fuelled the very fabric of the universe. It spun the threads which stitched together every plain of reality. God as physics. Far removed from the facile imaginings of old men and their holy books designed to subjugate women and perpetuate fear and distrust. The myth of Us and Them.

So why had he dismissed Abigail's question so bluntly? Because he'd been on the wine. Drunk and in no mood to offer hope. Not when he'd lost his. He remembered the sadness in his daughter's eyes.

And made a promise to cut back on the wine. He launched the empty bottle far into the darkness. An act sure to incur the wrath of the Gods: The God of Neglected Bottle Banks, the God of Litter Free Coastal Environments, the God of Empty Yet Potentially Reusable Vessels... But it was the God of Satisfyingly Distant Splashes who answered him.

A shooting star sliced across the sky as though it had been fired from the moon. The scar healed before he could give it a second thought.

First Sylvia. And now Abigail. Lost. Gone. And Tom? Well, he'd become more and more of a stranger to him. Jonathan's family had ruptured. The good ship Squall had lost its rudder and would soon sink beneath the waves.

He stepped knee-deep into the welcoming tide. Despite the never-ending heatwave the water felt surprisingly cold. Undeterred, he continued onwards. The sea rising to his waist. And then to his chest. Deeper still into the all-consuming blackness. A blackness full of hidden threats. Full of bites and stings. When the sea spilled over his shoulders and his feet lost contact with the sandy bed, Jonathan began to panic. He imagined all those mouths and tentacles closing in. He twisted to face the shore. Drifting further away, the lights of the promenade dipped in and out of the swell. Jonathan clutched desperately at an object glinting and bobbing in the turmoil thrown out by his floundering arms.

CHAPTER FOURTEEN

AUTOTUNE

All the lights inside the Squall family home were off. No cars parked outside. No sign of any activity within or without. Abigail checked the neighbouring windows for twitching curtains. Satisfied she was free from prying eyes she hurried over. The front door was firmly locked. She picked up an ornamental frog squatting by the garden path, tipped it up until it regurgitated a key into her hand and blessed the naive trust of a small community.

Door unlocked, she crept into the hall. Waited... Silence... She moved carefully into the lounge. The room welcomed her with a comforting warmth infused with all the familiar scents of home. Again she waited until her eyes adjusted to the darkness long enough to confirm there was nothing lurking behind, between or beneath the dark contours of the furniture. Abigail placed her radio on the coffee table and released the aerial to scratch an itch under her woolly hat.

FLASH!!!

Dazzled half blind, Abigail blinked repeatedly until her vision flickered, jerked and finally settled on the bizarre scene in front of her. The bright lights of a TV studio flared above the lounge where two camera operators and a floor manager kept a keen eye on events from their positions behind the three-piece suite.

'And he joins us now from our Westminster studio...'

The voice, clipped with perfect diction, belonged to a blonde, middle-aged woman, tanned and svelte in a smartly pressed Chanel suit. Abigail recognised the newsreader sitting cross-legged and straight-backed in Jonathan's favourite armchair but couldn't quite recall her name. Emily... something.

Twiddling a BBC pen in her fingers, Emily Something swivelled to address the huge face projected across the entire wall above the mantelpiece; a stern, wary face softened only marginally by a supercilious twist at the mouth. According to a caption superimposed across his puffed up chest, this was Timothy Barwell MP. With Big Ben looming over his shoulder, the parliamentarian's demeanour quickly began to lose its self-satisfied gloss as Emily unleashed a salvo of hard-hitting questions.

'According to the latest figures, violent crime has risen yet again on your watch.'

'Those figures have to be taken in context,' Barwell squirmed, evasively.

Emily Something poked a finger against the coffee table. 'But in the context of your manifesto promises you have quite clearly failed to deliver.'

The MP's cheeks blossomed. 'These things take time. We clearly underestimated the scale of the mess we inherited from the previous Labour administration who...'

Smelling blood, Emily quickly cut in; 'And as I recall you wasted no time in calling for your predecessor to resign. Is it time for you to resign Mr Barwell?'

'My priority, as ever, is focused on tackling the issues which have...'

'Is it time for you to resign minister?'

Barwell exploded. 'If you would *please* let me finish!'

The outburst prompted a wry smile on Emily Something's face. Victory.

Abigail snatched the aerial. The lounge immediately returned to its natural state. A dark cluster of silent shadows.

Feeling a little freaked, Abigail backed away and tiptoed through to the dining room.

So hungry...

Once she was sure there was no-one waiting to pounce, she padded across the kitchen and opened the fridge. Her eager face shone in the radiance spilling out from the treasures inside. KitKats, éclairs, a plate of cold meat covered in cling film (*Yeuch!*), mushroom pate, coconut yoghurt... Thinking with her stomach she made the mistake of releasing the aerial as she reached for the fattest, creamiest, chocolatiest bun.

FLASH!!!

'This is a truly naughty but luscious sticky toffee pud,' said a rich, sumptuous voice.

Abigail turned to face the equally luscious TV cook standing behind the kitchen worktop surrounded by all the ingredients necessary for said sticky toffee pudding. She recognised the woman instantly but again struggled for the name. Bella? Bella... thingamajig?

Like a wonky hologram Bella Thingamajig flickered and faded momentarily but steadied herself with a swish of her luxurious chestnut hair. She dipped a finger into the pudding mix and sucked the sweet glossy brown gloop clean away.

'Hmm,' she purred, 'I can't wait to lick the bowl.'

~ *Hmmm,* ~ the radio murmured salaciously, ~ *Very nice. She can lick my receptacles any time.* ~

'Granddad!'

~ *Whoa! Did I say that out loud? Sorry Pookie.* ~

Abigail grabbed the radio. Bella vanished and the kitchen fell into silence once more. The light from the fridge revealed a worktop disappointingly free of chocolate pudding. Keeping one hand on the aerial, Abigail made short work of the éclair and several KitKats.

Upstairs next.

She paused on the landing. Extra caution required in case the bedroom doors hid a sleeping Squall or two. She listened intently. No snoring to be heard. A good sign as both Jonathan and Tom were masters of the art. She crossed the deep pile carpet and, wary of her own bedroom door's propensity to squeak, opened it just enough to allow her to enter.

The blinds had been drawn leaving the room in complete darkness. She noticed a trace of unfamiliar perfume in the air. She'd had a visitor. Rather than risk turning on the light she opened the blinds and filled the room with moonlight instead. Her heart sank. Someone had ransacked her keepsake box and scattered the contents all over the floor. Everything had been tipped out. Her unopened present from Sylvia, her photos, her beachcombing mementoes... Her diary was missing! Who would do this? Jonathan? Tom? Both? How could they do this to her?

~ *Don't be too hard on them. The police probably asked them to search for a clue to help figure out where you might have run off to. They'll be worried about you don't forget,* ~ reasoned Granddad.

Abigail tucked everything back in the box. 'I suppose,' she said.

~ *Meanwhile, you have more important things to worry about. Don't forget the plan.* ~

Abigail turned to the window nodding in agreement. She peered through the blinds to the dark spike poking from the distant hilltop. The moon was in serious danger of being punctured if it dipped any lower. She watched a small red light blinking at the transmitter's summit. A warning to low-flying aircraft and visually impaired owls.

~ And I'll bet there's a bloody stupid moth nutting that light as we speak. ~ Granddad muttered.

'What is it with you and moths?'

~ Don't like 'em. ~

Abigail stepped in front of the wardrobe mirror. She had to admit she looked ridiculous. She leaned forward for a closer look at her face. A distressing sight. She stared at her blotchy, aching eyes and pressed at the crease cutting into her forehead; symptoms of the relentless pain. Not much she could do about that right now but as for those hideous clothes...

Abigail opened the wardrobe, selected an outfit and laid the items on the bed. She braced herself knowing she would need both hands to change.

~ Ready? ~

'Ready,' said Abigail. She took a deep breath.

~ Okay. After three... One... Two... Three! ~

Abigail put the radio down and pulled her boots off...

<A SUICIDE BOMBER KILLED FOURTEEN...>

She yanked off her hat and said goodbye to Rudolph as the skull-stretching torture intensified.

<BY ANY MEASURE, I'LL GIVE YOU PLEASURE...>

Buttons flying across the room, she tore away the pink shirt and stripped to her socks...

<WHY NOT CONSOLIDATE YOUR DEBTS INTO ONE MANAGEABLE SUM...>

The pain hacksawing at her optical nerves, she tugged on a pair of black combats...

<HOLD ME FEEL ME SQUEEZE ME BABE...>

Strength draining rapidly from her arms, she wriggled into a plain black hoody...

FLASH!!!

And suddenly a hummingbird, big as a pigeon hovered in the centre of the room dipping its slow motion tongue into the flute of a beautiful orange and yellow flower. A familiar voice narrated the scene for her...

- THE HUMMINGBIRD'S WINGS BEAT AT TWO HUNDRED TIMES A MINUTE USING UP AN EXTRAORDINARY AMOUNT OF ENERGY AND FORCING THIS TINY,

DELICATE LITTLE BIRD TO SPEND THREE QUARTERS OF ITS WAKING LIFE SEARCHING FOR NECTAR... –

Mesmerised by the beautiful, iridescent bird she slipped into her boots and tied the laces. The image flickered, pulsed, then died. One blink and inexplicably Clint Eastwood had taken the hummingbird's place. Clint aimed his gun at Abigail's head...

- NOW I KNOW WHAT YOU'RE THINKING. DID HE FIRE SIX SHOTS OR ONLY FIVE?... -

~ *Love that movie,* ~ said Granddad.

Abigail, snatched the radio. Clint disappeared. Fully dressed in stealthy black, she left her room and slipped silently through to the landing.

~ *Looking good Pookie. Like a ninja assassin.* ~

'Thanks Granddad,' she whispered.

Passing Tom's room, she stole a quick peek inside... Empty. Same with Jonathan's room. Same with the bathroom. Where was everyone?

~ *Out looking for you I expect.* ~

Abigail waited under the loft and listened hard. No suggestion of any movement up there either. Caught in two minds she remained rooted under the hatch.

~ *Need to move on girl. They could be home any minute.* ~ Granddad warned.

'I just want a quick look. I might not get another chance.'

~ *Aye you will Pookie. Stick to the plan...* ~

But Abigail had already pulled down the ladder and begun to climb.

Once inside the loft she needed a moment to sit and recover. The climb had sapped what precious energy she had left. She sympathised with that busy little hummingbird. Eat. Fly. Fly. Eat. Fly. Higher and higher. She looked at the stars caught in the square of night framed in the open skylight. The telescope awaited her. Abigail gathered herself and put her eye to the viewfinder. A minor adjustment and there it was.

Saturn...

'So beautiful...'

~ *It certainly is. But then they're all beautiful. You wouldn't believe what's out there Pookie. The universe never fails to astonish.*

There is so much wonder! You need an eternity to appreciate it. But when it comes to our own little system, Venus is my favourite. I like to spend time there. And with the Moonlings of course. A very hospitable and accommodating bunch. And boy do they know how to throw a party! ~ Granddad boasted.

'Thank you Granddad but I stopped believing in the Moonlings not long after I learned the truth about Santa and the Tooth Fairy,'

~ I see. Well, Moonlings aside, everything else I said is the God's honest truth. ~

'You're telling me you've actually been to Venus?'

~ Absolutely I have! Some like it hot as they say! When you're dead, there's nothing to stop you going wherever you damn well pleasey. No stupid body to hold you back see? The world is your oyster, the solar system is your limpet and the universe is your scallop! ~

Abigail pondered this mollusc-themed revelation for a moment. Then a thought struck her.

'Where does Mum like to go?'

~ She likes it right here. And I must say I don't blame her. Despite the fact the world is full of eejits hell bent on tearing it apart, there really is no place like home. ~

Abigail felt her skin prickle. 'Is she here? Now? Can I speak to her?'

~ She'll be here soon I promise. Now Pookie, we really shouldn't linger. We have a job to do. So let's grab some tools. ~

Lifting the key to the shed from its hook in the kitchen, Abigail left the house via the patio doors and darted across the garden. She quietly unlocked and removed the shed's padlock but no amount of care could stop the hinges creaking wildly as she opened the door. The pale moonlight slanting through the opening picked out a few shadowy details; instruments belonging to Tom's band, Abigail's bicycle perched against the wall at her side, Sylvia's workbench. One of her mother's unfinished sculptures still remained on the bench; the beginnings of a steel pine cone.

A big sturdy wooden chest took up most of the space underneath the bench. Inside she found her mother's tools; welding torches, small canisters of oxyacetylene, files, grinders, cutters, drills... She found a dusty old canvas holdall and filled it with all the implements she thought might prove useful to her quest. A seriously chunky staple gun gave her an idea. Clenching the aerial in her teeth she removed her hoody, cut the lead apron to shape and stapled it to the inside of the hood.

She pulled the top back on, flipped the modified hood over her head and let go of the aerial. The results were slightly disappointing. The signals flurried back in a mashed up thrum of static. Annoying but a workable short term solution and certainly comfier than the tight, scratchy wool hat.

~ *Does it work?* ~ Granddad asked once she took hold of the radio.

'Not perfect. But I can live with it.'

~ *Then let's go cause some damage!* ~

Hoisting the hefty tool bag over her shoulder Abigail turned to leave. Her heart stalled with fright when she collided with the stocky silhouette blocking her exit.

'What do you think you're doing?' asked a cold, female voice. The woman stepped in and flicked on the light.

Abigail retreated a step. 'Aunt Gemma! What are you doing here?'

Gemma closed the shed door with a sharp tug. 'You little bitch,' she hissed, enjoying the startled panic on her niece's face. 'Running away like a silly schoolgirl. You've had us all worried sick. Have you any idea the amount of hurt your little charade is causing Jonathan? Selfish brat. He's a complete mess thanks to you.'

'But... I'm sorry. I'm not trying to hurt anyone. I just need to fix...'

Gemma stepped closer. 'What have you got in that bag?'

'Nothing. Just some things I need...'

'Don't you dare insult me young lady. So, you're a thief as well as a liar.'

'I'm not stealing anything! And I'm not lying!' Abigail tried to reach the door but Gemma shoved her away so hard she tripped over a stray guitar pedal and tumbled to the floor. The radio slipped from her grasp and span across the gritty concrete.

The screaming tumult reduced her aunt to a glutinous smear of beige and pink with a little mouth popping away at the centre of an angry fleshy blob. Pain slicing at her eyeballs, Abigail desperately tried to retrieve her radio but Gemma beat her to it, plucked it from the floor and hurled it aside where it bounced against the wall and cracked wide open.

'No!' Abigail wailed. 'Please no!' The radio transmissions piled noise upon grinding noise, peal after seething peal, shattering and fracturing the onslaught of television images trying to overpower their stronghold. The entire broadcasting world wanted to conquer her headspace and would not rest until they'd successfully cleaved it in two.

Gemma slapped her hard across the face. 'Stop it! I for one am not going to fall for your pathetic games. Now pull yourself together. You and I are going to have a little chat.'

Abigail managed to pull the hood over her head. The clamour dipped to a bearable rush of white noise. Gemma opened a small book in front of her face. Her diary. Abigail's heart deflated further.

Gemma glared down on Abigail, eyes blazing with contempt. 'Why does your diary suddenly stop right after your mother died?' she demanded. 'I'll tell you why. It's because you're trying to keep a secret from us, isn't it? You know something don't you? Something you didn't want to commit to paper because you knew it would incriminate you. Meanwhile you're happy to let everyone believe it was a simple hit and run accident. How convenient. Well I for one remain far from convinced. You're guilty of something. I just know it.'

Abigail rushed over to gather the broken radio. The aerial had almost snapped in two at the middle. She held it tightly in both hands.

'Granddad! Granddad!'

Nothing...

'Granddad please speak to me!'

A closer inspection of the damage left her in arrant despair. The guts of the unit dangled hopelessly through a fatal split in the casing. Abigail hugged the radio to her chest, tears dripping.

'No... Don't go...'

Gemma stomped across and slapped her again. 'Stop playing the imbecile! Listen to me. You need to stop this act. I am not stupid. Why do you always have to behave like a sideshow freak? Your mother was far too soft on you. Far too indulgent. If you'd been my daughter I promise you, I would not have tolerated any of your nonsense. Now, tell me. What *really* happened to my sister, hmm?'

Abigail tried to force the eviscerated wires and circuit board back inside the wound 'Granddad make it stop,' she pleaded. 'Please... Mum?'

Losing what little patience she had left, Gemma grabbed fistfuls of Abigail's collar and dragged her into a chair.

'It's not too late you know. Make a full confession now and maybe God will forgive you despite your many sins. Tell the truth Abigail. For the sake of your soul, tell me the truth.'

Abigail twisted the radio's tuning dial. 'Mum, are you there? Help me...'

Gemma wrested the radio from her hands and threw it to the floor. 'You can have your toy back as soon as you put an end to this performance and start talking.'

'Please...' Abigail begged through sodden eyes. 'Let me go. I have to stop the noise.'

'You are not going anywhere young lady until you talk to me. And I'm perfectly willing to stand here all night if need be.'

*

Tom closed the camper's sliding door and slapped the window. Wizz responded with a brief toot before driving off with the rest of the Hell Spawn Avengers. Susannah waved from the rear with a killer smile. Tom replied in kind, their eyes locked until the van disappeared around the corner. He stood rooted to the spot until the engine faded into the night and all he could hear was the faint, caressing shush of the breeze.

Susannah... The way she'd held him at his mother's grave. Close and warm. Without saying a single word. No misguided platitudes or ill-conceived clichés like those he'd been subjected to by everyone from teachers, classmates and neighbours, to people he didn't even know. Susannah rose above all that falseness. She understood. He'd laid bare all his raw naked grief for her to see and she hadn't flinched. Anyone else would have run a mile leaving him crippled with shame and embarrassment. But not Susannah. She must have held him for a full fifteen minutes or more until he eventually ran out of tears and composed himself. Then finally, it was time to leave Sylvia in peace.

Susannah lifted his head, wiped his eyes on her cuff and kissed his brow.

They returned to the van. She never mentioned his breakdown to the others and merely confirmed their search for Abigail had proved fruitless. And off they all went. The rock gods and seekers of the lost. Eventually the yawning gods decided to postpone the search until tomorrow when, as Kris had put it; 'If Balemouth Bay doesn't reveal Abigail to us, then the town will discover to its cost, that Hell hath no fury like an Avenger spawned.'

Tom still had no idea what the bloody hell Kris was on about. Neither had Wizz who, by way of an explanation, had directed Tom's attention to the empty can at Kris's feet. One beer. The magic potion which never failed to transform the usually taciturn guitarist into a blethering enigma.

Throughout the drive home, Susannah had sat with her arm slotted through his. Rather than say anything that could be overheard by the band, they exchanged texts:

- U OK?
- Yep
- I'm here 4 U
- Thanx
- Can we go out? Just me + U?
- That'd be great!
- Let me know where + when
- Will do!

And as he stood there, scrolling back through the conversation string with a grin as wide as the bay, his phone pinged again:

- Nite. XXX

He thumbed his response:

- Nite. XXXXXXXXXXXXXXXXXXXXXXXXX

His chest thumped like a big bass drum. The kiss they'd shared in the van. He could still feel it playing on his lips... *Can we go out? Just me + U?*

That had to be, without question, the best text he had ever received. A date! With Susannah! Where should he take her? He checked his wallet. Fifteen pounds. Where could he take her for fifteen pounds? The options zipped through his head as he closed the front door behind him. Nobody home. He made straight for his room and slumped on his bed dead beat but elated. He couldn't recall ever feeling like this before. Like the weight of the world had been lifted from his shoulders. He was no longer alone. There was someone else out there who understood him. Exhausted though he was, sleep would have to wait. He needed more time to properly study the selfie she'd taken and forwarded to him. Her head resting against his. Crystal clear eyes smiling. God, and so was he! Tom and Susannah. Susannah and Tom. Sounded cool. Sounded perfect. Tom and Susannah Squall. Even better!

The battery died. He got up and reached for the charger on the windowsill. The phone chirruped happy for the fresh juice. The display lit up and reflected against the glass photo frame perched beside it on the sill. A picture of himself with Sylvia and Abigail. He was ten years old. On the beach. The three of them standing by one of Mum's brilliant sand sculptures. A crocodile. All teeth and menace. Tom straddling its head, Sylvia and Abi behind him, all grinning for Dad's camera. To think he used to hide this picture whenever his bandmates visited, worried they might find it too soppy. Well not anymore.

Yes, I do miss you Mum and yes, I do care about you Abigail... So where the hell are you?

He stared out through the window. The full moon cast a ghostly veil over the rear garden. Then he spotted a different source of light. A thin yellow fleck glowing from under the shed door.

*

Gemma's lurid pink nails clasped Abigail by the jaw forcing her niece's eyes to meet her own.

'Doesn't Daddy give you enough attention sweetums, hmm? His delicate little princess? You may have fooled Jonathan but not me. I know this is all an act. The doctors couldn't work out what's wrong with you because there *is* nothing wrong with you. So tell me the truth. What did you see? Did you see the car? You were standing right next to her. You must have seen something? So why are you keeping it to yourself? Did you see the driver? Did you recognise the driver?' Gemma waited but Abigail said nothing. Growing ever more furious she moved her grip to Abigail's throat. 'Answer me! Are you protecting the driver for some reason? Is that it? Or are you protecting yourself? Was it all your fault? Did you *push* Sylvia in front of that car? That's it isn't it? You pushed her! Didn't you? Tell me!'

Eyes squeezed shut, Abigail shook her head rapidly.

Gemma stepped back and forced herself to calm down. Time to try a different approach.

'I only want to know the truth Abigail,' she said, her voice cotton soft now. 'Is that so wrong? You're my niece and I love you but I don't like secrets. Only the devil benefits from secrets. People should be open with each other. Don't you agree? Open and honest. No secrets. Nothing hidden. Everything out in the open. For example; wouldn't you like to know what's inside here?' She removed something she had tucked in the waistband of her skirt and held it in front of Abigail. The unopened birthday gift from Sylvia. Gemma put her nose tip to tip with Abigail's. 'Shall we find out together?'

Abigail tried to snatch the present but Gemma stepped smartly out of range. Smiling sweetly, she lifted the tag and looked at the inscription. 'Now then, what does this say: *Happy Birthday Abi! Your life is ready to sparkle! Love Mum.* – How sweet! And she's added two little kisses at the end there. That's nice.'

'Don't! Please…' begged Abigail, distraught. 'I promised I would wait…'

'Tell me the truth and I'll stop. After all, confession is good for the soul.' Gemma slowly began to peel away the wrapping paper. Abigail launched herself from the chair in one last frantic effort to stop her. 'Sit Down!' Gemma shoved her back into the seat with such force the hood flopped from Abigail's head.

<THE MARKETS TOOK ANOTHER POUNDING TODAY> <*OH LITTLE ANGEL LIGHT MY WAY*><WHO HAVE WE GOT ON LINE TWO? MICKEY FROM LEAMINGTON SPA! MICKEY, WHAT'S ON YOUR MIND MATE?><*DON'T DROP ME, DON'T DROP ME, DON'T DROP ME NOW*><YOU'RE LISTENING TO UP ALL NIGHT WITH ROB><*HOLD ME, FEEL ME, SQUEEZE ME, BABE…*>

The vision of Gemma slowly opening the gift dissolved into the pulsating morass engulfing Abigail's anguished mind. An image of Sylvia lying broken and dying on the wet tarmac flickered briefly…

<A TRULY ONE-SIDED AFFAIR, UNITED WERE SIMPLY TOO STRONG><*SUCH A FESTIVAL OF LIES*><FORCED TO RETREAT UNDER A HAIL OF PETROL BOMBS AND> <*OOOH HOW CAN LOVE BE SO CRUEL?*><REMEMBER YOU CAN DOWNLOAD OUR PODCAST NOW><*BEDTIME TOY, BEDTIME TOY, TIME FOR BED NOW GIRL...*>

Abigail fumbled for her hood and tugged it on in time to see Gemma tear away the last shred of wrapping to reveal a wooden box.

'Last chance Abigail,' said Gemma, her fingers closing around the lid.

Abigail held out her hands pleading for the box. 'Don't do this. Tell me what you want me to say and I'll say it.'

Gemma scowled contemptuously. 'Are you deaf? I want you to tell me the truth!'

'But I'm not lying to you...'

Gemma flipped open the lid. She put her hand in the box and removed a beautiful, delicately constructed suncatcher. Holding it up against the bare bulb hanging from the rafters she watched as handmade discs of polished metal span, sparkled and looped around a large berry red crystal.

'Pretty, if a little pointless,' said Gemma far from impressed. 'Always had busy hands your mother.' She let the ornament drop to the floor. When Abigail tried to retrieve it, Gemma slapped her across the face. 'I told you to sit down!'

'Hey! Don't you dare hit my sister!'

Gemma wheeled round startled. Tom glared at her from the doorway.

'Don't interfere Tom. She needs to be disciplined. Your dad has been far too lenient with her. With both of you. It's not his fault. He has far more important things to worry about than the two of you. But fortunately he has me now. So things are going to change in this house. I suggest you both get used to that fact.'

Abigail slumped to the floor clutching her head. Tom rushed to her side.

'You're sick do you know that?' he said, staring furiously at his aunt. 'You're not welcome here! Wait till I tell Dad about this!'

'Jonathan will understand. He needs me. He can't cope on his own. He knows I only want to make him happy. Unlike his children who insist on making his life a misery.'

Fastening her hood tightly around her head Abigail managed to push herself upright. The noise under control but the pain escalating, she rescued the broken radio and the suncatcher and stuffed them both inside the holdall.

'Sit back down! I'm not finished with you!' Gemma hollered, trying to drag Abigail back to the chair.

Tom wrestled Gemma away from his sister and pinned her against the workbench. 'What is wrong with you? Leave her alone!'

Seeing an escape route open up, Abigail grabbed her bicycle and rushed from the shed. Gemma tried to wriggle from Tom's grip. 'Come back here!'

Abigail rode across the garden, the front wheel wobbling alarmingly under the holdall slung weightily over the handlebars. Off the grass and on to the smooth path leading to the front of the house, she finally tamed her bucking steed and began to build momentum. A clunking change of gear and the ride became much cleaner, much speedier. She clattered off the kerb and into the road... Full steam ahead…

Tom hared into the street. 'Abi! Stop! Please! I won't let that old bat hurt you!' he yelled at the quickly diminishing rider. He managed to sprint halfway to the junction at the end of the road before his battered ribs forced him to give up. Holding his aching side, he watched Abigail swing her bike and pedal swiftly out of sight.

'Abi...!'

CHAPTER FIFTEEN

SIGNAL LOSS

Another beautiful morning in Balemouth Bay. Air thick with all the aromas of a seaside summer. Hot sand. Sugary treats. Tanning lotion. Fast food and fresh coffee ... The promenade buzzing with tourists and locals. Joggers weaving through the throng. Infants dozing in droopy sunhats. Old timers puffing at the old harbour wall offering nuggets of advice to the young lads casting their crab lines. Dogs bounding from the water to shake and spray their soggy coats over shrieking sunbathers. And the ever present gulls on the mooch, watching the whole merry performance from their lamp posts and railings.

But not everyone appreciated the heatwave. Those spoilsports at the Water Board had followed through on their threat. Not that Valerie Hobbs gave two hoots.

'Long may it continue!' she beamed.

'God willing!' Mr Zurawski chuffed, swapping a bag of iced buns for a five-pound note. 'Sun equals ice cream and ice cream equals a happy till and a happy till equals a happy Mrs Zurawski. And when Mrs Zurawski is happy, life is good!'

'To hell with them and their hosepipe ban, that's what I say. My garden will just have to suffer. So let the sun shine as long as it wants. I mean is there anything finer than feeling the warmth of the sun against your skin, hmm?' said Valerie.

'To hell with them Valerie. If the water runs dry I shall fill my taps with cold beer instead.'

'Now that is quite possibly the most brilliant idea I've ever heard. Cheerio!' waved Valerie.

'*Do widzenia* Valerie!'

Crouched behind the rear of a parked Volvo, Stevie Morton watched the woman exit the bakery pouring some change into her purse then, with a spring in her step, she went straight into The Green Grocery. No-one else in sight. Now was his chance. He checked with Jamie and Ben hiding in the bushes close by. His brothers egged him on. Stevie bolted across the car park towards the fruit and vegetable laden tables. Grabbing a fat marrow the size of a rugby ball he heard a brief shrill of warning from the bushes. His brothers signalled urgently for him to take cover. He struggled to see the danger at first but soon spotted PC Godwin ambling towards the shops. Stevie ducked into the cool shade under the tables and hunkered up against the shop front hugging his marrow.

With no other customers to negotiate and no-one manning the counter, Valerie briskly roamed the empty aisles adding fresh handfuls of big bright colour to her basket. *He must be out the back somewhere* - she thought, humming merrily away to herself; a silly tune she'd heard on the radio and now couldn't get the damn thing out her head. Some teenybop keech about being held and squeezed like a toy.

'I'm making one of my legendary summer salads,' she said cheerfully addressing the open door to the storeroom. 'Feta, sun-blushed tomatoes, olives, peppers, celery; the works! I always make far too much for myself. So I was wondering, if you're not too busy obviously, maybe you'd like to join me? I have a decent bottle of Malbec ready and waiting. Do you like walnuts? Or would you prefer… oh!' Valerie stopped mid-flow when a woman she'd never seen before appeared from the storeroom.

Gemma smiled a frosty blade of a smile. 'You were wondering if I'd prefer what exactly, madam?'

'I'm sorry, I thought you were Jonathan.'

'Jonathan is indisposed.'

'Indisposed? Is he ill?' asked Valerie.

'No, he's not ill. Not unless you regard chronic naivety as an illness. He's trying to find that daughter of his. He's been out all night searching for her.'

Valerie looked puzzled 'Searching for her? I thought she was in hospital.'

'Not anymore,' said Gemma. 'She's run away.'

'Run away? That doesn't sound like Abigail. When did she run away?'

Taking a seat behind the counter, Gemma minutely studied the intruder in ascending order; all the way from her shoes to her ponytail. 'The night before last. And how would you know what Abigail sounds like, if you don't mind me asking?'

Valerie offered her hand. 'I'm Valerie, Valerie Hobbs. I'm a friend of the family.'

Gemma deigned to brush the tips of Valerie's fingers then folded her arms under her bosom. 'Valerie Hobbs,' she repeated, pursing her pink mouth into a wrinkly smudge as though she'd swallowed something distasteful. 'No. Never heard of you. And I *am* family. Abigail is my niece.'

'Oh, I see. You must be worried sick.' said Valerie.

'As I keep saying to Jonathan, there's really no need to be worried. Abigail will turn up soon enough. And she's quite capable of looking after herself.'

'Poor thing. She's a sweet girl'

'Do you think so? I've always found her to be somewhat sour. She has her dad wrapped around her finger and she knows it. So it's no wonder she behaves like a spoilt, attention seeking little madam at times.' Gemma stood abruptly and turned to the flowers displayed on the shelf behind her. 'Beautiful aren't they?' she said, pointedly fussing over each stem. 'Jonathan bought them for me. A little thank you gift for all my help. He asked if I could stay with him for a few days. Inconvenient for me but how could I refuse? My family needs me. Personally I prefer azaleas but I'm happy with tulips. And to his credit, he did choose the Linifolia. He obviously likes a touch of class. A touch of style,' she said facing Valerie, her flinty smile back in place. 'He's a man of taste. He's not interested in bland, run-of-the-mill blooms.'

Valerie tried to conceal her irritation. 'I'm sure Jonathan's very grateful for the help.' She placed her basket on the counter. 'So, Sylvia was your sister?' she asked, desperate to change the subject.

'She was. And still is. Anything else you'd like to know?'

'Oh, I'm sorry. I didn't mean to... I'm truly sorry about what happened to Sylvia.'

Gemma dismissed the apology with a wave of her hand and totted up the bill. 'That'll be seven-pounds and sixty-pence please... And the answer to your question by the way, is no.'

'I beg your pardon? Which question?' said Valerie, fishing a note from her purse.

'You asked if Jonathan likes walnuts. He doesn't. He's allergic to them. The anaphylactic shock would kill him. So I'd say he's had a lucky escape. Who knows what other poisons may be lurking inside one of your undoubtedly *legendary* salads?' Gemma placed Valerie's change in her palm then added a little condescending pat on the wrist. 'Oh, come now, there's no need to look so upset sweetheart. I'm only teasing you. Nevertheless, it's probably much safer for all concerned if Jonathan eats with me tonight, wouldn't you say?'

Stevie stroked his prize. Cold, heavy and green. He couldn't wait to throw this beauty off the bridge. He poked his head out from from under the fruit and veg table and peered across the car park. His brothers, still crouched in the bushes opposite, motioned furiously for him to join them. The shop bell chimed just as Stevie shuffled forth. He skittered back under and waited in the darkness cradling his precious marrow. He watched a pair of white canvas espadrilles pace quickly from the shop. They suddenly stopped in the bright sunshine, the toes mere inches from the shadows where his own scuffed black trainers were hiding. He heard a woman mutter scornfully under her breath. She was wearing a long skirt. Sky blue. The hem within touching distance. Sorely tempting to reach out and sneak a peek. Sorely tempting...

The woman tutted in irritation. A pound coin bounced on the ground at her feet. Stevie pulled his fingers away from her skirt and cowered deeper under the table. The woman crouched, her hand chasing the little gold wheel as it rolled into the shadow. Heart bouncing against the marrow Stevie held his breath while the coin traced a leisurely arc around his feet. More of the woman folded into view; knees, thighs, hips and a blouse matching her skirt tucked in at her waist... One hand balanced her shopping on the pavement while the other stretched beneath the table, fingers sweeping the ground millimetres from his legs.

Momentum fading, the coin wobbled back into the sunshine.

'Gotcha!'

Stray cash clasped safely inside her purse, the woman straightened up, collected her bag and walked off. Sucking air into his starving lungs Stevie slumped to the ground in relief. Over in the bushes Ben and Jamie were signalling; *wait... wait...wait...* The moment Valerie turned the corner the signal changed... *Now!*

Stevie shoved the marrow up his jumper and bowled out from under the table to join his brothers in a race for the bridge.

'Nice one bro! What did you get?' Ben grinned admiring his younger brother's pregnant belly.

Stevie proudly lifted his jumper and gave birth.

'Ooh aye! That's a beauty. What is that thing?' asked Jamie admiring the bulbous green offspring.

'Dunno,' Stevie admitted. 'It's heavy.'

'Let's have a feel... It is heavy innit?' Jamie concurred holding the vegetable in both hands.

'Looks like a big cucumber thing.'

'How are you supposed to eat that?'

'It's a bloody watermelon ya donkeys,' Ben concluded with authority.

'Naw,' said Stevie taking it back. 'Watermelons are round, in't they? This thing looks like a giant knob.'

Jamie laughed. 'Knob! You're right, it does look like a giant green knob!'

'It's a bloody watermelon I'm tellin' ye!' Ben insisted.

'Knobmelon more like.'

'You two are the knobs. Right, whose turn is it?' asked Ben as they charged on to the bridge.

Stevie petulantly snatched the marrow from his brothers. 'Mine!'

'Aye well, get on wi' it then. I'll give ye a pound if you smack someone right on the heid. Like I did wi' that blonde tart.'

'Aye, that was a proper smack that was,' Jamie nodded in appreciation.

The three Mortons gathered together at the railing and looked down to the bus stop directly below. 'Arse! There's no-one there,' scowled Ben.

'Hold on, what about him?' Jamie pointed to a cyclist powering along the road. A few more seconds and he would be right under their feet.

'A pound you say? Easy money,' said Stevie. In a sure sign he'd switched to full concentration mode, he poked his tongue through the corner of his mouth, made some minor adjustments to his stance and hoisted the marrow over the railing.

The cyclist coasted closer... closer... closer... closer...

'Bombs away!'

Eager to track every plummeting inch of the projectile's trajectory, the brothers craned as far as they dared over the railing. The cucurbit missile exploded against the cyclist's handlebars spattering fleshy green slop all over his face. His yellow jersey and shorts decorated in a buckshot of moist seeds, the shocked rider clamped his brakes. The front wheel locked, twisted and smacked hard into kerb, ejecting him from the saddle and into the undergrowth at the roadside. Mission accomplished, the brothers hightailed it to safety laughing hysterically all the way.

A bead of sweat cooled by the breeze, slowly wound its way down the nape of her neck and continued on to follow the ridge of her spine. Valerie had to admit the heat wasn't quite so blissful when carrying a week's supply of shopping. Not that she lived far from the local shops. A five-minute hike. Long enough for her thoughts to mine a rich new seam of paranoia and guilt. Who did that godawful woman think she was? How could Jonathan let someone like that stay with him? If he needed help why didn't he just ask? She would gladly have dropped everything to help him. He can't be thinking straight. He must be at his wits end with Abigail. So what possessed her to think she could cure all his woes with a bloody salad? She was such a fool! He needed practical help not a plateful of rabbit food. She should be at his side helping him look for his daughter. Poor Abigail…

Valerie pushed open her garden gate. Halfway up the path she suddenly dropped her bags. Frozen with fear, she stared at the sleeping vagrant slumped on her doorstep unsure whether to run off screaming for help or to attack the man head on with whatever she had to hand. The latter option quickly lost its appeal after she considered the choice of weapons on offer. How much damage could she do with a handful of radishes and a stick of celery?

Another tentative foot forward and she realised the shambolic heap blocking her front door was Jonathan. He looked dreadful. Unshaven, crumpled and snoring. She prodded a toe against his knee. He grumbled, snorted and turned on his side. Valerie prodded him harder. He snuffled, shuddered and finally woke.

'Jonathan? What are you doing here?'

Rubbing his groggy eyes, Jonathan hoisted his creaking body upright. 'Val? Sorry. I didn't know where else to go.'

'Look at you. You're a mess. Let's get you inside.'

Jonathan sheepishly followed Valerie into her bright airy kitchen where she dumped her shopping on the dining table and helped unload a bag full of vegetables. 'A nice Red Brunswick,' he said, holding up a purple bulb. 'Organic. Locally sourced. Versatile. Good for cooking but sweet and mild enough to be used raw in salads. You clearly know your onions.'

Valerie ignored his smile. 'Sit,' she ordered. 'Are you hungry? I was planning to rustle up a salad. But then I met your sister-in-law and boy, did I lose my appetite? Charming woman. Took great delight in showing off the tulips you bought for her. You're a man of class and taste apparently. Which is news to me.'

'Tulips?' said Jonathan, perplexed. 'I never bought her any bloody tulips. Where did you meet Gemma?'

'In your shop. I was in a perfectly good mood, full of the joys of summer and then I'm served by this one-woman cold front and suddenly winter has arrived. How can you even bear to have that woman in your house?'

'I didn't invite her!' Jonathan protested. 'She just barged her way in and I was too preoccupied to say no. Thing is, she's like the mildew on my bathroom ceiling, she's really difficult to shift.'

Valerie shook her despondent head. 'Don't do that.'

'Don't do what?'

'Don't try and make me smile. I'm not interested in your mildew.'

Jonathan watched her sweep back and forth banging cans on to shelves and dumping vegetables in the fridge, doors flying open and slapping shut. 'If this is a bad time I can always come back later.'

Valerie's frustration boiled over. Banging a fist against the granite worktop she fixed Jonathan with a desperate stare. 'Why didn't you tell me Abigail was missing? I would have helped you look for her. You know where I am. You know I'll always help you. So why didn't you *ask* me?'

Jonathan covered his face in his hands and let them slide down to his throat. He could still feel the sea's gelid embrace sliding around his skin. He shivered, remembering how close he had come to meeting his end. And how badly he had wanted to. But mercifully, the instinct to survive took full command of the controls and somehow he managed to kick for shore. He had a vague memory of lying there, on the beach, staring at the moon and the stars with the empty wine bottle in his hand. At which point he must have fallen asleep.

'Because,' he sighed, 'I thought I could cope on my own. But I was wrong.' Jonathan rose from his seat and took Valerie's hand. 'I've missed you so much.'

'Don't do that. You've got no right.' Valerie snatched her hand away.

'Then tell me to leave.' Eyes welling, Valerie turned her back on him. Jonathan took her gently by the waist and pulled her close. 'Valerie?'

'What do you want me to say?' she asked.

'I want you to say you've missed me too.'

Valerie furiously shook herself free. Hands trembling, she wiped her eyes and tucked away a stray lock of hair. 'Isn't it obvious? Why do you think I visit your shop so often? I could buy these things anywhere. I go because I want to see you. To see how much longer I have to wait. But the way you look at me sometimes. Like I'm an inconvenience.' Valerie moved towards him eyes blazing with hurt. 'You needed time and space. I understood that. You needed to look after your children. You needed to grieve. I understood. But it was so hard. Don't you get it? I had no-one. No-one to understand what *I* needed? And I needed *you*.'

Jonathan tried to take her hand again but Valerie backed away. 'Val, please...'

'I hate feeling like this Jonathan. How can I possibly compete with a dead woman? I'm constantly treading on egg shells. She's been gone over a year but she still has this hold over you. Over me. Everything! She's still keeping us apart. I'm not a fool Jon. You loved her, you loved her very much. But I'm not to blame. I never asked for any of this. It's not my fault she died.'

'Of course it's not your fault,' said Jonathan.

'Then why do you make me feel like it is?'

Jonathan moved to the window and searched the sky beyond as if the right words were hidden somewhere in its bright blue vastness. 'We were only twenty-one when we married,' he said finally. 'Just kids really. And you're right, I did love her. Very much. But after eighteen years of marriage, my feelings changed. And I'm sure hers did too. They're bound to aren't they? Christ, it's impossible to maintain that stupid youthful infatuation forever isn't it? But I'd made my decision. I was going to spend the rest of my life with Sylvia and the kids. Because it was the common sense thing to do. Because we were content. And what is so wrong with just being content? Why do we always have to look for more?'

He saw Valerie reflected in the window, watching him. So much hurt. 'But then I met you and common sense went straight out the window. I was ready to give it all up. All of it. And then she went and died. She died before I had the chance to tell her about us. After all that time together the very least she deserved was the truth and... I never gave it to her.' He turned to Valerie and wiped a tear from her cheek. 'And the truth is... I'm in love with you.'

Jonathan wrapped Valerie tightly in his arms. This time she made no attempt to break free and rested her head against his chest. She listened to the quick, steady beat of his heart.

'I never knew you were allergic to walnuts,' she said.

'I'm not. Who told you that?'

'Doesn't matter,' said Valerie. 'By the way, you do realise you stink like rotten seaweed, don't you?'

'Do I?' Jonathan sniffed his shirt. She had a point. 'Sorry.'

Valerie's smile closed in on Jonathan's mouth.

'Forgiven,' she said.

They kissed. Softly at first...

CHAPTER SIXTEEN

AMPLITUDE MODULATION

Mr Zurawski pulled the shutters down on the bakery. Another day, another dollar. Quite a few dollars if truth be told. He offered a thumbs up to the sun. As long as that big yellow beneficent ball continued to grace the sky then the good folks of Balemouth Bay would continue to treat themselves to picnics at the beach or along the promenade. And those unfortunate enough to be working would continue to enjoy extended al fresco lunch breaks in the meadows or in the park. Hampers and lunch boxes packed with sandwiches, filled rolls, pastries and cookies. His smile drifted to the far side of the car park where a shimmering mirage rose from the scalding tarmac. Yes, another day, another fistful of dollars. Well, a till full of pounds at any rate. Real money. Not that toy Euro stuff. Bring back the zloty! Shutters secured he headed for his car. A modest old Volvo. Trusty but growing tired. He liked that new Nissan from the TV adverts: Take the City – Take the Country - Take the Road! Perhaps he should try to convince the wife they could afford a splash of recklessness in this time of plenty. Yes, he would broach the subject at the dinner table.

At the rear of the building, Henryk dumped the last of the rubbish into the bins before locking the back door. Another busy day consigned to the trash. Time to go home and repair his moped. Oil leak. Shouldn't be difficult. Change the sealing washer, tighten the sump plug and he would no longer have to rely on the old man for a lift. He brushed the dirt from his hands. A car would be so much better. Maybe he should try and convince the old man to give him a pay...

'Henryk! Help me!'

Startled out of his skin, Henryk backed up against the door looking all around for the source of the strained whisper.

'Henryk, it's me.'

Dressed completely in black, a slender, hooded figure appeared from behind a recycling dumpster brimming with cardboard. She had a bicycle with her. A heavy looking khaki holdall dangled from the handlebars.

'Abigail! Oh my God!' he cried when a patch of daylight revealed her sunken, bloodshot eyes. 'Look at you. I'm calling your dad.'

'No!' Abigail leapt forward, grabbed Henryk by the arm and pulled him down. She pressed a finger to his lips before he could utter another syllable. 'Please don't. You mustn't tell anyone. Please,' she said, her voice hoarse and brittle.

Henryk stared closely at the desperation framed within the black oval of her hood. 'I don't know...' he whispered unsure, thumb poised over his mobile phone. 'Everyone's looking for you. Everyone's worried. Look at you! Look at your eyes. You look terrible. Are you hurt? Maybe I should call an ambulance.'

Abigail cupped a hand over his phone. 'Henryk. You have to believe me. If they take me back, you'll never see me again. Ever. I'm serious. They want to cut open my head. You can't let them do that to me! Please. I need your help. I need somewhere to hide.'

Hearing an ageing engine turn in towards the delivery bays, Henryk quickly unlocked the back door. 'Quick! Get inside!' Helping her with the holdall he steered Abigail safely into the bakery. 'I'll be back as soon as I can.'

Henryk twisted the key in time to see his dad pull up with a sharp toot of the Volvo's horn.

'Another day, another dollar, eh son!' Mr Zurawski said cheerily as they drove off.

'Aye,' Henryk smiled innocently at his dad. He managed one final, anxious glance to the bike propped by the bins before the car turned and headed for home.

Abigail shuffled her way through to the little cafe area near the front of the store. She dumped her bag on the corner table and sat down. Too tired to lift her head from the back of the chair, she watched motes of dust drift and dance in the arrows of sunlight piercing the shutters and float over cabinets and shelves laden with an array of cream-filled, cherry-topped, sponge temptations. The air smelled warm and sweet. The dull throb of noise continued its maddening attempt to prise apart the plates of her skull. She massaged her aching temples, not that it made the slightest difference, and soon gave up.

Abigail sat forward, lifted the broken radio from the bag and laid it carefully on the red and white checked table cloth. The damage looked fatal. The casing cracked almost in two, the circuit board dangling loose, the aerial bent and split. Brushing away tears she threw her head back in despair and felt her hood slip to her shoulders.

FLASH!!!

'Listen up my hungry little shoppers! You will have to move faster than a cheetah on steroids if you want to bag a pair of these little beauties!'

Abigail squinted hard at the hyper-enthusiastic, heavily made-up woman who had suddenly materialised behind the counter. An information graphic listing a price tag, P&P rates and a telephone number, hovered in the air just above her right shoulder. With ice bright teeth and hair sprayed to a solid immutable flourish of candyfloss, her quick hands fluttered eager to sell, sell, sell!

'These items are making their debut on *Shop Till You Drop TV*,' the presenter beamed, 'And I guarantee they'll disappear quicker than a Saharan snowflake!' She pulled on a pair of grey woollen gloves and waggled her hands making sure her audience could admire them from every possible angle. 'I know it's the height of summer right now but in just a few short months time you'll wish your hands were tucked inside a pair of these clever little gems. How handy - excuse the pun - are these going to be? Now, I know what you're thinking, sitting there in your cosy, tastefully furnished little sitting-rooms, - *But Nikki, surely that's just an ordinary pair of gloves you're wearing?* - Well you could not be more wrong my deeply huggable friends. Look!' She raised a palm for the invisible camera to zoom in to. 'What's this stitched in to the palm of my glove? My God can it be? But how? But wait! But yes! It is! Your eyes do not deceive you. Sadistically simple yet devilishly clever! It's a built-in heat pad!

'Imagine. It's six a.m. on a cold and frosty winter morning. You're freezing your perfectly manicured pinkies off and you'll be late for the office unless you clear that pesky ice from your windscreen toot sweets. So what do you do? Start rummaging hopelessly in your boot wondering where you put that clumsy and completely ineffective scraper? Oh no! Not with these babies! Just press the button on the thumb and wham! Instant heat. Slap your toasty paws on the windscreen and watch that frosty evilness melt away. These Hot Mitts are just genius and only £9.99. And what's more, if you buy the left hand we'll throw in the right absolutely free…!'

Shaking her head fiercely, Abigail hurled a sugar dispenser at the presenter but in a blink the woman was wiped away and the dispenser crashed harmlessly into the bread trays behind the till.

She flipped the hood back into place. Something glinted in her bag, sparkling wildly in a shard of sunlight. Abigail lifted the suncatcher free and held it up. The discs dipped and weaved, bouncing the light reflected and refracted from the central crystal. The colours split into tiny rainbows. Mesmerising. It must have taken her mother an age to construct something so delicately beautiful. She stood on a chair and tried to hang it from the light fitting but as she reached up, the weighty, lead-lined hood fell away again.

FLASH!!!

Once the burst of sheer white faded, the room grew steadily darker... and darker. The space juddered, stretched and flickered to a soundtrack of short wave static and beeps.

Abigail retreated against the wall. A dot appeared in the darkness no bigger than a marble. The little sphere quickly expanded until its swirling mass filled the entire shop and took on the glorious, unmistakable form of Saturn. The globe spun slowly, gracefully in front of her. So beautiful! She reached out to touch the planet's rings. Her fingers passed through the belts of ice and rock feeling nothing.

A voice, clear, distinct and authoritative cut through the profusion of beeps and white noise:

- AFTER THIRTEEN YEARS OF PATIENT STUDY THE CASSINI PROBE ENDED ITS MISSION BY PLUNGING HEADLONG INTO THE PLANET'S MYSTERIOUS DEPTHS. THE INTREPID LITTLE PROBE MAY HAVE UNLOCKED SOME OF THE GAS GIANT'S SECRETS BUT THERE ARE SO MANY QUESTIONS LEFT UNANSWERED. QUESTIONS WHICH WILL KEEP SCIENTISTS BUSY FOR YEARS TO COME. BUT THERE'S NO RUSH. SATURN IS NOT THE KIND OF PLACE TO DO THINGS IN A HURRY. AFTER ALL, IT TAKES THE PLANET ALMOST THREE DECADES TO ORBIT THE SUN... -

Then, inexplicably, Saturn disappeared leaving Abigail in total darkness. The void bristled with a persistent hiss. The hiss of heavy rain...

Abigail's skin crawled at the sound of screeching brakes...

And then the scream. That awful scream.

Her mother's scream.

Pealing on and on within the endless blackness.

And then came that horrible thud. The sound that signalled the end of a life.

She heard her mother's voice.

'I love...? One love...? I love...? One love...?'

'Mum!' Abigail cried.

The darkness lifted. The splintered blades of sunlight returned. The bakery reappeared exactly as before. Abigail sat down and fastened the hood tightly before the chaos could erupt and split her mind again.

She was so tired. So, so tired... The noises gurgled away somewhere in the background. Thanks to the nullifying effect of the hood, she was learning to ignore them. Gathering the radio and the suncatcher close, she folded her arms on the table and rested her head.

So... so... so... tired...

'I love...?'

Jonathan heard the raised voices even before he put the key in the door.

'Oh God, what is it now?' he muttered. Readying himself for battle he pushed on through. The argument raged from the kitchen.

'Why are you still here?' he heard Tom yell. 'Don't you get it? You're not welcome. And we certainly don't need you!'

'I beg to differ young man,' came Gemma's defiant response. 'You're a spoilt brat. Someone has to teach you how to behave and that someone may as well be me.'

'You're an interfering old bag! Piss off!'

Jonathan hurried through. 'Hey! Enough! Apologise to your aunt.'

'No way.'

'Apologise to her!'

But Tom remained resolute, staring furiously at Gemma. Gemma tapped her feet, crossed her arms and matched his stare with a smug smile as she waited for an apology that was clearly never going to come.

'You see Jonathan? This is what happens when you allow your children to run riot?' she said, her eyes firing daggers into Tom. 'I know how difficult things have been since Sylvia passed away but there comes a point when you have to stop mollycoddling them. There's nothing wrong with showing a firm hand when it's required.'

'Gemma please, I'll deal with this. Tom, I'm not going to ask you again. Apologise to your aunt.'

'She's the one who should be apologising after what she did to Abigail.'

Jonathan noticed Gemma's mask slip. Just a little. 'What are you talking about?'

Tom finally shifted his stare from Gemma to his dad. 'When I came home last night Abigail was here. In Mum's shed.'

A knot of hope tightened in Jonathan's chest. 'Wait. Abigail's here? Why didn't someone call me? Where is she?'

'She's gone! That's my point. I came back and found Abi in the shed. And *she* was yelling at Abi. She slapped her in the face. Hard. And Abi ran off again. And I don't blame her! I've been trying to call you but it keeps going straight to voicemail.'

Jonathan checked his phone. Dead. Moisture leaked from the charging port. The sea had managed to claim a victim after all. He turned to Gemma who shook her head in disdain.

'This merely serves to prove what I've been trying to tell you all along. You've been too soft on him. This is why he thinks he can get away with such barefaced lies.'

'It's true! Abigail was here! She hit her!' Tom persisted, pointing unequivocally at his aunt. 'She went mad saying all kinds of mental stuff. She even accused Abi of killing Mum!'

Gemma dropped her head, her face a portrait of despair. 'That is truly despicable,' she sniffed, fighting and failing to hold back the tears. 'To use the memory of your dead mother, my treasured sister, just to get yourself out of trouble. I... I can't believe you'd stoop...'

'It's true! That's what she said. And she would have slapped Abi again if I hadn't stopped her.'

Jonathan examined their faces. His son's full of righteous anger, his sister-in-law's a dejected well of sorrow.

Who to believe...

'Get out.' He said eventually.

Tom scowled in disbelief and made to storm off but Jonathan pressed a hand to his chest stopping him in his tracks.

'Not you. You stay here.'

Gemma looked truly affronted. 'I beg your pardon? You're telling *me* to get out?'

'That's correct.'

'Let me get this straight. Are you seriously taking his word over mine?'

'Correct again Gemma. Now get going.'

'You are making a colossal mistake Jonathan. You will regret this.'

'Missing you already Gemma.'

Her bluff called, Gemma ditched the fake hurt and tears. She snatched her handbag and coat. 'You are a weak little man,' she hissed into Jonathan's face as she made for the hallway. 'Whatever Sylvia saw in you is a complete mystery to me.'

Placing a guiding hand on the small of her back Jonathan shepherded her to the front door, feeling her fury swell with each step. 'Thanks for stopping by Gemma. Drive safely now.'

'You're hiding something aren't you? Why else would you behave like this? Why else would you treat someone who's done so much for you like a petty criminal? Your own kith and kin! You must be hiding something.'

'Allow me to get the door for you.' Jonathan released the latch and swung the door wide open.

'If Abigail didn't kill Sylvia maybe you did,' Gemma spat, determined to fight to the last. 'Yes! You killed her didn't you? You say you were at work but where's your proof? And even if you were, you could easily have hired someone to run her over. I'm right aren't I? You can't fool me. Rest assured, I shall be speaking to the police!'

'Bye Gemma.' Jonathan closed the door. He peered through the peephole watching her half run, half walk to her car parked by the gate. Hurling her bag in the rear, she thrust herself behind the wheel, revved hard and growled off. Jonathan rested his back against the door and expelled one long, stress cleansing blast of a sigh.

'Good riddance,' he said once he'd calmed down. 'Mad as a sack full of itchy monkeys that one. Where did Abi go after you saw her?'

'I don't know,' said Tom, still somewhat stunned by this unexpected turn of events. 'She took her bike and rode off down the street. I couldn't catch her. Sorry Dad.'

'You've got nothing to apologise for. I should have been here,' said Jonathan, ruefully stroking his stubbly chin.

'Are you okay, Dad? You don't look well. And to be honest, you don't smell too great either.'

'You need to work on your bedside manner Tom but thanks for your concern. A quick shower and a shave and I'll be fine. Once that's done I'm going to look for Abi. Want to help me?'

'Sure.'

'Good,' Jonathan nodded before plodding wearily upstairs.

Abigail's eyes fluttered. Closed... Fluttered again. Closed... Opened...

She pulled focus on a landscape of snowy pink peaks and cratered, chocolatey plateaus formed by a mountain range of doughnuts rising high above the red and white checked plains. A cup of coffee slid across the table in front of them. Steam rising. Looked hot. Smelled delicious. Abigail raised her drowsy head and watched Henryk take a seat.

'Coffee and doughnuts. There's all kinds there - cinnamon, custard, chocolate iced, strawberry cream. I thought you might be peckish. I know they're not exactly the healthiest option,' he said with an apologetic smile. 'But then people go to your shop for the nutritious stuff don't they? There's gingerbread if you'd...'

But Abigail had already crammed half a custard doughnut in her face. Another bite and it was gone. Between a few slurps of coffee, a second doughnut suffered the same fate and was demolished in a flash. Mouth messy with sugar and jam she grinned at Henryk, chewing furiously.

'Enryk, ees are orjuss! Ow mong av you bin eer?' Henryk couldn't decipher a word. Abigail gulped down a clod of sweet mush. 'Sorry. How long have you been here?' she repeated and edged closer to concentrate fully on Henryk's voice over the constant jabber pestering her headspace.

'A while,' he said. 'I thought I'd better let you sleep. You looked so exhausted. I'm surprised I didn't wake you sooner with all the noise I was making. It's funny how when you try really hard to be quiet, everything you do ends up sounding like a grenade going off or something.'

'What were you doing?'

'Fixing your radio. I hope you don't mind. I think I've sorted it. I mended the board, soldered the loose connections, realigned the speaker and straightened the aerial. The casing is still cracked but I've glued it as best I can, so it should hold.'

Abigail's ecstatic heart sang. She took the precious radio from Henryk, turned it on and clutched the aerial in her eager fingers. The noise in her head died completely.

~ *That was close, eh Pookie?* ~

Abigail hugged the unit overjoyed. 'Granddad!'

~ *You didn't think you'd get rid of me that easily did you? How are you feeling? How's that head of yours?'* ~

'Messy. Getting messier. But much better now you're here!'

~ *Hmm... we better maintain radio silence. We're getting some funny looks.* ~

Abigail slapped a hand to her wayward mouth. She turned to Henryk, cheeks scarlet. From his small, puzzled smile and the look of outright alarm she could tell he was itching to get online and order a straightjacket with next minute delivery.

'Sorry. I think a lack of sleep is making me hysterical,' Abigail smiled at him. 'It's just that Granddad's old radio means so much to me. Thank you, thank you...' She put a hand behind his neck and pulled him in for a big kiss right on the lips. 'Thank you!'

Henryk sank back in his chair stunned and baffled but ready to die a happy man. He cleared his throat, eyes locked on Abigail's lips as she sat cradling her radio like a precious child.

'S'okay,' he ventured once he'd regained the power of speech. 'Don't you think we should tell your dad you're safe?'

'I will. But not yet. There are some things I have to do first.'

'Need some help? I can carry your bag for you.' Henryk hoisted the holdall off the floor and instantly regretted the offer. 'Jeez, this thing weighs a ton. What do you need all this stuff for?'

Abigail let go of the aerial.

<HOLD ME, FEEL ME, SQUEEZE ME BABE, LET ME BE YOUR BEDTIME TOY...>

She clasped the aerial again killing the irritating ditty dead.

'Can you seriously not hear that?'

'Hear what,' Henryk asked, looking ever more perplexed.

'Never mind. Thing is, I have to clear my head and those are the right tools for the job,' said Abigail with a nod to the holdall.

~ *Well said Pookie! Are you ready?* ~

Stuffed full of doughnuts and a renewed sense of purpose Abigail stood, stomped her foot, and grinning sharply at Henryk pronounced, 'I'm ready!'

*

With Tom at his side in the passenger seat, Jonathan powered The Green Grocery van over the River Bale, swung a U-turn at the junction by the ruins of St Luke's and headed back across the bridge for yet another circuit of the town. Checking doorways, bus stops, alcoves, benches, alleys... Tom wound down his window. The warm dusk air flowed inside carrying the swish of passing cars and snippets of boisterous conversations. They passed the crowded bars and busy restaurants. The smokers puffing on the porches of the hotels and the B&Bs. The beach dotted with lovers ambling this way and that. The teens gathered by the fountain. The young family studying a map of the town on the Tourist Information board; the mother holding a child in each hand while the father pointed at the You Are Here dot. The elderly couple sitting by the promenade sharing a bag of chips, one wooden fork between them, watching a little fishing boat putter for home.

All those faces and not one of them belonged to Abigail.

*

PC Godwin decided to take a stroll through the square. One last patrol before shift's end. All the shutters were down. The Green Grocery had removed all the produce from the exterior display tables, all that was, except for a solitary and slightly sorry looking melon. Cursing Jonathan's carelessness, he dropped the fruit in a bin.

He continued past the bakery, the newsagent, the florist, the fishmonger and the butcher. All quiet on the Western Front. He would catch them. Those Morton reprobates. Their days were numbered. He'd already spoken to the parents. A finer example of potty-mouthed, grease-fuelled, work-shy, soap-dodgers you'd never hope to find.

'Where's yer proof?' Maw Morton had demanded, her face pinched like a pug's. 'You cannae accuse oor boys of that stuff. Oor boys are good boys. Why is it whenever somethin' bad happens it's always oor lads to blame? Police brutality that's what this is! Now fu...'

Proof? Aye. Definitive. He needed to set a trap to catch the wee wastrels in the act. Aye, their days were numbered for sure. The people were demanding justice. He would sweep the dirt from the fair streets of Balemouth with the long broom of the law. The latest victim, Jimmy Stokes, had been knocked off his bike after being bombed with a marrow. They could have killed the poor bugger. Why did Jonathan insist on making it so easy for them? He'd have to have another word with him. Not yet though, poor sod had way too much going on at the moment.

He took the path leading down to the bus stop where he'd left his squad car. Abigail Squall. Where could she be? Wee tyke. Bless her. Perhaps tomorrow he'd find her. Only so many hidey-holes to be had in this wee town after all. Aye, tomorrow he'd have a damn good hunt. North, South, East, West. No stone would be left unturned. Right now though, his day was done. Time to drop the car at the station, book off with Control, then grab a fish supper on the way home. A large portion to share with the missus. And a battered saveloy. Oh aye, a battered saveloy would secure him extra brownie points.

Nearby, squeezed inside a telephone box, three sets of scheming eyes watched PC Godwin saunter off.

'Hurry!' urged Ben. 'If we're quick we might get him.'

Jamie made a dash for the bin, rescued the melon and followed his brothers as they ran for the bridge.

'See? *That's* a melon,' said Stevie. 'What we had yesterday wasn't a melon.'

'Aye it bloody was!' Ben argued. 'It was a bloody watermelon. That's a different *kind* of melon Jamie's holding.'

'What kind is this one then?'

'It's a bloody organic melon, ya tit. Look at the bloody sticker on it! *Or-gan-ic!*'

'Hey, you two gonnae shut it, aye?' Jamie snapped as they approached the bridge. 'He'll bloody hear ye!'

The three brothers scrummed together at the railings and leaned over to look down on PC Godwin. The ample policeman puffed towards his car.

'Don't miss him!' whispered Ben. 'You get extra points for a copper!'

One eye shut, Jamie slowly raised the melon and took careful aim.

The Mortons were so engrossed in their target not one of them noticed Henryk and Abigail steal up from behind, each sporting a bicycle D-lock. Henryk quickly snapped his lock around Jamie's left ankle and Ben's right. In the same instant Abigail slapped her lock through Jamie's right ankle encapsulating it with Stevie's left. Feeling the sudden bite of steel clamping their feet tight, the alarmed Mortons spun to confront their captors but, with all three tugging in different directions, they tumbled helplessly, palms splaying against the deck of the bridge.

'Ooyah, my ankle! I think I've bust my ankle!'

'Oi!'

'What the fu...' Ben's fury died in his throat when Abigail, armed with a fully loaded plastic spray bottle, leaned down and squirted a fine mist into his face. Toting his own atomiser, Henryk sprayed a dose into Jamie and Stevie's eyes.

'Agh! That stings! I cannae see!'

'My eyes! What is that stuff?'

'Acid! It's an acid attack!'

Henryk quickly dragged the blinded heap of wriggling limbs against the railings and held them there while Abigail yanked a heavy duty chain from her bag, looped it around the brothers' necks and padlocked them securely to the bridge. Down below she saw PC Godwin squeeze into his car and drive off towards the town centre.

'Take these friggin' locks aff or I'll bloody kill ye! Now!' Ben yelled, rubbing his streaming eyes.

The D-locks proved a nice snug fit and try as they might, none of the Mortons could pull so much as a toe free.

'Shoosh boys. We're in charge now,' said Abigail with a calmly malevolent glint in her eye.

Stevie tried to lunge for her but the chain held him firm. He tried kicking out instead.

'OOya!' Jamie wailed. 'Mind ma foot. That bloody hurt! I think my ankle's definitely bust.'

'Let us go now or we'll bloody shank you proper! Don't care if you're a girl or what!' Stevie snarled, tears dripping from his chin.

Unimpressed, Abigail raised her spray bottle and tightened her fingers around the blue plastic trigger. All three brothers twisted wildly, desperate to keep their badly leaking eyes away from the menacing nozzle.

Henryk searched their pockets and found Stevie's knife. He showed the blade to Abigail.

'I didnae mean it! Honest! Don't acid me, I'm beggin' ye,' Stevie howled.

Abigail squirted a shot into his crimpled face. 'It's lemon juice, idiot,' she said, taking the knife from Henryk. 'This looks sharp. I wonder if it's sharp enough to cut off a nose.'

The terrified Mortons tried to squeeze everything under, through or over the railings, frantically tugging, pushing and even biting the chain, but it was all hopeless.

'Cut Ben's nose off! Cut Ben's! His is the biggest!'

'Stevie, ya wee bastard! Yours is way bigger!'

Jamie held up his hands in submission. 'Please. Don't do this. We promise we won't ever come here again. We'll do whatever you want.'

Abigail crouched to collect the badly bruised melon lying at his fettered feet.

'I know you will,' she said and began to cut the fruit in half.

*

Inverness. The long drive home had done nothing to dampen Gemma's ire. She sat silently in her living room sipping sherry and fuming over an old family photo of the Squalls. Jonathan and Sylvia on their wedding day. Gemma the maid of honour at her sister's side clutching a big bouquet of posies. They all looked so bloody happy! What a sham! How dare Jonathan turf her out like that! After all she'd done for him! After all that cooking and cleaning. All that *caring*! Moron! Let him rot. Let them all rot. In Hell. Him and his retarded kids. Yes, let them rot. How *dare* they. They were all up to something. She could tell. The deceit was written all over their scheming faces. The lies. She had most certainly hit a nerve when she'd accused Jonathan.

There they were, in the palm of her hand. Husband and wife. He could have killed her. Easily. Or he could have paid someone to do it for him. Yes. Easily. Why though? Didn't matter why. The money. The thrill. He was evil. Look at the way he treated his own sister-in-law. Evil. They all were. Abigail, that little attention seeking witch, she was the focal point of the whole conspiracy. Tom as well. *Evil.* All you had to do was look at that boy. Covered in piercings. His bedroom smothered with demons and hell-sluts. Evil! And that music he played. The Devil's work. Yes, they all connived in Sylvia's death. Either that or Sylvia deliberately stepped in front of that car. Unable to live a moment longer in the midst of such evil, she took her own life. Who wouldn't? Curse them all.

No, Jonathan killed her. He positively stank of guilt.

Gemma took a pair of scissors from the dresser at her side and proceeded to snip all the way round Jonathan's head until the blades paused at his neck. The final slice… and off with his head!

Satisfied, she picked up the telephone and dialled 999. She shuddered. From her angle it looked like she was dialling the number of the beast.

God would surely prevail.

*

Jonathan opened his window hoping to clear the condensation fogging the windscreen. The wisps of steam rising from their coffees and hot burgers made good their escape and drifted into the night. The Beach Boy Burgers kiosk on the esplanade represented the last hope for anyone suffering a severe bout of the munchies at this time of night. Picking through palms heavy with coins, a smattering of teens from the fountain gang formed a healthy if disorderly queue alongside a swaying trio of drunken pals, a taxi driver and a dog walker on rollerblades.

Takes all sorts, mused Jonathan.

A particularly annoying song bubble-gummed from the radio.

Hold me, feel me, squeeze me babe...

A couple of bars later and both he and Tom were reaching for the dial...

'Go on,' Jonathan deferred. 'You choose a station. Anything but this... Or country music.'

Tom wasted no time in locating a slab of hard rock. Ripping a mighty bite from his quarter pounder he suddenly grinned.

'What's funny?' asked Jonathan tucking into a cheeseburger.

'I was just imagining the lecture we'd get from Abigail if she saw us eating this stuff.'

Jonathan nodded, smiled and offered an affectionate impersonation of his outraged daughter: '"How could you eat that? That meat has been pumped full of growth hormones, steroids and antibiotics!"'

'Tastes good though doesn't it?'

Jonathan laughed at the sight of Tom's chipmunk cheeks grinding away at the Frankenstein meat. 'She always hates it when you say that to her.'

'I have to get my own back sometimes. She's forever winding me up.'

'Ah well, nothing wrong with a bit of sibling rivalry.' Jonathan found himself staring at the bruises staining Tom's face and neck. 'They look sore.'

'Looks worse than it is.'

'Did you manage to mess up the other guy's face?'

'A bit.'

'Good.' Jonathan dropped what remained of his burger back in its plastic tray. It didn't taste that good to be fair. Difficult to tell which component tasted less like a weapons-grade chemistry experiment; the meat, the cheese or the bap. A safe bet that none of the ingredients had ever been within a country mile of a farmer's field. 'Listen Tom,' he said, after a moment spent searching for the right approach. 'I owe you an apology. I know we haven't exactly been on the best of terms recently. It seems all I ever do is snap at you rather than actually, you know, talk. And, if I'm being honest, I can't really say why that is. But I do know you deserve better. I'm sorry.'

Tom stopped chewing and swallowed. He looked warily at his dad. 'That's okay,' he drawled, suspecting a trap.

'No. It's not. I've been so wrapped up in my own problems I haven't taken the time to listen to yours. Which is inexcusable. What do you say we call a truce and work together from now on? Me and you, as a team. Deal?' Jonathan held out his hand. Tom narrowed his eyes. It was a deeply suspicious gesture. He carefully examined Jonathan's imploring gaze and the outstretched hand but as hard as he tried, he couldn't detect any hint of an ulterior motive and so shook it, firmly.

'Deal. Don't you want the rest of that burger?'

'I'm trying to be the caring, sharing father here. You're bursting my bubble,' said Jonathan.

'I know. I appreciate it. I can be a stubborn git too sometimes. Must take after my old man. So, yeah. Clean slate. Onwards. Do you want that burger or not?'

'Take the burger.'

Tom shovelled the cheesy-beef-dough concoction into his mouth.

'You're a regular waste disposal unit, do you know that?'

Tom, cheeks bulging again, offered a thumbs up in response.

A loud rat-a-tat-tat on the roof of the van left Jonathan clutching his heart. A tall, broad policeman leaned to the window.

'Jesus Archibald Christ! You trying to put me on the transplant list Stewart?' Jonathan puffed. It was Stewart Tully. The youngest son of Gail Tully, his old maths teacher from way back. A few years younger than Jonathan, Stewart possessed the kind of height and physique that commanded instant respect. Yet, imposing as he undoubtedly was, to anyone who knew him Stewart was the archetypal gentle giant.

'Sorry Mr Squall sir. Didn't mean to startle you.' He said with a pained expression.

'What's happened? Have you found Abigail?'

'I need you to come down to the station with me Mr Squall, sir.'

A wave of panic raked Jonathan's already fragile nerves. 'What's going on? Is it Abigail? Tell me. Is she okay? Please, just tell me she's okay?'

'We still haven't located your daughter as yet sir. This pertains to another matter.'

'What matter? What's going on?'

'It's all a wee bit awkward sir,' said Stewart opening the van door. 'If you'll kindly step out of the vehicle and come to the station with me please.'

'Step out of the vehicle? Stewart, tell me. What's the problem? The van's in good order. Passed its MOT only last month. It's taxed and insured. I have the documents right here if you need to see them?'

'Please, Mr Squall. My Sergeant's instructed me to arrest you if necessary. I told him there'd be no need for that. I told him we'd be able to sort this without any undue fuss.'

Tom sprang from the car. 'Arrest him! Why? What for? He hasn't done anything. He hasn't even had a drink. Not for a few hours anyway.'

'Thanks Tom. I'll handle it,' Jonathan chipped in before Tom could dig an even deeper hole. 'Please, Stewart, I don't wish to be obstructive but I'm not going anywhere until you tell me what the hell's going on.'

Plainly finding the whole episode quite distressing, Stewart stared down at his polished size twelves and grimaced. 'Well, the thing is, we've received new information in relation to the death of Sylvia Squall, sir.'

'New information? What new information? Wait. Don't tell me you've located the driver after all this time?'

'No sir, nothing like that. An accusation has been made. Regarding yourself. And your possible involvement in your wife's death. But I'm sure it's all a misunderstanding. We just need you to come down to the station for a voluntary interview, then I'm sure this will all be done and dusted in five-minutes. So if you wouldn't mind stepping out of the van.'

'Hold on. An accusation? Someone's accusing *me* of being involved in Sylvia's death? But that's absurd!'

'Mr Squall, will you please step out of the van. I really, *really* don't want to have to arrest you.'

'Stay in the van Dad! Don't listen to him.'

Seeing Stewart reach for the cuffs Jonathan decided it would be prudent not to test the human tower block's patience any further. 'Okay, I'll come. But let me follow you in the van. I don't want to leave it here.'

Stewart didn't seem happy with this suggestion. He retreated to his squad car where he leaned against the roof rubbing his furrowed brow while chatting into the radio hooked to his uniform. Conversation over, he returned to the van.

'Sorry sir, the Sergeant insists you travel with me. He's seems to think you might do a runner if I let you out of my sight. I told him you're a man of your word and that you'd never do anything that stupid, but orders are orders. So, if you please sir.' Stewart opened one of his shovel-like hands, inviting Jonathan out.

'Fine, you win.'

Tom forced himself between the lofty policeman and the van, blocking Jonathan's exit. 'You can't do this!' he glowered up at Stewart. 'Where did this accusation come from? Whatever it is, it's bollocks!'

'Don't make things worse Tom,' warned Jonathan. 'It's a misunderstanding. I'll sort it.'

'Your dad's right. It's just a formality. I'm sure we'll have it cleared up in no time. But I need you to step aside, now please.'

'Do as he says Tom.'

Tom reluctantly obliged. 'Can't you at least tell me who's accusing Dad of this bullshit?'

'I'll give you one guess,' said Jonathan as he climbed into the back of the squad car.

Tom rolled his eyes in disbelief. 'Aunt Gemma? But she's a psycho!' He made a last ditch attempt to make Stewart see reason. 'You can't believe a word she says. She's completely mental!' Stewart shrugged an apology and folded himself behind his steering wheel. Tom watched on helplessly as the police car reversed away from the van and pulled into Shore Street. 'You can't do this!'

He heard someone chuckle. The teens crowding the burger van were gawping and snickering. In fact, the entire queue and even Mr Beach Boy Burgers himself, were having a good old infuriating stare.

'Why don't you take a picture. It lasts longer!' Tom fumed.

A lanky girl in a pink tracksuit held out her smartphone and did exactly that. She shared the picture with her coven who cackled and pointed scornfully at Tom.

He quickly retreated to the sanctuary of the van and thumped the dashboard.

CHAPTER SEVENTEEN

TONE

'It's no good. It's punctured, see?' Henryk plucked the offending article from the front tyre of Abigail's bicycle. An RNLI badge pin. Abigail took the little lifeboat and examined it under the pool of the streetlight. Pleased with the find, she fastened it to her cuff. They had reached the end of the road. Literally. She stood with one foot on smooth tarmac and the other planted on the baked earth of a rutted track which curved steeply upwards through the quiet darkness of the woods.

'Leave the bike here. We can fix it later,' she said.

'That's okay. I don't mind pushing it. We can still use it to carry the bag. I don't think we're allowed to go that way though,' said Henryk with a tentative nod to the big, no nonsense sign fixed to the nearest tree - *Private: No Through Road.*

'Oh don't worry about that. We'll be fine.'

'Aren't you going to tell me where we're going yet?'

'You'll see!'

Henryk watched her bound fearlessly on through the trees holding her radio tightly to her chest. He looked behind him. They had reached the summit of Inch Point Road, the last residential street on the hill overlooking the southern end of the bay. His thighs burned. It had been a punishing climb, riding the bike up here with Abigail on the back and the holdall slung across the handlebars. Lovely view though. Balemouth Bay at night. The sweep of the promenade dotted with a necklace of lights. An expensive view judging by the size of the properties they'd passed and the parade of BMWs, Audis, Jaguars... He'd have to work for a hundred years just to raise enough cash to slap a deposit on one of those red sandstone mansions. A whole lot of bread-making to make the bread for a house on the hill, a room with a view, away from the riff-raff and the rabble.

Henryk suspected he'd seen one or two curtains twitch as they cycled by. What must they have looked like? Him, in the middle of the night with a bag full of tools, giving a backie to a girl dressed like an assassin hugging a badly damaged vintage radio. He was certain the police would arrive any second. But it was fun! Whatever she was up to, it didn't matter. He was hooked. Happy to help her on her crazy mission. No turning back now, especially after what they'd done to those Morton dunderheids. What a thrill that had been! Those boys had met their match in Abigail that was for sure. She was like some avenging Marvel heroine. She certainly looked the part. All in black. Hood up. *Radio Girl*! *She'll tune you in and spit you out*!

And Radio Girl had kissed him. His lips still tingled. He closed his eyes and tried to replay that moment back in the bakery in super high resolution slo-mo. A moment he would never forget. A kiss he would never let go. Ever.

A gull keened sleepily from the streetlight. He peered into the shadowy woods. Abigail had been swallowed up by the trees. Henryk adjusted the holdall's strap, tightening it across the handlebars and wheeled after her.

He caught up with her at the brow of the hill, where the track broke from the trees to meet the moon's lopsided smile. A fence on one side of the track bordered a field sheltering a herd of highland cows. A few shaggy, horned humps lifted their dozing heads when they heard the bike bounce and clatter over the bumps and stones. A drystone wall ran along the other side. A few feet beyond the wall the bluff tumbled sharply to the rocks nipping at the sea. The water looked as smooth and black as slate.

Abigail pointed to the bottom of the slope where the track veered towards a cluster of white buildings clinging to a thumb of rock. 'He lives down there, in the lighthouse.'

'Who?'

'Tony V. We're going to say hello.'

'Tony V? You mean the singer?'

'Yup.'

Henryk angled his watch to the moonlight. 'It's getting late. He might be in bed.'

'Then we'll wake him up,' said Abigail, her pace quickening.

'I don't think we should be bothering him at this time of night Abigail. Why don't we come back tomorrow?'

'No, it has to be now. Trust me. He'll be fine.'

'But he might have a really big guard dog or something. He might have two really big guard dogs,' said Henryk wheeling the bike alongside her.

~ *I like your boyfriend,* ~ Granddad piped up. ~ *He seems like a good lad.* ~

'He's not my boyfriend.'

Henryk stared at her, puzzled. 'Tony V? I didn't think he was. I mean he's a pop star and a rubbish one at that. He wouldn't be interested in you...'

Vigorously shaking her head, eyes pressed shut, Abigail kicked her boots into the ground sending up a burst of dust as she skidded to an abrupt standstill. She sneaked a wary peek. The baying, howling pack of Formula One cars she'd seen unleash from their starting grid in a screaming eruption of smoke and rubber had vanished leaving the track as quiet and empty as before. Apart from Henryk who was standing in front of her, holding the bike and looking deeply embarrassed about something.

'Not that he shouldn't be. Interested in you that is,' he said picking awkwardly at a loose thread on the bag's strap. 'What I'm trying to say is pop stars only want to date other pop stars don't they? Not that I'm saying you can't sing. I've never heard you sing. So I can't say for sure. But I bet you've got a great voice - Oh God where am I going with this?' He pressed a despairing palm to his forehead and looked at the moon. 'I didn't mean to upset you. I'm not suggesting for one second he wouldn't find you attractive. Any man with functioning eyes would find you attractive. And I'm not saying blind men wouldn't find you attractive, I'm sure they would too, because it's not just about your looks. It's everything.'

Henryk stared at Abigail and gulped, cheeks blazing. 'Please stop me talking. None of this is coming out right. My point is, any man who isn't interested in you is a fool. And Tony V is a fool. You are way too smart for him.' Henryk bit his babbling tongue and waited for Abigail to respond. She watched him silently, a small smile growing wider. Henryk looked at the bag tangled around the handlebars and wondered if there was room inside for one more tool.

~ *Listen to him bumbling away there!* ~ chuckled the radio. ~ *Only a smitten heart can reduce what was once a perfectly fine, upright and erudite young man into the blethering car wreck you see before you now. He's keen on you. That's a fact. You could do worse Pookie. Look at him. He's a healthy bugger. Handsome. Maintains a good level of personal hygiene. Slightly weird hair but that can be fixed. Sturdy teeth. And he works in a bakery no less! Think of all the free buns and muffins you could get!* ~

'There's more to life than buns and muffins,' said Abigail flatly.

Henryk seemed a little hurt. 'I know. I'm sorry. I'm not claiming to be any better than Tony V. Obviously you'd rather go out with a pop star than a baker. You'd be mad not to. Oh God! Not that I think you're mad! Because you're not. You're perfect. Oh please stop me talking! Can we pretend the last five minutes never happened, rewind and start again? Make that ten minutes to be on the safe side. Thing is, I don't want to work with my dad forever. I'm not complaining mind. I like working there. It's just, like you say – there's more to life than buns and muffins. You see, what I really want to do is go to college. Study engineering.'

~ *Hear that? Engineering! The lad's a boffin. The baker boffin! Handy with a soldering iron too. That repair job he did has worked wonders. I think I sound even better than before. Like I've been digitally remastered. I'm telling you Pookie, he's a keeper.* ~

'Really?' Abigail set off briskly down the track, a big grin on her face.

Henryk pulled the bike after her. 'Absolutely! I've always been fascinated in how machines and structures work. How components fit together and come apart. What about you? What do you want to do with your life?'

~ *The lad's asking you what your ambitions are.* ~

'You know what I want to do.'

'No, I honestly don't. I don't know much about you at all. Sure, we say hello to each other most days but that's pretty much it. I've always wanted to get to know you. Like, properly. But I totally understand if you'd prefer to keep things as they are. I wouldn't want to upset your boyfriend… If you have one... Do you have a boyfriend?'

~ *And there it is!* - Granddad exclaimed. ~ *The single most terrifying question a young man will ever ask. He wants to know if you have a boyfriend Pookie.* ~

Abigail tiptoed over a cattle grid and on to the gravel moat surrounding the thick white boundary wall of the lighthouse complex.

'A what?'

The bicycle rattled noisily over the metals strips. 'A boyfriend,' Henryk repeated, his throat dry with anticipation.

~ *A boyfriend!* ~ Granddad affirmed. ~ *A significant other!* ~

'No I don't. Why do you ask?'

Henryk cleared his sandpapery throat. 'No reason. Well, not true, there is a reason. I was thinking that maybe, when you feel better, you might like to go out somewhere? With me? It's okay if you say no. I'll understand. No problem.'

~ *He's asking you out!* ~

'Out? On a date?'

'Yes a date. Anywhere you like. Your choice. I'm buying.'

~ *Yes a date! Anywhere you like apparently. Your choice. He's paying. So choose something expensive. Make his wallet beg for mercy.* ~

Abigail suddenly pirouetted to face Henryk. The beautiful broad grin illuminating her face did nothing to make him feel any less vulnerable. Like the condemned man waiting for the blade to fall.

'I'd like that. I'd like that very much.'

Henryk's chest bloomed with a warm rush. His knees buckled forcing him to lean against the wall for support. 'Oh thank God! I was lying when I said it would be no problem if you said no. I think I would've died right here, right now. That would've been it. Game over! Where would you like to go? Cinema? Theatre? The gallery? We don't have to stay here in Balemouth. We could take a day trip. How about Skye or…?'

'He's coming! Quick, hide!'

A Range Rover grumbled over the rise, its headlights wobbling and jostling as it followed the track's uneven descent. Abigail hauled Henryk and the bike to the seaward corner of the wall where they crouched out of sight. She peered around the whitewashed stone and watched the vehicle clatter over the cattle grid and pull up in front of the main gate. The Range Rover's interior light came on. Tony V lifted a flask to his lips, swallowed a mouthful of something potent and aimed a small gadget out of his window. She heard a faint beep and the tall black gate cranked open. Tony drove inside.

Abigail crept round to the front. Henryk watched her go and punched the air with joy. She had actually said *yes*!

Staring through the gate, Abigail watched Tony V park up beside an even larger vehicle. Big, black, boxy and built like a tank. Looking a little unsteady on his feet, he stepped onto the crunchy gravel and fumbled a key into the door of the lightkeeper's cottage. Abigail looked up at the dormant lighthouse prodding at the stars, expecting it to explode into life at any moment and ensnare them in its merciless glare while sounding an intruder alarm that could be heard all the way to Reykjavik.

Instead, all she heard was another faint beep… and the gate began to close.

With Tony safely inside Abigail beckoned Henryk to follow her through the shrinking gap.

Keeping low, she shimmied between a clutch of outbuildings and stopped outside the shiny black door of the cottage.

Henryk edged the bike carefully up behind her. 'We could go for a meal,' he whispered. 'There's that new Italian place; Bellucci's. Or maybe you'd prefer Chinese? Or Indian? Thai maybe? Fish and chips. Or even just a burger?'

Abigail's radio burbled oddly.

~ *Shut up baker boy. You're making my stomach growl,* ~ Granddad moaned. ~ *What I'd give to sink my teeth into a nice juicy steak.* ~

'Yuck! You do realise meat is pumped full of growth hormones, steroids, antibiotics and antiparasitics? Can I have the bag please?'

'You're a vegetarian? Quite right,' Henryk nodded, unhooking the bag from the bike and handing it over. 'I've been considering giving up meat myself. A veggie diet has to be healthier doesn't it? I could cook something for you. When you feel better. When you get your head sorted. A mushroom risotto or something? I make a mean chana masala if you'd prefer.'

~ *Chana masala! What are you waiting for Pookie? Marry the boy!* ~

'Shh! Quiet! I need to concentrate.'

'Oh, sorry; yes. Things to do. I'll be quiet.' Henryk made a show of zipping his mouth shut and watched Abigail's busy hands rifle through the tool bag. His delight changed to unease when she started setting aside some worryingly lethal looking implements.

'I thought you just wanted to say hello?'

Tony V poured himself a generous measure of Glenmorangie, downed it, then poured another. The moment of truth. He'd been avoiding it long enough. Long enough to sink several pints of Dutch courage. Time to find out if all the hard work had paid off. Docking his smartphone into the stereo, he opened the Official Top 40 Chart Countdown podcast and swiped to the business end of the progress bar.

'*...At number five, down three places, it's Adele...*' the DJ crowed over a thumping backing track designed to heighten the suspense. '*At number four: Clarissa Deep climbs three places with One Happy Day, One Happy Girl... At three: it's a non-mover for The Keyrings and Festival Fiasco...*'

Tony gripped his tumbler a little firmer. 'Come on... come on... come on...'

'*And at number two: this week's highest climber, up thirteen places, it's The Halcyon Days with Angel... And here it is...*' said the DJ lowering his voice a notch to show that Things Were Getting Serious... '*This week's number one on the Official UK Top Forty is...*'

Tony V shut his eyes and gulped his glass dry... Come on!... Come on...!

'*Yes! He's still there! Seven weeks at the top of the pile: it's Jake C and Sweet Sunshine Smile!*'

Before the first bar of the flouncy pop smash managed to wiggle into his ears, Tony V picked up the stereo and bowled it across the living room hoping to see it smash in a satisfying explosion of electronic guts against the wall. To his disappointment it bounced wildly off the sofa, tumbled and span over the zebra skin rug, flinging the phone from the dock. The phone somersaulted to a skidding halt at his feet where Jake C's aggravating, tinny falsetto sang into his toes:

'*... Peaches and ice cream and sugar coated daydreams...*'

'Bastard!' Tony screamed stamping on the phone. 'Bastard! Bastard! Bastard!'

'*... Beaches and hot steam and diving into mountain streams...*'

Tony kept on stamping until the screen cracked, splintered and died under his heel. How he wished it were Jake's head! He hated absolutely everything about his former bandmate. He detested that voice. Despised his stupid floppy fringe. Loathed his smug pretty boy face. 'Bastard! Bastard! Bastard!' He booted the shattered remains, sending shards of plastic and glass under the drinks cabinet.

Tony snatched up his retro Thirties style telephone and dialled. 'Hoy Billy! That twat is still Number One! What the hell happened?

Where the hell is Bedtime Toy?' He heard a weary sigh at the other end, a pause, then Billy Spink cleared his throat.

'Tony. No need to be upset. Bedtime Toy is a slow burner. Like the perfect soufflé it will rise slowly.'

'Billy! I can tell you're watching The Great British Bake Off! I can hear that Paul bloody Whatshisface in the background, so cut the soufflé crap! What number is Bedtime Toy?'

'Straight in at number ninety-four no less! It's a promising start,' said Billy trying to sound upbeat. 'I've got a few nightclub gigs lined up for you next week. It's a DJ smash! It will tear up the charts once we get a club remix cut... Tony?... Tony? You okay?' Billy could hear his client's breathing growing increasingly erratic.

'Ninety-four! A new entry at ninety-bloody-four! After everything I've done. After all the crappy promotion you made me do? Ninety-four! People will laugh at me Billy! Jake will be laughing his, ooh-so-baby-smooth, twatty little face off! You said we'd set the charts on fire! Well it looks like we ran out of bloody matches doesn't it?'

'Tony, Tony, calm down. You have to trust me on this. We're playing the long game. This time next year Jake C will be Jake Who? Whereas you will be riding the crest of a massive wave. A Tony tsunami! Who cares if Bedtime Toy's sales are a tad disappointing at the mo? The momentum is on our side.'

'A tad disappointing? Just how many copies has it sold Billy?'

'Bear with me a sec, I have the figures here somewhere... Ah! Here we go. Six hundred and fourteen downloads plus seven hundred and thirty streams.'

'Billy. Are you honestly telling me the thing hasn't even managed to reach a thousand downloads?'

'Not yet Tony. And I emphasise the *yet*. Perhaps it's my fault for securing so much airplay. It might've been a mistake to let people actually hear the song before they bought it. I guess the public aren't quite ready to handle such adult subject matter. But give them time...'

'What do you mean it was a mistake to let them hear it? And what do you mean - "adult subject matter?"'

'I'm talking about the core message of the song Tony. It's central message.'

'What central message? What are you on about?'

'Seriously Tony? Have you not read those lyrics?'

'Billy. I sing the bloody words. You can't expect me to read them as well. I'm not interested in any hidden meanings!'

'Hidden meanings? It's not exactly a carefully crafted metaphor Tony. You're singing; *Hold me, feel me, squeeze me babe. Take me from your drawer. Let me bring you bedtime joy.* Tony! It's a song about a dildo!'

Stunned, Tony's world wobbled for a moment. More whisky...

'You what?' he swallowed. 'Are you kidding me?'

'No Tony. The central message of Bedtime Toy is that you are a dildo. But that's irrelevant. What you need to do right this instant, is relax. If all else fails – which it won't –then I'm confident I can get you a slot on Strictly Come Dancing or that celebrity jungle thingy. So chill Tony. You're my main man. Now I really must go. Paul's about to sample Helen's flan.'

'Hey! Don't you dare! Why do I listen to you Billy? I am *not* a singing dildo! Why in God's name do I *ever* listen to you? You said Bedtime Toy was a cast iron guaranteed Number One! *Numero Uno*! Consider yourself well and truly fired you useless... Hey! Don't you dare hang up on me! I haven't finished yelling at you yet! ... Billy...!'

Tony tore the phone from its socket and hurled it after the stricken stereo. Draining the last measure of Scotch into his glass he heard the doorbell chime. 'I'll kill 'em. Whoever it is I'll kill 'em!' He stomped through the hall and wrenched the door open.

With Henryk standing nervously at her side, Abigail smiled at Tony's thunderous face.

'Hello,' said Henryk politely offering his hand while Abigail ignited her blowtorch.

Tony glowered at both of them in turn. 'Who the bloody hell are you?' he growled, ignoring Henryk's hand. 'Bugger off, I'm not in the mood. Do you honestly expect me to sign your bloody blowtorch? Why do I always get the nutters?'

Henryk leaned forward. 'I don't think she wants your autograph,' he said apologetically before turning to Abigail whispering; 'I am right, yeah? You don't want his autograph?'

'So what does she bloody well want then?'

Abigail bobbed her head from side to side singing; '*Let me be your bedtime toy...*'

'In your naughty wee dreams sweetheart,' Tony scowled. He shifted his glare to Henryk. 'Listen buddy. Take your girlfriend home. I understand she might want a thorough seeing to, more than you're capable of supplying, but I can't oblige every little teenybopper that comes knocking on my door. Comprende?'

'I hate that song,' said Abigail stepping in front of an increasingly bemused Henryk. 'I need you to help get your song and all this other noise out of my head, for good.'

'You need help all right doll, but it's not the kind of help I'm qualified to provide. Expert loony doctors, that's what you need.'

Abigail moved closer. 'Sorry. I'm not making myself clear. I don't have the words to tell you just how much I *hate* your song. And you are going to help me get rid of it.'

'Get lost and stop pestering me you deranged mentalist!'

When Tony tried to shut his door Abigail leapt forward and fired the blowtorch into his whisky. The glass ruptured in a spray of dripping flames. Tony flung the blazing liquid to the floor and reeled backwards into the hallway. He stumbled over a Scottie dog doorstop and fell flat on his back.

'Abigail! Jesus!' Seeing the fire spread rapidly across the carpet, Henryk tried to grab her arm but Abigail yanked herself free and moved in for Tony.

Fearing for his life, Tony scrabbled away from the advancing, black-hooded pyromaniac. 'Get away from me you psychofreak!'

Abigail kneeled, gathered Tony by the collar and aimed the small blue tongue of sizzling flame close enough to let him feel the heat tickle his chin. 'You switched it on. Now you're going to help me switch it off,' she ordered calmly. 'Agreed?'

Convinced he detected a whiff of burning stubble Tony sobered up quickly and took the sensible option. 'Agreed. Anything you say,' he said, his voice rigid with fear.

'Good. Drive me to Thrapsay Hill.'

Henryk charged frantically up and down the hall, pouncing on every scrap of fire he could find. The unfortunate Scottie dog's tartan tail burned steadily. Henryk snatched the doorstop and ran through the hall trying each handle until he found the toilet. He dropped the sorry looking dog down the pan and charged back into the hall. More flames had taken root near the stairs. He darted to the front door, snatched up the welcome mat and began beating at the floor until the mini wildfire had been thoroughly quelled.

'Oh, jeez that was close,' he breathed slumping against the wall, satisfied he'd won the battle... If not the war... More smoke curled blackly towards the ceiling. The fire had opened up a new front. A last errant flame had seized an expensive looking wall hanging; a full length, faux Warhol style tapestry of Tony V grinning under sparkly sunglasses. Henryk ripped it from its hooks and jumped on Tony's multi-coloured heads until he killed the blaze completely.

'I didn't realise you hated his song *that* much,' he said breathlessly after triple-checking every inch of the hall. Only then did he realise Abigail and Tony had left the building. Hearing the low, guttural rasp of an engine he dashed outside the cottage. The Range Rover was still there but the Hummer was on the move, already on the other side of the gate which was swinging to a close.

'Abigail wait! Wait! Where...?' Henryk sprinted through the courtyard but arrived too late to stop the gate clanking shut. Through the bars he watched Abigail in the front of the monstrous truck aiming her blowtorch at Tony V. The ashen-faced singer carefully steered them across the cattle grid and up the dirt road.

With whisky burning in his belly and the blowtorch threatening to do the same to his petrified face, Tony V guided the Hummer through the woods, down Inch Point Road and on into town. He hadn't driven the Beast for a good long while and struggled initially with the gear stick and clutch control. When she'd forced him from the cottage at flame-point he'd automatically headed for the Range Rover, but this psycho-groupie had insisted on the Hummer, saying its power could come in handy. Handy for what he didn't dare ask.

Balemouth was dead. No-one around. Not one person to blast the horn at or scream to for help - 'Call the police! There's a maniac trying to burn my face off!' – Not one soul. Not even another set of wheels on the streets. He was on his own. Solo. Number ninety-four. How much more humiliation could one man take?

Only when they'd cleared the traffic lights and headed inland via the High Street did Tony finally brave a detailed look at his kidnapper. The girl was truly insane. Red-eyed and shivering. Through anger or cold, he couldn't tell. She kept the blowtorch flame steady and true by resting the grip on the edge of his headrest while her other hand alternated between keeping her hood snugly in place and fiddling with the ancient looking radio tucked tightly under her arm. She gripped the aerial again. Tony glanced at the unzipped bag taking up most of the space between them.

'Sweet baby Jesus! What have you got in there? Are those bombs?' he wailed, spying a pair of gas canisters the size of her thighs.

Despite having a firm grasp of the aerial and her hood up, the burgeoning noise inside Abigail's head refused to be hushed. 'What?'

'In your bag. Are those bombs? Please tell me you're not one of those terrorists!'

Granddad had to raise his voice in order to be heard above the uproar. ~ *He's asking if those canisters inside your bag are bombs! And, he wants to know if you're a terrorist!* ~

'No. They're not bombs. Their oxyacetylene canisters. For welding and cutting metal. And, no, I'm not a terrorist. I'm a freedom fighter.' She tried for what she hoped was a menacing smile but her head hurt too much to keep it up.

'Oh Jeez. This is not good! What do you need those hacksaws for? And is that a chisel in there? Oh God, listen, there's no need to torture me. I'll do anything you want. Anything. Anything but pain. I don't do pain. Or blood. Please don't cut any bits off! I'm begging you,' Tony howled, his voice rising another octave.

'Just drive to Thrapsay Hill or I'll cook your cheeks medium rare!'

'If it's money you're after I'll give it to you. Every penny. It'll have to be a bank transfer though. I'm a bit short of cash just now.'

'I can't hear a word you're saying Tony! Just drive to the hill!'

Tony fixed his teary eyes on the road ahead. 'Okay, okay! Only, please don't hurt my face. Please not my face!'

'Drive to the hill!'

'I am! I am driving to the hill! This is me driving to the hill!'

'Belt up!'

'Right. You got it. I won't say another word. You're the boss. This is me belting up!'

Frustrated by the din's inexorable attempt to occupy every spare nanometre of headspace Abigail wound her fingers around the aerial so tightly it began to bend. 'I can't hear... What's he saying Granddad?'

~ He's saying he won't say another word! You're the boss! This is him belting up! – Granddad yelled hoarsely.

Abigail glared at Tony V. 'I meant your seatbelt, numpty!'

~ Quite right Pookie. Safety first! ~

Tony clicked his belt into place and eyed the small bottle of blended in the glove compartment, its contents sloshing with every bump and turn in the road... Tempting... His emergency whisky. He'd forgotten it was there. It must have been hiding in there for over year. Ever since...

'Why me? Why are you doing this to me? That's all I want to know. Then I'll shut up. Promise. What have I done to upset you like this?' Tony asked, then wished he hadn't when she began muttering to her radio again, talking to it as though it were an old friend. Like a full on Hannibal Lecter.

'Granddad I'm really struggling to hear a thing right now. What's going on? What's he saying?'

~ He's asking why him? Why are you doing this to him? ~

'Because you switched it on Tony!' she yelled. 'Now you can switch it off!'

Tony hurriedly wiped his eyes dry. He had to calm down. Compose himself. Contain his fear. Placate her. Time to change tact and hit her with the old Tony V charm offensive. Never failed. He offered her the full seduction package; the toothpaste ad smile, the brows arching over twinkly come-and-get-me eyes and the smoother-than-bathing-in-warm-chocolate voice.

'Look, there's no need for this to get out of hand or anything. It's a beautiful night. We still have a few miles to go. We should use this time to get to know each other. I for one, would love to know everything there is to know about you. We can be friends. That'd be good wouldn't it?'

~ Look at him! ~ said Granddad with a note of purest disdain. – *Look at those stupid veneers! Look at him sitting there with his rugged good looks, sunbed complexion and freakishly luxuriant hair... The big jobby! ~*

'You already know my name. How about you? What's your name, angel?'

~ Now he wants to know your name! And, oh dear, oh dear, he called you angel. *~*

The Hummer whacked a pothole. The hood slipped from Abigail's head. The increase in volume knifing into her brain almost made her faint.

<TAKE ME FROM YOUR DRAWER...><WITH THE LOSS OF OVER ONE THOUSAND JOBS...><I'LL LEAVE YOU BEGGIN' FOR MORE...>< CONTROVERSY TODAY IN THE JUNGLE WHEN JACINTHA LICKED THE TOILET BOWL THEN KISSED...><MOIST AND ON THE FLOOR...>

Abigail thrust the hood back and gripped the aerial. The noise level dipped but nowhere near as much as she'd hoped.

'My name is Abigail Squall. And I am nobody's angel.'

'Abigail Squall,' repeated Tony, ignoring the rebuke and rolling her name around his tongue as if he were sampling the finest of wines. 'What a beautiful name. What an utterly gorgeous name. Abigail please believe me – I am truly sorry for whatever it is I've done to upset you. So let me do what I can to put it right. Maybe I didn't sign a CD for you. Was that it? Or did I refuse to let you take a selfie with me. But fair's fair Abigail - you have to understand I can't sign every little thing that's handed to me, or smile into every phone that's shoved in front of my face. There's not enough time. There's not enough *me* to go around. Seriously, I wish there was...'

~ *Listen to him! The egocentric maniac still thinks you're after his autograph and his bloody picture. Tony V. What does the V stand for uh? Vain? Vacuous? Vacuum? All of the above? That's it! Tony the vain vacuous vacuum!* ~

'I am not interested in your stupid autograph.'

~ *You tell him Pookie. Probably doesn't know how to spell V anyway.* ~

'I see,' Tony nodded thoughtfully. 'I think I get the picture. You wanted a bigger prize, something more substantial than a signed CD. Something that would've left your girlfriends moist with envy. So, let's think. Did I spurn your advances? Maybe after a gig? In a hotel? Listen, sweetheart, I'm really sorry. I wish I could oblige all my groupies. Especially the babes. But hey listen, I can book us into a hotel right now and we can spend the whole night in bed together. To be honest with you, being kidnapped by a fan like this is a bit of a turn on in a freaky kinda way.'

~ *It gets worse! The big eejit thinks you're after his body! Now he's offering to whisk you off for a night of Premier Inn passion!* ~

Abigail's mouth curled in disgust. 'Don't flatter yourself.' She tweaked the blowtorch, adding another half inch to the flame. Tony looked in his rear-view mirror and saw a twist of smoke spiralling from his singed sideburn taking his whole charm offensive with it.

'Please! Abigail! Don't! I'm begging you. Not my face,' he whimpered. 'I've got a photo shoot tomorrow. It's for a double spread feature in Teen Beat magazine.'

~ *I think you should melt his nose off!* ~

'My radio thinks I should melt your nose off.'

With raw, unbridled fear in his eyes, Tony V glanced at the lunatic girl at his side. 'Please, don't take advice from your radio. I don't think you can trust a word it says. But you can trust me. You said you wanted me to switch something off. What exactly do you want me to switch off? Just point me to it and it's done.'

~ *What a tube! He's asking you what exactly it is you want him to switch off. Unbelievable. The man has the IQ of a pickled moth with learning difficulties.* ~

'I want you to switch off the Thrapsay Hill transmitter. You switched it on. So now you have to switch it off.'

'The transmitter. Thrapsay Hill. Of course I'll switch it off. Not a problem. Anything you want.'

~ *Finally he gets the ...ssage! He says he'll t... you to the t....mitter. He'll... sw... off... Any... ng... you... Listen Abigail...I'm losing power!* ~ Granddad hollered, desperately trying to stave off the aural mush battering into Abigail's headspace. ~ *Turn me off!* ~

'What? I can't! I need you now more than ever!'

Tony V dared to land a sympathetic pat on her thigh.

'And I'm here for you Abigail. Anything you want. Just don't damage my face.'

Abigail slapped his hand. 'Keep your hands on the wheel! I'm not talking to you!' She grasped the aerial, twisting it in every direction, hoping to pick up a stronger signal. 'I won't switch you off Granddad. Don't ask me to do that.'

~ *My ...tteries ... dying! You must conse... them! You can swi... me back ... when you've dealt ... the ...smitter! Please Pookie. Trust me...*

You need to be stro... You can do this. I know ... can. You're going to beat this ...ookie! Switch me off! We'll spe... oon. ...ise... ove you!...~

Her heart broken, Abigail switched the radio off. Tears streaming, she tightened her hood but the lead apron stapled inside offered zero defence against the drilling barrage of sound. Tony's mouth flapped like a bird in distress but she couldn't distinguish a word. She took the blowtorch in both hands focusing her attention on the intense blue point as the Hummer sped out of town and on towards a single dark peak.

Slipping down through the gears, Tony steered them on to the service road at the foot of Thrapsay Hill. Halfway to the summit a break in the trees allowed Abigail a glimpse of the transmitter's stark silhouette thrown against the moonlight. A red warning beacon winked from the apex. Her pain intensified with each bludgeoning, vision-smearing pulse of the flashing cherry. The blowtorch trembling in her hands Abigail fought hard to ignore the flickering mesh of images playing out on the windscreen. The TV signals firing into her head had her hurtling through deep space at hyperspeed one moment then ploughing through a rubble strewn street, scattering a small army of menacing rioters, faces hidden under scarves, the next. The rioters vanished in a blink to be replaced by a herd of wildebeest charging across a blazing African plain.

She shook her head faster and faster... The wildebeest disappeared amidst a rapid fire collage of fuzzily jolting blipverts; washing powder, sofas, chocolate, shampoo, crisps, tyres, double-glazing, car insurance, paint, bleach... A disorientating profusion of shiny new cars, perfect whiter than white teeth, processed snacks, spotless bathrooms, bouncing babies, fast acting painkillers, lifetime guarantees, satisfaction or your money back... Promises, promises, promises.

She shook her head until her neck nearly snapped. Adverts cleared, she looked at Tony V... And shrieked in terror. A big round, yellow cartoon of a head, sat on his shoulders. Two big eyes and a big smile. Tony V had morphed into an emoji. His big sunbeam face flickered through a glut of emotions: anxious, angry, perplexed, surprised, sleepy, upturned mouth, downturned mouth, grimacing, winking, love hearts for eyes, ZZzzz... Abigail banged her head against the headrest. Tony's real face popped back. Mouth continuing to flap he flicked the

Hummer's headlights on full beam and concentrated on the track rising steeply in front of them.

But Abigail couldn't see the road ahead for the reams of SMS messages streaming across the windscreen in an incoherent alphabetti spaghetti, all accompanied by a fractious, stratified soundtrack of conversations, songs, jingles, ringtones and white noise...

/OMG!/FFS WHERE RU?/OMG! YTTT/LOMLAS/BOBFOC IMHO/LOL/WHERE RU?/DQMOT/PMSL/THANX/LUV U/ IGWS/ROFLMAOASTC/YGTBK/2DLoo!/

Looking back to Tony she screamed at his new devil face. A demon emoji, purple with horns and an evil smile. She banged her head again. The texts cleared from the screen and Tony's face returned to its normal bronzed hue.

They approached the summit. The headlights levelling out as the track broadened and swept them towards a security gate beyond which lay the transmitter compound. Tony slowed down.

'Don't stop!' Abigail yelled.

'But...'

'Drive through it!'

Nostrils detecting another whiff of burnt hair Tony stamped the accelerator and smashed through the gate. The padlock snapped from the chain and smacked the windscreen. Unable to see through the fine mosaic of cracks, Tony slammed the brakes. The Hummer skidded to a halt showering the maintenance hut in a cloud of dust and grit. Abigail snatched the ignition key before Tony could gather himself. Hauling the tool bag, she stepped down from the Hummer and hurried round to throw open the driver's door.

'Out!' she ordered. The dazed singer slid out of the cab, hands raised. 'Lie down!' Tony dropped to the dirt. Abigail pressed a knee into his spine, 'Hands behind your back!' She took a roll of duct tape from the bag, tore off a strip and bound his wrists together.

Tony lifted his chin and watched Abigail use a pair of bolt cutters to snip the lock securing the door of the hut. The skeletal outline of the transmitter mast criss-crossed high into the sky above her head. 'Please don't hurt me,' he moaned.

She opened the jaws of the cutters around the base of Tony's neck 'Get in!' Tottering like a newborn foal he pushed himself to his feet and into the hut. Abigail searched the wall by the door until she located the light switch and flicked it on. Illuminated by a single fluorescent strip, Tony found himself standing at the centre of a bewildering array of fuse boxes and control panels. Abigail clutched at the endless, ear-shredding explosions splitting her skull. The agony like two hot thumbs spoiling to push her eyes clean out of her head.

'Which one is it? Which one turns it off?' she screamed.

Tony scrambled from panel to panel utterly confused. 'I don't know!'

Abigail snatched up the blowtorch and increased the flame to full blast. 'Turn it off! Now!'

Fingers waggling frantically at his back, Tony reversed from one unit to the next, pressing and throwing every button, lever and switch he could find. 'I don't know which one it is!' he wailed.

'There!' Abigail pointed to a big green plastic button mounted on a lectern tucked away in the corner. She dragged it out and banged the button repeatedly. 'It's green for Go people! That's what you said! Why isn't it working?'

'You want to know why it doesn't work?' Tony kicked the lectern to the floor and prised the button off with a toe. 'See? It's stuck down with a bit of Velcro. It's not connected to anything. That thing I did with the mayor? That was just for show. It's just a useless big plastic button. It doesn't do anything, honest.'

Abigail stared at Tony's bright yellow emoji face. Perplexed. Confused. Frustrated. Grimacing. Upturned. Downturned. Straight. Open... But all she could hear, all she could feel was the noise. Burrowing into the very core of her being, renting her apart, cell by cell. She sank to her knees in despair. The sheer weight of sound threatened to smear her into the coarse concrete floor.

'Make it stop! Please!'

Tony watched the deranged girl curl up into an agonised foetus. She had no fight left in her. He seized his chance and kicked the blowtorch from her grasp. He crouched down and carefully worked his wrists close to the hard blue flame. A brief smell of burning plastic and glue and his hands were free again. He fingered the strands of scorched hair by his ear. His left cheek felt a little hot and raw. He pressed at the soreness then looked at his fingertips. No blood. Tony returned his attention to the girl squirming on the floor. He squatted beside her and hovered the flame over her face.

'You crazy wee bitch. Let's see how you like it.'

He aimed for her ear. Her perfect little ear... but the flame sputtered and died. Out of fuel. Disappointed, Tony ditched the blowtorch, retrieved his keys from Abigail's pocket and left the hut.

Trying to clear the pulsating interference from her vision Abigail butted her head against the floor. She saw Tony approach the Hummer parked just a few feet from the open door. She could see the number plate... The noise in her head screeched and hissed...

*

... The hiss of heavy rain...
   ... The awful screech of brakes... unable to stop in time...
   ... A thud...
   ... And then the deep roar of an engine accelerating...
   ... Fading... fading...
Time slowing to a crawl...
Running to her mother's side...
The blood leaking from Sylvia's head...
Sylvia's eyes struggling to focus on her daughter...
'I love...?'
The red smear of the vehicle's tail lights racing for the corner...
And the registration comes into focus...
1 LUV...
Sylva's dying words...
'I love...? One love...? I love...? One love...?'

*

Tony pulled open the driver's door, reached inside and took the whisky from the glove compartment. He unscrewed the cap and filled his mouth with the sweet amber burn. The stress slipped away the moment he swallowed. He raised the bottle for a second helping. An inch from his welcoming lips the bottle exploded showering him in glass and alcohol. Something slammed into the black metal of the Hummer's roof missing his scalp by a hair's breadth.

'Give me the keys.'

Abigail marched towards him, dragging her tools behind her with one hand, while the other aimed a nail gun in a worryingly erratic grip. She fired again. The nail obliterated what remained of the windscreen. Tony's guts spasmed launching a packet of bile infused whisky into his mouth. He forced the acrid measure back down and handed over the keys.

Abigail's eyes blazed with hatred. 'What are you waiting for? Get back inside!' Tony hurried inside the hut with his arms raised. Abigail slammed the door shut and punched several nails around the edge, pinning it to the frame. Tears clouding her way, she moved to the front of the Hummer and crouched beside the number plate. She wiped her eyes then slowly traced her wet fingers along each angle and curve of the black lettering...

1 LUV...

Abigail climbed inside. Turned the engine. The vehicle tremored with the pent-up fury of an angry rhino. She swung the animal round and parked its nose against the door of the maintenance hut.

With Tony safely contained, Abigail killed the ignition, stepped out and dragged her tool bag to the nearest of the transmitter's four legs. As though aware of what was coming, the red beacon at the tip flared with a new intensity. And the transmissions screamed and wailed and rang and shrieked, louder and fiercer than ever...

<WITH THE HEATWAVE SET TO CONTINUE WELL INTO NEXT WEEK><*LET ME BE...*><FOR YOUR CHANCE TO WIN...><*LET ME BE YOUR...*><TEXTS COST 50P PLUS YOUR STANDARD NETWORK RATE><*LET ME BE YOUR BEDTIME TOY...*>

Abigail pulled the oxyacetylene canisters from the bag, connected Sylvia's cutting head and ignited the flame. Donning a pair of goggles, she started on the first incision; opening a slow, deep tract into the steel. A white hot wound of blinding sparks and molten blood, dripping and slicing through the transmitter's ankle...

Tony threw his weight against the door. And again. And again... Shoulder versus door. His shoulder gave way first. A little popping noise deep in the joint followed by a hot stabbing pain. Conceding defeat, he sat in the dust to nurse the damage.

'Ya mad mental wee whore!'

He saw himself reflected in the polished metal of the panel opposite. What a mess. His suit covered in whisky, dirt and flecks of glass. Tony moved in for a thorough examination of his face. His left cheek looked pink and tender thanks to the blowtorch but no lasting damage had been done. A smidgen of foundation would do the trick. And a minor trim would soon fix his frazzled hair. But there was a little cut by the corner of his mouth caused by the exploding bottle. The photographer would have to shoot him from the other side. His right side was his best anyway. Tony turned his head to admire the prettier aspect of his face. He pouted and raised a sultry eyebrow. Yes, he still had it. Far better looking than that mega-twat Jake. Bastard! Number one! Someone needs to smash his Sweet Sunshine Smile teeth in!

Tony punched the panel crumpling his own furious face. His split knuckles sang with pain. He groaned. Now they'd have to photograph him with his hand hidden in a pocket or behind his back. Then again, a bandaged hand would look pretty cool. Give him a hard edge. Tony V, tough guy. The more he thought about the idea, the more he liked it. But if he didn't get out of this hole, there'd be no photoshoot... Number ninety-four! Would they still want him?

He hunted through his pockets then dropped his head with a despairing sigh when he remembered his phone was back at the cottage somewhere under the drinks cabinet and various other places.

He back-pedalled across the floor, huddled himself in the corner and listened to the strange crackling and buzzing sounds coming from beyond the door. Tony hugged his knees and began to sob.

CHAPTER EIGHTEEN

DEAD AIR

The sea to his left held a mirror to the stretching sun, heralding the beginning of yet another scorcher. Not a breath of breeze to be had. Nothing to soothe Henryk's hot sweaty face and tired limbs. He'd spent the night searching the entire town, discovering alleys and backstreets he never even knew existed. Apart from a milk float and the odd delivery van, the roads were deserted. Where was everyone? He'd tried the Squalls' house. No-one home. No lights on. No answer when he'd knocked the door. Several times. He'd tried The Green Grocery. Shutters down. He'd called the hospital in Inverness: No - Abigail Squall had not been located. As far as they were concerned she was still missing. And no - no-one by the name of Tony V had been admitted overnight.

Henryk wheeled the crippled bike along the promenade. Its shredded tyre flip-flapping uselessly over the pavement. Damage he'd exacerbated whenever a downhill slope proved irresistible. Anything to give his aching ankle a rest. He'd landed heavily after scaling Tony V's gate. A mild sprain. Enough to curtail his speed to a brisk limp.

He checked his watch. He should be helping his dad open the bakery in less than an hour. The old man would be less than happy to find himself flying solo on what would doubtless prove to be another busy day at the ovens. Never mind. He was on an important mission. Mission: Abigail. Mission: *Radio Girl*.

Where the hell had she taken Tony V? And what was she planning to do with him? And almost setting fire to his house! He could think of better ways to say hello. He didn't like admitting it, but it was all so painfully obvious. Abigail was not well. More than that - she was a wee bit unhinged. Okay - more than a wee bit. Why else would she have agreed to go out on a date with him? A sane Abigail would have politely but firmly rejected the idea. He really should have contacted her dad the moment she appeared behind the bakery bins. She had to go back to hospital. If anything happened to her it would be his fault. Idiot, idiot, idiot!

Henryk forced his leaden legs up the High Street. He saw the police station a hundred yards up ahead and kicked himself. The one place he hadn't checked and straightaway, even from this distance, he recognised two vehicles parked outside. The Green Grocery van and the unmistakeable Hell Spawn Avengers camper.

Tom stared at the clock. The slim red second hand completed another circuit. Susannah lay against his shoulder fast asleep. Rick snored in the seat nearest the police station's main door. Kris had opted to lay down across several seats using his jacket as a pillow. Wizz was wide awake thumbing her smartphone through yet another level of *Space Koala Mayhem!*

Since they invaded the place en masse late the previous night, the Station Duty Officer manning the reception desk had repeatedly tried to persuade them all to leave. And on each attempt the lady had been put straight with the Avengers rowdy battle cry; 'Free the Balemouth Bay One!' But as the hours rolled on, the Avengers began to fall asleep one by one. Wizz, ever the night owl, left the station for a short while. She returned holding a large piece of cardboard on which she'd written the group's battle cry in big, bold letters. From then on, whenever the woman returned to the front desk to ask them to leave, Wizz quietly raised her makeshift placard so as not to wake anyone up.

The security door leading to the bowels of the station buzzed open. Wizz wearily raised her placard expecting another visit from their arch nemesis but sat up straight when Jonathan came through with Valerie Hobbs at his side.

Puzzled by Valerie's presence, Tom gently lifted Susannah's head from his shoulder and rose to meet his tired but relieved looking dad.

'What happened?'

'They asked some questions. I answered them,' Jonathan whispered, noting the sleepyheads all around. 'I think they know your aunt is full of nonsense. Valerie kindly helped put them straight.'

'And how did she do that?' Tom asked. Valerie diverted her gaze to Wizz who was ruthlessly moving in to rouse her dozing bandmates.

'Avengers up! Rise and shine people,' she clapped and harried.

'I'll explain later. Any news on your sister?' asked Jonathan.

Tom shook his head despondently.

Wizz stepped over. 'Before young Tom told us of your predicament we, that is the Hell Spawn Avengers, were out searching all over town Mr Squall. No sign of Abigail I'm afraid. But no fear, we'll keep looking.'

Jonathan allowed himself a weary smile. 'Thank you. Hell Spawn Avengers, uh? Is that your band's name?'

Tom nodded fearing ridicule.

'That's a brilliant name,' Valerie grinned.

'Thank you!' Wizz hugged Valerie tightly, catching her completely off guard.

'It's a good name. I like it,' Jonathan concurred. He too received a fulsome squeeze from Wizz.

'Thank you Mr Squall. And we will find Abigail. I know we will.' The security door buzzed and in came PC Godwin, a big gaping yawn stretching his face. Wizz's mood flicked to rage. 'You should be ashamed of yourself! Locking up an innocent man!'

'Hang on!' Godwin protested. 'Whatever it is, it's nothing to do with me. I'm just starting my shift here. What on earth is going on?'

'Come on Jon. Let's get you home.' said Valerie taking Jonathan's arm. She turned to Tom. 'Your aunt has gone hasn't she?' Much to her relief Tom affirmed with a nod.

Taking their cue from Valerie everyone headed for the exit but before the door had fully parted, Henryk charged in.

'Mr Squall! Sorry. I've been bloody everywhere looking for you. Your house, your shop. Checked the beach, the park, the cemetery. Gone through every single street. Even checked the church in case you were praying. I've been calling your phone. Landline and mobile...'

'Henryk. Take a breath. We get the picture. You've found me. What do you want?'

Henryk gulped down a lungful. 'I've seen Abigail.'

'You've seen her?'

Henryk took a step back slightly alarmed when everyone closed in, anxious to hear his news.

'Where?' urged Tom.

'With Tony V. I think she's kidnapped him.'

Wizz's eyes widened. 'Kidnapped Tony V? That is just about the coolest thing I've ever heard.'

Jonathan remained perplexed. 'Who the hell is Tony V?'

'He's a pop star. Used to be in Hi-Jump,' Susannah explained, taking Tom's hand.

'A pop star? You're telling me you think my daughter's kidnapped a pop star?'

'She threatened him with a blowtorch and nearly set fire to his house,' said Henryk.

'Oh wow!' Kris clapped his hands together. 'That is truly awesome. It's about time somebody did.'

Looking all the more incredulous, Jonathan inched closer to Henryk. 'Why on earth would she kidnap a pop star and threaten him with a blowtorch?'

'I'm guessing you haven't heard Bedtime Toy, Mr Squall?' said Rick.

'She was acting a bit strange,' Henryk continued. 'Which is understandable considering, you know, she's not well at the moment. I heard her say something like – "You switched it on and now you're going to help me switch it off," – I was busy trying to put the fire out at the time. And the next thing I knew they were driving off in his Hummer with Abigail pointing the blowtorch at his face.'

'Tony V? Isn't he that vacuous plastic man who switched on the new transmitter?' asked Valerie.

'Aye, that's the one,' Tom confirmed.

'She had a whole bag of tools with her. Not just the blowtorch. She had cutters, grinders, gas canisters and god knows what.'

'Oh, this is extra special!' Wizz beamed at Henryk. 'She's going to slice and dice Tony V!'

Jonathan shook his head. 'It's not him she's looking to cut down. I think we'd better get ourselves to Thrapsay Hill, and soon.'

PC Godwin suddenly shoved his way through the crowd barking urgently into his radio. 'Sierra-Golf-One-Six to Control. I've received information that the missing person Abigail Squall could be on Thrapsay Hill. Believe she is in the company of one Tony V and may be holding him under duress. I'm making my way there now.'

'Phil! You leave my daughter alone, d'you hear me?' warned Jonathan, but the paunchy cop was already halfway across the car park.

'Let's go Avengers! To the Spawn-mobile. Quick, quick, quick!' Wizz and her band dashed to the van.

Rick slammed the camper's side door shut. 'Am I getting this right? Are we seriously thinking she's gonna try and pull down that transmitter?'

Kris grinned. 'This is intense. We just have to dedicate our debut album to Abigail.'

Watching PC Godwin prepare to reverse from his space Wizz turned the ignition, squeezed the accelerator and slid the van up behind the squad car blocking his exit. 'I think we can go one better,' she said. 'Why don't we call the album *The Hectic Headspace Of Abigail Squall*?'

'Inspired,' said Kris. Through his window he saw the others climb into Valerie's Saab and speed off down the High Street.

Godwin angrily banged his horn then hauled himself back out and stamped across to Wizz's window. 'Move this piece of junk now!' he bawled.

Eyeing the keys left dangling in the police car's ignition, Tom snuck out of the van. Wizz put on a fine show of key twisting and pedal slamming. 'Sorry, the thing's stalled. I can't seem to fire it up officer,' she shrugged helplessly. Behind Godwin's crimson scowl she saw Tom ease the keys from the policeman's car. Susannah anxiously motioned to Tom: *Hurry up!* Tom sneaked back on board jangling his prize. Mission accomplished.

'Young lass, you are deliberately obstructing a police officer in the course of his duty. That's a criminal offence which could lead to a...'

The camper van's engine suddenly grumbled into action.

'Oh look! She's started,' beamed Wizz. 'We'll be on our way then officer. Bye now!'

She floored the accelerator and the Hell Spawn Avengers zoomed off.

PC Godwin hurried back to his car cursing them all. He panicked. No keys. He checked every pocket until the penny finally dropped. He glared at Tom waving impudently from the back of the fast disappearing van...

*

<**-@////~~~///~~///+-)o...///AA¬¬¬///xx...../// xx....:)☺☺☺☹;) ///¬¬¬```¬¬¬`^^///****zzhhhzhhh!!::::::""""@$$HHHHhhheehe sshhshshhshhshshhsOoo/>

She cut a crippling wound through the last of the transmitter's supports. Her rattling, screeching headspace felt ready to erupt into a fountain of fire. It was as though the transmitter was amplifying its own agony directly into her every last, frazzled neuron. The torture of a patient undergoing multiple amputations without anaesthetic.

<///oo;)))))):_____.....///~~~~|||||\\\\wwwww...tro~~~~#///\\...cccrrcrrrrrrrroiloily-->

Five inches from completing the surgery, the fiery scalpel sputtered and died. Abigail smashed the welding kit against the mast's concrete foundations. The canister rolled free and clanged into its partner. Both now spent.

She threw off her goggles and screamed up at the red light blinking from the top of tower. 'I am not giving up! Do you hear me? I am not giving up!'

<...///....\\\@@@@+☺☺☺lollollollollolBLASH!zip##blame\\\~~CIVILUNREST/to@sHEY!!{}FIVELIVE!'''CC~~...WINNNNN NNNNN:}}}}JOOOOOLLLSSSS>

Abigail ran to the Hummer and opened the rear. Buried under a pile of dirty looking rags and old car magazines she found a coiled length of thick rope. She quickly tied one end to the tow bar then secured the other around one of the mast's severed limbs...

<***--.~~*LET ME BE, LET ME BE*@@@//// //@@@...wwww. /*BEDTIME TOY!!!!!!!!!* SHHHHH HHSSSSSSSSSSS...*TIME FOR BED NOW* /~~assshhhh+>

She clambered inside, brushed the windscreen fragments off the seat and turned the key. Twisting the steering wheel on full lock, she spun away from the hut and aimed for the downward slope. Full speed ahead... The rope yanked taut, halting the Hummer in its frothing tracks. The fat tyres rasped and spun, chewing at the loose gravel and peppering the maintenance hut in a torrent of stones and dirt. Abigail stomped on the accelerator pushing it hard to the floor with all her weight... But the tethered vehicle refused to budge another millimetre.

<///☺☹;0::☺);///!!!*BEDTIMETOY!!!SSSSSSHH*☺*;9*......++/ *TOY! !SHHHHHH SSSSS SSS!* \!\!\!|!|*SSSSSI SSSSSSS!!!!!T*....*O*....*Y* ...*EEEEEEEE EEEEHHHHH??ISSSSS*///###@*LOL*/...~~~~ffff OWWWWW☹#hurtttttttttssss~~FFS=>

The Hummer slithering sideways, Abigail shielded her smarting eyes from the flaring sun. She could see the whole town laid out before her.

'Come on!'

<TTTBED....:)☹;)☺☹☺)://\\\OOESSOOOTIMETIMeTIME☺###~~~EEEEEEEEEE!!!!/HiTIME☺(:...////!!///*TIMETOY! //...*PLEASE GAMBLE RESponsssss:o0Ooo.>

'I am not giving up! Come... ON!'

She heard it. Even above all the internal mayhem. The horrible, prolonged screech of metal rending from metal. The Hummer ploughed forward and punched through the perimeter fence. Hitting the slope Abigail's stomach lurched. She floored the brake pedal and pulled the handbrake hard in both hands.

<*...YoTOYYYY///EEEEBEDDD!!!OY!!!!SSSSSSSSSSSS*☺☺☹*~~~//////!!!\>SSSEEEEEE??///+++T... LET MEEEEEEEEEEEE BEEEEEEEEEE!!!/...>*

The skidding Hummer veered and scooped against a half-buried boulder. The huge stone bit hard into the chassis...

<*///HOLDMEFEEEEEEEELLLL!!!!!!TOY!!!...//////!!!SEEEEEE EEEEEEEEEE???///...>*

The world span and tumbled. The sun arced in a spiralling, violent blur. The trees melted into the sky. Everything smudged and smeared. In gold and green, in blue and black. The truck flopped over on to its side, sliding several yards before a tree stump brought its descent to an abrupt halt.

<*//////SQUUEEEZZEEEEEEEETOYBED////!!SSHHHHH...//...FEE EEEEEEL>*

Abigail felt a warm trickle roll from her ear and over her neck where it dripped to the pillow of earth and shattered glass pressing against her head. Outside, the world was a tilted confusion of dust and shivering sunlight...

<*//TOOOYOOYOYOYOYBEDTTTTSSSSISSSSSBEYOURRRR RRRR////SSS!!!!/TOY!//BEDTIME*☺☹*////!!LETMEBEEEEEEEEE EEEEEE!!!!////BAAAAAABETOY!!!*☺☺*////!!OYOYOY!!EDTIME!!/... LETMEEEEEEEBEEEEEEEEE!... luv>*

The screech gave way to a thunderous snap... Abigail looked through the upturned passenger window to see ribbons of flickering shadow streaming across the sky.

CRASH!!!!!!!!!!!!!!!!!!!

A storm of dust and debris swept inside, coating every surface in a dry brown film. A red glow came and went. Abigail untangled her feet from the pedals and pulled herself over the dashboard. Choking and gasping, she tried to lever her way through the empty void of the windscreen but something blocked her escape. A huge metal strut, gunmetal grey and pocked with rivets. Abigail collapsed back inside.

Through eyes drooping towards sleep, she watched the suffocating fallout drift away. And as it melted skywards, it carried with it a dying series of static infused beeps…

~   .‒‒ . .‒.. .‒..   ‒.. ‒‒‒ ‒. .   .‒‒. ‒‒‒ ‒‒‒ ‒.‒ .. .   ~

*

A series of thuds and bangs pounded the door from within. The frame shuddered, trembled and cracked as nail after nail gave way.

'Come... on.... you... BASTARD!'

The door splintered and broke. Tony V hobbled into the sunshine trying to keep the weight off his sore, battering ram foot. His face stiffened in shock at the carnage which greeted him. The transmitter lay on its side. Felled and toppled. A big gap in the sky above four ragged stumps. Tools were lying everywhere but there was no sign of his tormentor. Tony limped alongside the crumpled and tangled corpse.

'Oh no, no, no. What the hell have you done to my wheels?' he groaned when he found his precious truck wedged under the tip of the transmitter. The shattered beacon pulsed weakly.

Diesel trickling around his feet, he peered cautiously into the overturned wreckage. There she was, trapped inside, unconscious. A smear of blood leaking from her ear. He smiled, satisfied with this turn of events.

'You're a deranged schizo, d'you know that? Sod you! This is no more than you deserve.' He started off down the hill feeling quite pleased with himself. His pride and joy was a write-off but there was a silver lining in the form of a nice fat wedge from the insurance claim to look forward to.

Two vehicles charging up the track forced him to put his spending plans on hold. He ducked behind a tree and watched a dark blue Saab pull up by the wreckage. Three doors flew open. A VW camper van, its flanks and roof splashed in gory artwork, swiftly followed. The driver spotted him.

'Hey! Where d'you think you're going?'

Tony quickened his pace to a frantic waddle but Wizz, Kris, Rick and Susannah surrounded him in a flash.

'This has nothing to do with me!' Tony wailed. 'It's all down to that mad lunatic bitch back there.'

Rick grabbed him by the lapels. 'Nothing to do with you? Then why are you running away? What've you done to her?'

'I'm the victim here! Trust me, she'll be hearing from my legal team. Kidnapping. Assault. Theft. Torture. Everything! Look what the bitch has done to my wheels. She needs locking up.'

'Listen, knob-jockey,' Wizz growled into Tony's face. 'If you dare refer to my friend as a *bitch* ever again, I will take a blender to your private parts and make you drink the resulting soup through a straw. Capiche? And furthermore, if anyone needs locking up, it's you - for crimes against music. Meantime, you, Tony V, are in the custody of the Hell Spawn Avengers. Take him away.'

Leaving the others to drag Tony V into the van, Tom ran to help Jonathan and Henryk ease Abigail from the wreckage.

'It's okay Abi. I've got you. I've got you,' said Jonathan, trying to contain his distress.

'Oh God. I'll call an ambulance.' Valerie hurried back to her car. Cradling her in his arms, Jonathan carried his battered and bleeding daughter to safety. 'Everything's going to be fine. Help is on its way.' He set her down between the roots of a fine old conifer. Abigail stirred and looked into his eyes.

'That's the car,' she whispered.

'What's that sweetheart?'

Abigail straightened her aching back against the tree. 'That's the car that killed Mum. It was him.'

Jonathan turned to watch the unfortunate Tony V being bundled into the camper van. 'Are you sure?' he asked. A police car arrived to join the fray.

'I'm sure.'

Jonathan surveyed the bizarre scene. The mutilated truck. The toppled transmitter. The thrash metal teenagers taunting the pop idol. And a dumbstruck PC Godwin who plainly had no idea where to begin. A reassuring hand gently pulled his attention back to the tree.

'Dad. I'll be fine. Honestly. Don't let him get away.'

Jonathan kissed Abigail softly on the brow. 'I'll be back soon, promise.'

Tom watched him stride off to meet the bewildered policeman. He saw Susannah and smiled. She was giving Tony V a proper earbashing. The singer was going nowhere.

Henryk sat beside Abigail. She pulled him close to rest her head against his chest while he tenderly stroked her dusty hair. 'You forgot something,' he said and showed her the radio. 'Broken again. But I'm sure I can fix it.'

Abigail sat up and hugged him tight. 'Thank you! For everything.'

And then she suddenly realised. She'd heard every word Henryk had said with perfect clarity. There was nothing there to drown out his voice. She closed her eyes and concentrated... All she could hear was the gentle shush of the warm breeze swaying through the treetops. The noise had gone. Her headspace quiet. Clear. Nothing but blissful silence. No signals. No visions. Nothing... She picked up the sorry looking old radio and took hold of the aerial.

She watched a bird take flight and glide across the brilliant blue as a familiar voice spoke to her.

Her mother's...

Abigail smiled, closed her eyes and listened to the bird sing.

CHAPTER NINETEEN

SWITCH OFF...

Road testing her new trolley-bag Mrs Tully bustled towards the bridge. A thoughtful gift from Bill. – 'No more lugging heavy bags for you my petal!' – The bag was chock-full but the wheels rattling along the path made the load feel almost weightless. This summer! Too old for this heat! She stopped. Mopped her brow with a hanky. *Must Get home before Bill's Cornettos melt.*

She wheeled on. The curve of the bridge rolling closer. *That's strange... Very strange*! Three figures were propped against the railings, twitching and wriggling as she motored towards them. Moaning through gagged mouths the Morton brothers watched her draw nearer with wide, pleading eyes. The old lady slowed to halt. Their pitiful struggles with the chains and locks securing them to the bridge intensified. The boys were positively drenched from head to toe in sticky fruit pulp.

'Ooh, what have we here?' she cooed.

There was a sign fixed to the handrail above the older of the three. On a slab of cardboard someone had painted in large bold letters, the words:

WE ARE THE FRUIT DROPPERS

Each boy had a sack of rotten fruit perched on his lap. And on each sack someone had written the same invitation:

HELP YOURSELF!

Jamie Morton squirmed fearfully as Mrs Tully delved deep into his supply of squishy, festering decay and selected the slimiest looking peach she'd ever seen. She eyed him with a wicked smile...

'I don't mind if I do.'

ALSO AVAILABLE:

THE BUZZ BUILDING

Scott O'Neill

The prison doctor delivers the bad news. A tattered left ventricle. Haig Dumfries should have known. Every ten years Fate hands him a birthday present guaranteed to rip his life apart.

On his 20th birthday his father died in a bizarre construction site accident. Exactly ten years later Haig was wrongfully arrested for murder. Today is his 40th. He will not live to see his 41st.

Haig refuses to die in some grotty cell. There are so many wrongs that must be put right. Somehow he has to find his way home and pay one last visit to The Buzz Building, the secret sea cave where it all started. The place where, on his 10th birthday, he watched his best pal drown.

KILLER ESCAPES!… Despite a severe bout of man-flu it's up to Detective Inspector Craven to trace this killer. A killer who thinks he's dying thanks to a doctor's sick joke.

Someone else aims to beat Craven to the prize. Nick Dodds loads the boot of his car with everything he needs to make sure the man who murdered his wife dies a slow, merciless death…

ISBN: 978-1-78407-312-1

www.scottoneill.net

Printed in Great Britain
by Amazon